TO FACE A SAVAGE TIME

ALSO BY JOHN LEGG

Arizona Territory Series
Blood Trail Series
Buckskin Series
Colorado Territory Series
Mountain Country Trilogy
Mountain Times Series
Rocky Mountain Lawaman Series
Savage Land Series

TO FACE A SAVAGE TIME

SAVAGE LAND
BOOK 4

JOHN LEGG

WOLFPACK
PUBLISHING
— EST 2013 —

TO FACE A SAVAGE TIME

ONE

"LOOKS LIKE YOU DID WELL, Mr. Cooper," William Sublette said as he toted up what he was to pay Cooper for his three packs of plews. "Must've been a quiet winter for you in between good fall and spring hunts." He stared at Cooper, inquisitive.

Cooper managed to keep from chuckling, though some of his friends could not. "Mostly quiet. Just a wee fracas with Bug's Boys during the time we were winterin'."

"Oh?" Sublette's eyes raised in question.

Cooper fought off a sudden surge of loss at the remembrance of the death of his good friend Zeke Potts. "Just a run-in with some wayward Blackfeet."

"Lose any men? I don't see that loudmouthed young fellow, what was his name, Zack something?"

"Zeke," Cooper said tightly. "Zeke Potts. He went under at the Blackfoot's hands. Luiz Gamez, too," he added as an afterthought.

"Raise hair on 'em?"

"Not exactly, but we made wolf bait out of a few of 'em."

"*Mon Dieu*, 'Awley tell him the truth," Two-Faces Beaubien said from where he waited with his loaded mules a few feet behind Cooper

"Aye, laddie," Duncan MacTavish added from where he stood close to the half-breed.

"I did," Cooper said, half in anger, half in embarrassment.

"*Mais non.* 'E is not telling ze whole truth, M'sieur Sublette. 'E and M'sieur Potts and Sits Down..."

"That fat, lazy, good-for-nothing Nez Percé?" the trader asked, surprised.

"*Oui.* 'E showed 'imself to be a great warrior. The t'ree of them, they..."

"Shut your trap, Two-Faces."

"*Mais non*, 'Awley. This needs to be told, to M'sieur Sublette, and to ze whole rendezvous."

"Two-Faces..." Cooper warned.

"Close yer maw, lad," MacTavish said. "Like Two-Faces says, this needs to be told."

"*Oui.* Ze t'ree of them, they killed many, many of those fiendish critters. You may not believe, M'sieur Sublette, but they made wolf bait of more than two dozen of them demons."

"I do believe you're stretching the truth more than just a mite," Sublette said, his voice holding both accusation and amusement.

"'Tis God's truth, Mr. Sublette," MacTavish said, eyes narrowing at the challenge to his and Beaubien's report. "Aye. Damned Blackfeet were everywhere, ready to run o'er us after letting us a stew a bit. But Hawley and Zeke and Sits Down got behind their lines and took the fight to those *auld clooties*—demons. Had those damn savages thinkin' there was an army of mountaineers come up behind 'em. Kept 'em busy enough that the rest of us had little fightin' to do, holed up in a cabin as we were. And the three of 'em killed those bastards and left 'em lyin' scattered aboot the forest. What few were left were sent packin' out of that valley as fast as their ponies—the few of them they had left—could carry 'em."

Sublette looked from one to the other, trying to discern if anyone would expose this as a fanciful tale. He saw nothing of the sort. "You're tellin' true now, eh?"

"They sure are," Bill White said. "The Good Lawd strike me dead here and now if we're lyin'. Weren't for those three, the whole lot of us would've been dead, scalped and butchered, the women and children carried off, all our horses and plews gone. Yes, sir, those three saved our bacon sure as I'm standin' here."

No one noticed the annoyance and growing anger on Elson Brooks' face, He was standing a few yards away, having already traded in his plews.

Sublette cast his glance from one to the other of Brooks' men and saw no sign that they were lying. He nodded. "In that case, gentlemen, in honor of you boys riddin' the world of those devilish savages, I believe, though it's against my business nature, that you all are deserving of a pint of my finest whiskey and a pound of tobacco. Come 'round this evenin' to collect."

There were grins all around, but Paddy Murphy said, "Reckon we'd all rather have another quarter of a dollar a pound for our plews."

There was a rumble of agreement.

Sublette's face hardened some. "It wouldn't be wise of you to abuse my good nature, son."

"Had to try," Murphy said with a grin.

Sublette nodded. "Now, let's get back to business."

As the others sold off their plews, Cooper turned and headed for the mountain men's camp. He hadn't gotten far when he froze. He sat there watching Slow Bull coming toward him, leading a mule that pulled a travois loaded with tanned buffalo hides. The Shoshoni stopped a few feet from Cooper.

The latter nodded.

Slow Bull returned it.

"You seem well," Cooper ventured.

"I am well, yes. Winter was mild for us. We had a good winterin' place." He smiled a little, humor in his eyes.

"Wish we had."

"You had a bad time?"

"You could say that. Had us a run-in with a heap of Blackfeet itchin' to raise our hair."

"You're here so you didn't lose to them. You killed many?"

"Yep."

"Good." The warrior paused, then, "And the white devil you saved?"

"Son of a bitch caused us—well me and my woman mostly—a heap of grief. He paid for it, though." He sighed. "But we should've left him to you and your warriors," Cooper added with a rueful shake of the head. "I know that now, and regret that I didn't. And embarrassed you in the doin'."

Slow Bull nodded solemnly.

"You visited Cheyenne Killer's camp?" Cooper asked nervously.

"No. We arrived not long ago, made camp. I take buffalo robes to trade."

"You plan on visitin'?"

The Shoshoni shrugged. "Maybe yes, maybe no."

"And if you do, will you tell about our last meetin'?"

The warrior stared at Cooper for a few moments, then shook his head. "As you say, that devil took a life from us but you gave one back in not harmin' me. We are even. We are Shoshoni brothers."

"Glad to hear it," Cooper said with relief.

"Maybe all not well, though." At Cooper's questioning look, Slow Bull added, "I not tell. But some warriors from my village are visitin' with Cheyenne Killer now. Maybe they will tell of it."

"Damn." A look of despondency crossed his face.

"Maybe bad."

"Good chance of it." He hoped that Slow Bull would say that he would talk to Cheyenne Killer and explain things, but the Shoshoni said nothing. "Well," he finally said with a sigh, "I'm glad you are well. I hope the Great Spirit continues to look favorably on you."

Slow Bull nodded once and moved on. With a sinking feeling, Cooper continued his slow ride back to where he and the others had placed their camp a couple of miles from the trading tents. As he had thought, in the time he had been at the trading tent, the women had raised the lodges used by him and Goes Far; Beaubien and his two wives and their three children; Jacques Dubois and his wife and two children; Brooks and Potts' widow, Morning Song, whom he had taken in; and Bill White and his woman and child.

Cooper wore a forced smile when he arrived and Goes Far greeted him. They took care of his horse and the two mules and let the hobbled animals out to graze.

In the heat, Cooper sat a little away from the small fire in the tipi, appreciating the shade of the lodge and the light breeze that wafted across the interior through the rolled-up sides.

Goes Far handed him a cup of coffee. "No food yet," she said apologetically. "No time. Little pemmican soon."

Cooper nodded and sipped.

Goes Far fought back the urge to question Cooper. She knew something was bothering him but didn't think he would be willing to talk about it, and she was not sure if she should disturb him. She decided it would be better to wait, to give herself time to perhaps judge what was plaguing him.

Some of the other men began arriving in camp, most grumbling about what Sublette had paid for plews this year. As usual, it was not enough, even more so this year, though it was the same as the previous year. Cooper felt the same, though he was beginning to have an awareness that the trade was not as healthy as it had been. There had been talk the past couple of years that beaver was no longer being used for top hats, the way it had been for seemingly forever. Word was that silk was replacing beaver fur as the hat-making material of choice. It was disturbing and worrisome for Cooper. He knew nothing else but trapping. If the end was coming soon, he had no idea of what he would do in life, what he could do to support himself and his wife. He had never given such a thought to this before; the trapping had always been good, the yield both in furs and money more than adequate. But now he was not so sure what the future would hold for him. It was worrying.

He sighed inwardly. Such thoughts and those brought on by his brief chat with Slow Bull left him with a growing melancholy. His one hope was that none of Slow Bull's warriors had said anything to Cheyenne Killer or, if they had, that his Shoshoni father would accept that it had happened because it was the only thing Cooper could have done at the time. He suspected he would not be so fortunate.

He set the cup down and rose. Goes far, who had been sitting nearby mending a spare pair of Cooper's buckskin pants, looked up in question.

"I'm headin' to Cheyenne Killer's," Cooper said flatly. When Goes Far began to rise, he added, "I'll be going alone."

"Why?" she asked, surprised.

"I got business there that don't concern you."

"But I'll not see Pony Woman. She a good friend now."

"You'll get to see her another time."

"But..." she started, then stopped and nodded. "I get horse for you?"

Cooper smiled softly despite his inner turmoil. "No, Sally, I'll go get her. I get back, we'll see to gettin' you some foofaraw."

"I have enough," Goes Far responded, though her eyes glittered a little at the thought of some new geegaws she could show off to the other women.

"Hogwash," he said, trying for a little levity and almost succeeding. "Ain't never enough for what you deserve, woman."

She smiled, stepped up and hugged him, leaning

her cheek against his broad chest. "You good man, Hawley Cooper."

"And you're a good woman, Goes Far." He stroked her hair a few moments then pushed her away. "Now let's get goin'. I'll get you at the village before long."

"You sure you come back?" she asked only a little nervous. She trusted Cooper after their three years together, but there was always a small kernel of worry.

"Of course. You don't think I'd leave all my possibles here if I didn't plan to come back, do you?"

"No. I believe."

He kissed her, turned, and walked out. The gloom and...not really fear, but a feeling of pending loss, of almost doom, returned as he saddled his mare. Then he mounted and turned the horse's head toward where Cheyenne Killer's camp was set several miles down the valley. He ignored the jovial shouts of his fellow trappers, who were gearing up for the wild spree upon which they would soon be embarking.

TWO

HAWLEY COOPER'S sense of unease grew as he rode toward the Shoshoni village. He would be glad to see his Indian family and friends but he was concerned that some of Slow Bull's warriors had told the Shoshonis about Cooper's run-in with them last fall, which might make Cheyenne Killer's band reluctant to see him, if at all. He sensed a coolness among the people.

His concern deepened when his Shoshoni father, Cheyenne Killer, and his best friend among the People, Cuts Throat, were not outside the former's lodge to greet him as usual. Not seeing Pony Woman nearby increased his sadness. He dismounted and handed his horse's reins to a boy of about fourteen. "Don't stray too far with her," Cooper said.

With a sigh, he called for entrance to the tipi. His heart sank when he saw the stony faces of Cheyenne Killer and Cuts Throat and he was offered only a tin mug of coffee instead of a bowl of boiled buffalo or something. He left the cup on the ground where it had been placed.

"Say it, Father," he said quietly. "I figure I know what's comin' but it'd be best if I heard it from you right off."

"How could you treat a fellow Shoshoni like you did?" Cheyenne Killer said through gritted teeth. "To save the life of an evil white man."

"I couldn't find it in my heart to give over a white man to the People no matter what he did. Didn't like it, and after what he did later, I regret it. But it's too late for it now."

"So this evil man walks free?" Cuts Throat said more than asked.

Cooper glanced at him through clouded eyes. "That what you think?"

"What else are we to think?"

"That he has been taken care of as we told Slow Bull we would do."

"Has he?" Cheyenne Killer asked.

"Yes."

"You have his scalp to show?"

"Nope. Others stopped me from takin' it, but we left him alive for the wolves to feast on and shit out. Figured that was just as good."

"Better than lettin' him live," Cheyenne Killer grunted.

Silence grew until Cooper said, "I suspected you'd cast me over as your son, Cheyenne Killer, and I'm sorry it's come true. Don't blame you. I'll miss you and the People. I'll miss you, too, Cuts Throat. You've been as fine a friend as a feller could have."

"But you think more of your white brothers than your Shoshoni ones, eh?" Cuts Throat said.

"Seems that way to you, I reckon. But it ain't true. I just did what I thought was best at the time. Didn't have much time to reflect on it." He shrugged. "Would I have done different at another time? Don't know that. If I'd known what that scum would do later, I would have, yes. Can't change that now either." He rose. "I'm sorry it happened because it cost me the loss of my family and good friend. I'm obliged for all you've done for me since I became one of the People. Farewell."

He left, hoping they would stop him, and he was crestfallen when they did not. With a heavy heart, he rode back to his camp.

———

A SMILE BLOSSOMED on Goes Far's face when she spotted him, then fell when she saw the despondent look on his face.

"What is it?" she asked, worried.

"Nothin' for you to fret over," he said gruffly. He had kept quiet all along about what he suspected would happen with the Shoshonis. "You can go on over to the village and visit with your friends. I'll go spend the next few days here with Elson and the others."

Goes Far's eyes widened in shock and fear. "If you don't want me anymore, tell me. I not try to stop you."

"Who said I did want you no more? I sure didn't. You know I always spend most of rendezvous with the boys."

"Yes. But this time you don't look happy at bein' with them or havin' a spree here."

"I got things on my mind that ain't your concern."

He turned and started to walk away. She grabbed his arm. "I'm your woman. You treat me good, better than most White men treat their women. I do things for you. Many things. I'm happy to do them. But now you treat me bad, like other men do to their women. I..."

"Like I said, it ain't your concern." He shook her hand off. "I'll saddle your pony, then I'll ride with you to your village. You'll be happy to visit your ma. I'll be back to get you there in a week or so, instead of you stayin' here with the other women like usual." He turned and moved off, trying not to think of the hurt he was causing her.

He saddled her horse and they rode in awkward silence. He stopped just short of the village. "I'll be back," he said. "Don't you fret about that." He rode away, forcing himself not to look back. She would, he knew, be crying, or at least trying to hold back the tears, and he did not want to see that. His heart was heavy enough. He felt almost sick at the way he had treated her. After all that she had endured since she had been with him, it was, he knew, cruel to push her away like this. But he could not help it. Losing family and a friend was not something a man took lightly. He had friends among Brooks' group, Brooks himself, Two-Faces Beaubien, Duncan MacTavish, and Bill White, more than the others now that Zeke Potts had gone under, but they were different from Cuts Throat, he thought, though he could not really say why.

Riding along, he thought, *Maybe you need to be off on your own a spell. Bein' around people maybe ain't such a good idea*. Brooks and the rest of the men could celebrate just fine without him. Like as not, once they began roaring around the rendezvous, they wouldn't even realize he wasn't there. This would take some more thought, he decided. He stopped near a large, shady cottonwood and hobbled the mare. He sat with his back against the tree, mind awhirl with all that had happened.

———

HE AWOKE and rubbed the gritty tiredness from his eyes and looked around. A few feet away, Goes Far sat, sewing.

"What're you doin' here?" he asked, mind still a little foggy from the events of the day and the nap.

"Beadin' moccasins," she said, forcing herself to sound pleasant, not as frightened as she was.

"Go back to the village."

"No. I stay. My place is here, with you. You tell me what's wrong."

"I can't do that, Goes Far. It ain't your concern."

"You're not like most white men. You treat me special. I try to be not like Nez Percé woman in some ways, maybe too feisty at times."

"That's a fact," Cooper grumbled.

"So what affects you affects me. Unless you don't want me anymore. And you say that's not true. I believe you."

"Good thing, 'cause it is true. There's just some things I got to work out in my mind."

"I help. One way I'm not like most Nez Percé women, maybe not like white women—are there such things? I never saw one—either, is that I listen. You talk,

I listen. You feel better after. We face things together. Make things good again."

"You know, don't you, woman," he said with a sigh, "that you are a pain in my rump?"

"That is good maybe?" she asked innocently.

"You know damn well what it means, and it ain't good. You've been around me and the others to know that."

"Yes," Goes Far agreed. "But sometimes is good. Make you do things, like talk, when you not want to, but it will help."

"Lord a'mighty you're a damned nuisance." Cooper rested his head back against the tree trunk. Goes Far was wise enough to know to keep quiet. Then, almost as if in a dream, he began to explain. After the years together, she knew much of his relationship with the Shoshonis, but she had not been in Slow Bull's village, so didn't know what had happened, only that there had been bad trouble.

The woman was quiet as he talked, his voice shifting from anger to despair and back again. Until it reached the events of that day, when despair took over his voice completely.

Goes far moved up and sat next to him, resting her head on his shoulder. "You honorable man I think white men say, Hawley Cooper. You do right thing most times. Maybe don't work out sometimes but is right at the time. Your Shoshoni friends are fools to cast you out over such a thing. Slow Bull not hurt. You hurt no one else in village. You give Slow Bull his life. Webster is gone." She shuddered as his name brought back vivid images of the evil that the mountain man had done to her and Cooper as well as others.

"But..."

She placed a finger across his lips. "Shoshonis lose good man when they cast you out. They will be sorry someday. You see."

Cooper was quiet for a while, then let a soft, small smile drift across his face. "A few years ago, when me and El were at odds, you got me to thinkin' that friends shouldn't fight. I told El then that women—and I meant you—were sometimes a lot smarter than we men give 'em credit for. Same goes here. But I'm glad it's just me and you. It'd be embarrassin' for me to admit that you're a smart women in front of the others. They'd think I'd gone soft."

"Then you'd beat 'em into ground," Goes Far said with a small, tinkling laugh.

"Maybe I'd let you do that while I sat and watched." He chuckled. He felt a great burden lifting from him. His melancholy didn't go away, but it was suppressed enough that he could deal with it. He would miss his Shoshoni family and friend for all time, but he could look at it as if they had gone under. Always there in his heart and head and spirit even if not in the flesh. He knew, too, that there would be times for many months when the loss would become almost overwhelming. But he smiled a little when he realized Goes Far would be there to help him deal with such things.

Cooper put an arm around his woman's shoulders. "I think maybe I'll not celebrate so much this time. Maybe spend a little more time with an annoyin', sassy, feisty Nez Percé woman."

"Do I know her?" Goes Far asked brightly.

"A purty little gal I've seen around your village.

She's quiet and not sassy. Her name's Waitin' for Hawley, I think."

Goes far slipped an arm behind his back and squeezed him. "I ain't quiet and I am sassy, but I'm the one, and I not need to wait. Hawley is mine."

"Reckon I am, woman, reckon I am." He smiled as he rested his head back against the tree trunk. "But if you sass me anymore, I'll have to give you a good spanking."

"What is spanking?"

"I throw you over my knee, hike up your dress and slap your naked behind 'til it's red."

Goes Far stared at him in shock for a moment, then smiled. "I am redskin, white men say, so can't do."

"Well, then, I'll make it redder."

"Humph." Then she laughed. "You do, I'll do same to you."

He joined in the laughter. "I reckon you would, woman, yes indeed."

They hugged each other a little tighter.

THREE

THE FIVE OF them were riding sedately along, sweating under the hot sun and the mild hangover each had. There was, they had heard, a small herd of buffalo a few miles from their camp, and they needed fresh meat. They had pulled out of the trees lining the creek, and were more than halfway across the flat toward the same band of cottonwoods and willows where the creek curved around in an oxbow.

Suddenly a fierce pain ripped through Cooper's shoulder and side. A heartbeat later the crack of a rifle tore across the plain. "Damn," he muttered as he saw the half dozen Blackfeet come charging out of the trees.

He swung his horse around and galloped back toward the tree line whence they had left minutes before. The others, hesitating only a second until they realized what was happening did the same.

Cooper jerked to a halt, slid off his mare, kneeled, and fired. "Waugh!" he growled as he saw one of the Blackfeet fall. "How do you like that, boys?" he growled softly.

Then he was back in the saddle and racing on again. The whole thing had taken less than thirty seconds.

Jacques Dubois reeled in his saddle as two arrows appeared in his back, and it seemed as if a rifle ball had plowed into him as well. Two-Faces Beaubien and Duncan MacTavish were nearest and pulled up alongside the older mountain man as they tore along and managed to keep Dubois in his saddle, though he slumped.

Then they were in the thick string of trees. They dismounted, Beaubien carefully easing Dubois down and then laying him on his stomach, "'Old on, Jacques," the half-breed said.

Bill White grabbed the reins to all the horses and led the animals deeper into the trees.

"'Ow are you, 'Awley?" Beaubien asked as he took up a position behind a cottonwood near the edge of the plain.

"Right as rain," Cooper said as he hastily reloaded his rifle.

He fired, as did MacTavish and Beaubien. Two Blackfeet went down, and the others turned to the right and darted into the trees.

"T'ink you can sneak up on us, eh, you devils?" Beaubien said. "*Mais non*! Not if this 'omme 'as anyt'ing to say about it. And 'e does."

All three reloaded quickly.

"You plan to go lookin' for them, Two-Faces?" Cooper asked.

"*Mais oui*. I'm not going to wait 'til they come for us. *Non*, I 'unt them down like the *fils de putes* they are."

"My thoughts too. You ready, Duncan?"

"Aye, lad. I aim to have some Blackfoot hair hangin' from my rifle before another hour passes."

"Good. Bill, you stay behind and watch over Jacques and the horses."

"Why me?" the half-Black mountain man asked, peeved.

"Because you are like ze clumsy moose, crashin' through ze trees," Beaubien said.

"Reckon I got to agree with y'all on that one. You boys just watch yourselves. I'd hate to have to take care of all those demons by myself if they put y'all under."

"Won't happen, lad," MacTavish snapped.

They spread out as they moved forward, quickly at first, then slower as they neared where they thought the enemy had darted among the foliage.

Cooper sweated more heavily even under the cover of the leaves, which made it a bit cooler here, as the pain in his shoulder and his side, where the bullet had exited, began to slice through him. He pushed it out of his mind. He had faced worse pain before. He slung his rifle over his shoulder, wincing at the sharp pain, and cursed in annoyance. The rifle would be useless here in the close confines of the forest. He pulled one of his pistols, the weapon's heft comforting him a little.

Suddenly a gunshot sounded off to his left. It was followed instantaneously by a screech, and then a loud war whoop. Cooper smiled. That was Beaubien's victory cry.

Cooper spotted movement a short way ahead and stopped behind a large cottonwood and waited. He caught sight of a Blackfoot creeping toward where the gunshot and yell had come from. "Not so fast, boy," he muttered. He silently snuck a little closer. He paused, waiting almost patiently, as the warrior disappeared behind a tree and some brush. But moments later he reappeared.

No time like the present, Cooper thought. He brought the pistol up and fired. The ball smashed into the Indian's back, knocking him forward and down. The mountain men slipped up, took the scalp and shoved the bloody trophy into his belt.

Another gunshot came from farther to his left, and he waited anxiously.

A few seconds later, MacTavish's voice rang through the trees, "Damn ye, ye bloody goddamn savage. I'll raise yer hair right off, lad."

Cooper smiled, then fired his other pistol as he spotted a Blackfoot slipping through the trees. The lead ball thudded harmlessly into a cottonwood trunk. Before he could reload either pistol, the warrior was on him, knife in hand. Cooper stumbled backward and landed on his rump, with the Blackfoot almost on top of him., The mountain man struggled to get up but was having trouble with his one arm being almost useless.

The warrior lashed out with the knife twice, but Cooper managed to jerk himself out of the way just enough for the blade to hit dirt instead of his flesh. He was trying to reach his own knife with his good hand but having little luck.

Suddenly a shot rang out, and the warrior slumped on Cooper. The mountain man was trying to push the body off him, when Beaubien showed up and jerked the corpse off.

"About damn time, Two-Faces," Cooper gasped. He

tried to smile but could only grimace as pain shot through his shoulder and side. "Thank you, my friend."

"*De rein, mon ami.*"

"How many more are left?"

"Two, I t'ink."

There was another shot, followed by a shouted "Damn!"

Cooper and Beaubien saw MacTavish running toward the tree line trying to load his pistol as two Blackfeet, mounted on ponies, raced away across the prairie.

"Damn bloody Blackfeet," the Scotsman said as he stopped next to Cooper and Beaubien.

"Hard to believe they attacked so close to the rendezvous. Boys must be mad," Cooper said.

"Never can tell with Blackfeet," MacTavish said. "Ye should know that by now."

Cooper nodded.

They hurried toward where White waited with the fallen Dubois. "We're comin' in," Cooper called as they neared.

White slid his pistol away as his three companions arrived.

"How's Jacques?" Beaubien asked.

"Same as before. Maybe worse. I reckon it won't be long before he goes under."

"Well, we got to try to do something for him," Cooper said. He thought for some seconds, then said, "Bill, ride on to where the Nez Percé are. Tell 'em about this fracas and tell 'em there may be Blackfeet still about if they want to go lookin'."

"You givin' orders now, Hawley?"

"Yep. Plan to argue?"

White grinned, teeth white against his dark face. "Hell no. Just makin' sure."

"Git. Duncan, you..."

"Aye, I know, lad. Head back to the others and let them know."

"Nope. Head on over to where those missionaries are camped near Sublette. One of 'em's a doctor. Whitman, I think his name is. He's the one got that arrowhead out of Bridger's back last year after it'd been there three years or so. Tell him were bringin' in a badly hurt man who needs his ministrations."

"And where'll you and Two-Faces be?"

"Not far behind you. Got to figure out the best way to transport Jacques. And decide how fast to go. One thought is to ride like hell to get there as fast as possible. The other thought is that doin' so will be rough on him and might be worse than goin' slower."

MacTavish nodded. leaped on his horse and darted out of the trees.

"Well, Two-Faces?" Cooper asked when MacTavish had left. "What do you think?"

"I t'ink either way won't do him any good. I t'ink he won't live to make it to ze doctor."

"I think maybe you're right. But we've got to try."

"*Oui.*"

"Think we can hold him upright in his saddle?"

"*Non.*"

"Didn't think so. Lay him across his saddle, then?"

"*Oui.* It won't be dignified, maybe eh, but 'e won't care."

"All right, let's get to it."

They gently lay Dubois face down across his saddle and tied him down. The French Canadian groaned several times. Finished, Cooper said, "Reckon it's time to go."

"What about ze mule?"

"Leave it. I'll come back for it later."

"*Bon*. We go fast now, eh?"

"Reckon so. Maybe a canter, see how he takes it. That'll cover ground pretty fast."

"*Oui. Allons-y*—Let's go."

MACTAVISH AND DR. MARCUS WHITMAN were waiting outside the latter's tent when Copper and Beaubien pulled to a halt on frothing horses.

The two new arrivals gently lifted Dubois from the horse and held him upright as the physician stepped up and swiftly checked him back and front. He looked at the angle and depth of the arrows and the placement of the gunshot wound. He noted the amount of blood covering Dubois' shirt. Then Whitman shook his head. "He is beyond my help, gentlemen. His soul is in the hands of the Good Lord now."

"You sure?" Cooper asked.

"Sadly, yes. The arrows, I am sure, have pierced several vital organs as has the lead ball. I will pray for him when he is laid to rest."

Cooper nodded.

"You, though, could use my medical attention," Whitman said to Cooper.

"I'll be all right."

"Yes, you will—after I've tended to your wounds."

Cooper started to protest, but Beaubien said, "Do

what 'e says, 'Awley. It would be bad if you do not care for them."

"All right, then, get on with it."

The lead ball had gone clean through, so it was just a matter of the doctor cleaning out the wounds, poulticing them and bandaging them. "That should take care of you, Mr. Cooper," the physician said. "Just go easy for a few days."

"Obliged."

With Beaubien, he started to lift Dubois but MacTavish stopped him. "Take yer rest, lad," the Scotsman said.

Cooper nodded, relieved. He didn't feel too bad all in all, but he was weak with the trauma and loss of blood, so he was willing to let MacTavish handle this duty.

He and Beaubien carefully laid Dubois over the saddle again. His groans were fewer and far weaker. Cooper, Beaubien, and MacTavish mounted up, and with the body-bearing horse in tow, rode out.

A hungover Brooks and Paddy Murphy were the only men in camp.

"How is he?" Brooks asked, nodding toward Dubois.

"'Ow does 'e look, El, eh?"

"Not so good, I got to admit."

"Dr. Whitman says he won't be long before he's gone under."

"Reckon ye should put him in his lodge 'til the end comes."

"Don't reckon that'd be good with his woman and kids in there."

"Then what?"

"Don't know. I'll think of something."

"It makes no difference, 'Awley," Beaubien said. He had dismounted and was standing next to the horse carrying Dubois. "'E is gone."

Cooper nodded. "We'll put him behind my lodge under a robe 'til we can get him buried."

"*Oui*." Beaubien yanked the two arrows out of Dubois' back. "'E doesn't need those sticking out of 'im." He tossed them aside.

Goes Far edged tentatively up to Cooper, uncertain if he would want her nearby at such a time. But he smiled.

"You're hurt," she said nervously.

"Ain't so bad. Not even as bad as when me and Sits Down and..." He caught himself, "when we went against the Blackfoot during the winter."

"You not lie?"

"Nope."

"I tend horse?"

"Nah. I'll do so. Just make sure there's some food ready when I'm done."

Heedless of having an audience, she kissed him quickly and then disappeared into her lodge.

Cooper was glad the others took care of Dubois while he was talking to Goes Far. He and the others were tending their horses—Cooper realizing he should have allowed Goes Far to do it seeing as how dealing with the saddle was no easy task with his bandaged wounds—when White returned from talking to the Nez Percé.

"They were excited about the possibility of raisin' hair on the Blackfeet and were on their ponies and on the trail in minutes. How's Jacques?"

Cooper shook his head.

"Damn. He weren't the friendliest feller I ever met, but still, it never shines when one of us gets made wolf bait of by the damn Blackfeet."

THE FUNERAL WAS no big affair. MacTavish rode over and got Whitman, Paddy Murphy was less hungover than Brooks so helped Beaubien dig a grave under a spreading willow. Dubois was wrapped in a Hudson's Bay blanket, lowered into the hole, then covered up after Whitman gave a short invocation.

"WHAT WILL we do about Slow Calf now that Jacques is gone?" Brooks asked as the men sat around a fire that afternoon. He was still bleary-eyed.

The others in the group had drifted back into camp, word having spread of Dubois' demise. They were hungover but eager to get back to their festivities and so shrugged, not caring.

"We'll figure out something," Duncan MacTavish said.

Cooper gave a small smile, while the others nodded and headed back to the festivities.

FOUR

AS MOST OF the men were heading back toward the festivities with eager looks, Bill White looked at Cooper and jerked his head, indicating the latter should meet him behind the former's tent.

Wondering, Cooper did so. "What's up, Bill?"

"Nothin' to be hidden really. Just a word for you from Sits Down, and I'm not sure either if y'all want it known, at least yet."

"You saw him?"

"Yep."

"How is he?"

White grinned widely. "Fat, lazy and as slovenly as ever." He shook his head. "I don't know why, but he seems to want to everyone to think he's the same ol' Sits Down as he's always been."

Cooper nodded, thinking he understood. "He's well, though?"

"Yep. Wants to meet with you. Tomorrow an hour before dusk. At least I think that's what he meant. Had a little trouble understandin' him with all the excitement and commotion goin' on. Anyway, he said that three miles upstream there's a cluster of wind-twisted cedars atop a rough cliff. Says to meet him there, at the bottom."

Cooper nodded. "Obliged, Bill."

"Strikes me as mighty odd that he'd go back to bein' the way he was," White said with a confused frown. "Why would he do that after all he done with y'all and Ze...what the three of y'all did?"

"Ain't sure but I think I know. When I'm certain—if I ever am—I'll let you know."

White grinned widely again. "Well, time for this ol' chil' to do some more celebratin'. You comin' along?"

"Reckon not. Shoulder's painin' me some." He grinned too. "And I need Goes Far's womanly ministrations."

White laughed. "Far better'n downin' a bunch of Lightnin' under the circumstances." He trotted off, heading to where the horses were kept.

Cooper turned and stopped when he found himself facing Elson Brooks almost nose to nose. He took a step back.

"What was that all about, Hawl?" the latter asked.

Cooper's eyes rose. "What was what all about?" he asked suspiciously.

"That secret conference ye just had with Bill."

"Wasn't no secret conference. Just easier to meet here than elsewhere where all the rest of you were jabberin'."

"What were ye two discussin'?"

Cooper's ire started to rise. "I don't reckon that's any of your business, El," he snapped. "But since you're bein' a pain in my ass about it, I'll tell you. He just wanted to tell me that Pale Thunder was askin' about my health," he lied.

"And why would he do that?"

Cooper shrugged. "Reckon he heard about my wounds and such from the fight with the Blackfeet last winter."

"How would he learn that?"

"Dammit, El, what's gotten into you? It ain't like you to be askin' such questions, especially when there ain't no mysterious motive in what me and Bill were discussin' or why a Nez Percé chief I'm close to was askin' about me."

"How would he know you'd been so sorely used by the Blackfeet?" Brooks insisted. "We ain't been here that long."

"Bill rode over there to tell the Nez Percé that there were Blackfeet nearby if they wanted to chase after 'em," Cooper snapped, trying to keep his anger in check. "Doesn't matter anyhow."

"Well, I'm still booshway of this outfit, and it's my right to know what all's goin' on around me."

It took a few moments before Cooper could push aside his anger enough to answer almost civilly. "No, it ain't, El. And you damn well know it. You've been celebratin' since we got here, like usual, so maybe the Lightnin's talkin' for you. But I ain't fond of it."

"I don't give a damn what you're fond of, Cooper."

Cooper's eyes raised in surprise. "What in hell's gotten into you, El? You ain't been the same for the past couple, three months."

"Ain't nothin' got into me. I'm just doin' my duty as captain of our little group."

"You ain't doin' your duty, El, you're bein' a horse's

ass. Now get out of my way and go back to soakin' yourself in Lightnin' like you usually do at rendezvous."

"And ye don't?"

"Usually, yes."

"You're too good all of a sudden to join the rest of us boys in lettin' the wolf loose?"

"Nope. But with this shoulder, I need a night or two to recruit myself enough to join you boys in your little spree."

"I think you're lyin', Cooper."

"I don't give a damn."

"I think ye think yourself some big chief, braggin' about how ye defeated them hordes of Blackfeet mostly by yourself."

Cooper's eyes widened in shock. "Where'd you come up with such a damn fool notion, El? I've never done such a thing, not in the few days we've been here, nor in the time we run across some other mountaineers last month on the trail. It ain't of my nature."

"That ain't what I heard. Folks here, and some of the boys we met on the trail were talkin' about it."

"Don't know who you've been talkin' to, but if they're sayin' such a thing, they're pilin' up buffler dung higher'n a lodge. And you should damn well know it. 'Sides, how would those boys we met on the trail know anything at all about that fight?"

"Don't matter. I'm thinkin' you're the one lyin'."

"I ain't and you can go to the devil."

"You challengin' me?" Brooks demanded, eyes blazing.

"Not right now. El. My shoulder gets better, I'll be happy to knock you on your ass and do a war dance on your face. 'Til then, leave me be." He shoved forward, his good shoulder banging against one of Brooks'.

———

"I SAY BEFORE, you should not fight with friend," Goes Far said as she handed him a bowl of pemmican.

"You heard?"

She nodded.

"I ain't so sure he's a friend anymore," Cooper said with a sigh. "Not the way he's been actin'. He ain't been himself for a while now, like he's blackened his face against me, and it has me perplexed. Confused," he corrected when the woman looked quizzically at him. "But he accused me today of braggin' about the fight we had with the Blackfeet and my part in it."

"You not do, I think."

"Nope. I've crowed about some of my deeds, but that ain't one of 'em. If Zeke hadn't gotten put under and if Sits Down wasn't hidin' his identity as a warrior, I maybe would have. But that ain't the case."

"Maybe just firewater talkin'."

"Could be, but he didn't seem to be that much under the influence just now, and he certainly hasn't been on the last part of our journey here."

"I'll talk to Mornin' Song," Goes Far said. "Maybe she knows reason."

"That'd be..." He stopped when Two-Faces Beaubien called for entrance.

"Come on in, Two-Faces."

"You are right, *mon ami*," the half-breed said as he sat and thankfully accepted the bowl of pemmican from

Goes Far. "Ze ones on ze trail, they could know nothing. Ze ones here? Them neither."

"You heard?"

"Some."

"Damn, does everyone in camp know my
business?"

"*Non, mon ami.*" Beaubien grinned. "Just the inter-
estin' parts." He grew serious. "It is as you say, 'Awley.
'E 'as not been the same lately. And all ze men know it.
I don' know why though. Maybe it is as he said, 'e is
angry because he thinks you are ze 'ero of that big fight,
and not 'im, even though if 'e thinks about it, he will
know you're not that kind of 'omme. And if 'e 'as it in
his mind that you are tellin' everyone that, 'e 'as been
thinking bad things about you. Maybe that's it, maybe
not. But something is stuck in 'is craw and it's eatin'
at 'im."

Beaubien was surprised when Goes Far said,
"Maybe more. There is trouble, I think, between him
and Mornin' Song."

The two men raised their eyebrows at her.

"He took her to robes too soon, I think. She misses
her husband and ain't had enough time to grieve. I told
him so, but he not listen."

"But you told her to take to the robes with El."

Goes Far hung her head. "I wrong to do. She was
not ready. But he wanted..."

"I reckon I know what he wanted."

Cooper and Beaubien looked at each other. "Com-
bined with his accusations against me, I reckon this
could be makin' him crazy," the former said.

"*Oui.*"

"She say anything to you about it?" Cooper asked.

"No. But a woman can tell such things about another woman. She's not happy with things."

"But that don't make it sit any easier with me," Cooper said, annoyance creeping into his voice.

"Me neither. *Non.*"

"Any idea on what we should do about it?"

"*Mais non.*" Beaubien sighed. "I t'ink maybe we wait, see if 'e changes. Maybe 'is time 'ere lettin' 'is wolf howl for a spell, will clear 'is mind." If not..." He shrugged.

"Could be, but if he doesn't change, I'll find it mighty hard to ride with him again. I don't like that he might be havin' trouble with Mornin' Song. But that's 'tween those two. Unless he's abusin' her, I ain't about to get between a man and his woman. But I damn sure don't take a shine to him makin' accusations against me and tryin' to sully my name."

"I t'ink you are right about that. If you leave, I go wit' you, eh?"

Cooper nodded. "Reckon that wouldn't put me out none."

SITS DOWN HAD a small fire going and a haunch of deer hanging over the flames when Cooper arrived at the meeting place.

The mountain man hobbled his mare and turned it loose to graze. Then he sat. "Meat done?"

"If you like almost black on outside and near raw inside."

"Sounds about right." He sliced off a hunk of meat onto a piece of bark so he didn't burn his hand, took a bite, and chewed. "Good," he said with a nod. "You might make a Nez Percé woman a good cook someday."

Sits Down laughed. "You funny, Hairy Face."

"So how have you been?" Brooks asked.

"Good."

"You're lookin' like your slovenly old self. I'm surprised after you finished out the winter and part of the trip here as the new you. Why go back to the way you were?"

"The People don't know about what went on while winterin'."

"Didn't nobody say anything? The women maybe? Or I heard Two-Faces stopped by. He didn't say anything?"

"None of the warriors or chiefs believe women. Not when they look at me and see fat, lazy Sits Down. They not want to believe. And Two-Faces, he don't say anything. I think he knows I don't want him to."

"Maybe I'll go tell Pale Thunder when I visit the camp. After all, he is your pa and should know."

"You do and what Blackfeet did to you will be a fun thing compared to what I do to you," the Nez Percé said seriously.

"I don't think you would, Sits Down. But I don't reckon I'll take that chance. Besides, it ain't my place to go tellin' such things when you don't want 'em told."

"Good." Sits Down sliced off a large hunk of meat, shoved it in his mouth, and chewed with a look of pleasure on his face.

Cooper's brow wrinkled in thought, then he said, "Somebody must've said something. Hell, with Zeke not comin' 'round, many of the warriors would've noticed he was missin'. Couldn't help it with the tornado ol' Zeke was. And most would've believed Mornin' Song, and your sister certainly would have said something since she was with Brooks now, at least to her pa."

"Maybe they think she threw his possibles out of lodge and he went away."

"Mornin' Song turnin' out Zeke to join with Elson Brooks?" The foolishness of such a thing was thick in his voice.

Sits Down mouthed another hunk of meat. When he swallowed, he said, "Pale Thunder knows."

"You sure?" Cooper asked, surprised.

"Yes. You are right. Mornin' Song told our father."

"He hasn't told anyone?"

"I don't think so, no one treats me different."

"That'd be like him, I expect."

"Speaking of Mornin' Song. How is she?" Sits Down asked after a few more moments eating.

"She's fine. Sharin' the lodge with Elson, as you know."

"Not enough time for grievin'. I should've said something when he took her to his robes."

"Mayhap. But she needs a man lookin' after her. And a man she can look after. She still misses Zeke. You can see that in her face. But she knows life's gotta go on, so she's makin' do the best she can."

"Brooks treat her good?"

"Far as I can tell. Ain't seen sign otherwise."

"And you? How do you do?"

"Fine as I can be, I reckon."

Sits Down pointed at his bandaged shoulder and grinned. "You not fine unless you're wounded."

Cooper laughed. "Seems like, don't it? But several

Blackfeet paid for it. Again."

After some moments of silence, Cooper said, "You never did say why you went back to bein' the old you in the eyes of the People."

"I think they not believe if anyone tells 'em what I did. Not want to believe. They will think those people are mad, as you say. And if they do believe, then I'm expected to behave different all the time. Be a 'real' warrior, as they would think."

"Don't you want to be a real warrior in their eyes? Have everyone's respect, be well thought of?" He grinned. "Maybe get you a woman."

"Last would be good maybe," Sits Down agreed.

"You need a woman to care for you. Maybe we can find you one who can put up with you bein' someone you ain't, someone like you are now." Another grin. "There's that one ol' gal, Buffler Tail, might make you a good wife."

"She too fat and lazy," Sits Down said with a chuckle.

Cooper burst out laughing. "Sounds like she'd be perfect for you."

"Maybe."

They both ate in silence for a few minutes. Then Cooper said, "I think you should become the new Sits Down—the *real* Sits Down—the best warrior the Nez Percé have ever had. It's a waste of a good fightin' man for you not to be."

"I think on it." The big man sighed. "But is easier this way. No one expects me to do anything. They all laugh and make jokes. Insults roll off back like water off a duck. I live in peace."

"But..."

"And I still do like in old days—fight Blackfeet on own. Maybe follow other warriors sometimes, attack when they leave. Or maybe shoot buffalo, wait 'til night, bring meat into village and leave at someone's lodge. Maybe old woman who has no one to help her. Maybe to one of the chiefs, like my father. Make 'em all wonder where it come from. That's my joke on them. I do before. Will do again."

"You are one strange feller, Sits Down," Cooper said with a laugh. "I think you're foolish to let people make fun of you. I've seen what you can do. I've seen what kind of warrior you are. I've seen what kind of man you are. You deserve respect, deserve to be honored, not treated like a fool."

"Life easier this way." His eyes grew distant for a moment. "Like I say, if I change, people expect things of me that maybe I can't do or want to do. Better to be the fool and do what I want when no one looks."

Cooper shook his head. "Well, if that's where your stick flows, that's your business."

Sits Down nodded. "You keep watch on Morning Song?" he asked solemnly. "Make sure Brooks treats her right."

"I will certainly do so."

"You come get me if he don't."

"No, can't do that, Sits Down. But if he treats her poorly, I'll take care of it. He won't get away with it."

The Nez Percé stared at the mountain man for some moments then nodded. "It is good. I trust you."

"Good thing. You didn't, I'd have to stomp you into the ground."

The huge Indian laughed. "If any scrawny white man could do that, it is you, Hairy Face."

FIVE

TWO DAYS LATER, shoulder and side still bandaged, Cooper joined his friends in their festivities. He was well behind them in imbibing fiery Taos Lightning and in whooping it up in general, so he worked hard for a day or two trying to catch up.

But it was not the same, he realized. The rotgut and deviltry and contests could not replace the hole in his heart left by the loss of Zeke Potts and his abandonment by Cheyenne Killer and Cuts Throat, though he had tried hard to drink away his sadness.

But his attempt to party out his melancholy lasted only a few days. He tossed the remains of half a tin mug of whiskey into a fire, nodding at the brief flareup of flames it caused. He dropped the mug and staggered his way back to his camp.

Goes Far found him vomiting behind their lodge. She waited him out, then helped him back into their lodge, where he collapsed on the robes and almost immediately fell asleep, his breathing stertorous and ragged.

Morning found him bleary-eyed and suffering as he sat sipping coffee and trying to force down some buffalo-flavored broth,

Goes Far refrained from remonstrating him for the most part, not sure if she felt angry at him or sorry for him. But she did let him know that she was not happy that his carousing had started his wounds bleeding again, though just a little.

He finally rose unsteadily and headed for the flap.

"Where you go?" Goes Far demanded. "Back to the others? Drink more? Get sick more?"

"No. Just for a ride, get away for a spell."

"I go?" she asked hopefully.

"I won't be much company."

"I not care."

"Reckon I don't mend havin' you along." He tried to smile and almost accomplished it. "Long as you don't go botherin' me."

"I don't bother you, nope."

Cooper raised an eyebrow at her.

"Well, I can't promise, but I try," she said with a giggle.

They saddled their horses and rode out, crossing the stream and heading out into the open. Goes Far had enough sense to stay quiet, and let Cooper ride out the remains of whiskey shuffling through his veins and to overcome whatever beast besides the hangover was besieging him. They crossed the stream a few miles later, where it curved around, and they stopped. They loosened their saddles, hobbled the horses, and let them out to graze. Cooper kneeled and sucked down what seemed to be a couple gallons of warm water, then plunked down with his back against a cottonwood.

Goes far sat against another tree, facing him. "You go back to join friends again tomorrow?" she asked quietly.

"Don't think so. Things just ain't the same since..."

"I don't like to, but I say again, those Shoshonis who threw you away are fools."

"They may be, but I still miss 'em."

Goes Far nodded. "You have other family now. Me and..." She hesitated, then patted her stomach.

Cooper's head jerked up. and the back of it hit the tree trunk, eliciting a short exclamation. "You're sure?"

"Yes." She was nervous and showed it.

"You all right? Happy?"

"Yes. You?"

Cooper nodded. "If you're all right with it, after what happened, then I'm happy. Ain't no one gonna stop me from becomin' a pa now."

Goes Far smiled, relieved. She had not been sure how Cooper would take the news of her new pregnancy, not after the events of the past winter. She hadn't been sure of how she felt about it herself until she knew for certain that she was indeed with child. Then a feeling of joy had splashed over her, and the horrors of the past winter fled. She did, however, worry about how Cooper would react. And now that that had been resolved, she was happy.

"When will the baby come?"

"Maybe near the end of winter camp, *latiit'áal*— March as you say."

"You'll be all right 'til then? Need extra help or anything?"

"No," Goes Far said with a smile. "Not from you.

This is women's business. I handle. Other women help if I need."

Cooper nodded it and regretted it but the spinning stopped in moments. "Good thing," he said with his first real smile in some days. "I'd make a mess of things."

Goes Far laughed. "Men do in such things, yes. You stay away when the time comes."

"Don't need to tell me that," Cooper said, smile widening as he relaxed. Moments later, his eyes drifted shut and he dozed.

Goes Far watched, a pleased smile on her face.

"SORRY," Cooper said when he awoke and rubbed the sleep from his face. "Was I asleep long?"

Goes Far put aside the beading she was doing. "Not long. Few minutes. You feel better?"

"Some," Cooper agreed with a nod. He figured he should get up and head back to camp but he was mighty reluctant. He did not know what to do with himself if he were avoiding the others during their wildness. He sighed. He would have to face it soon.

Goes Far saw his hesitation. "Maybe we make meat?" she asked. "Maybe buffler not far?"

"Doubt there's any nearby," he said, glad for the reprieve. "Not with all the people who've been here two weeks or more already, but I reckon it won't hurt to go lookin' for a spell."

They cinched up the saddles, mounted, and were almost out of the cover of the trees when Cooper stopped. "Wait!" he ordered.

"Trouble?" Goes Far asked, voice worried.

"Could be, but not if I can avoid it."

The woman moved up and stopped her pony next to his mare. "Bad Indians?"

"Crows. Never can trust 'em."

"Crows are the ones who..."

"Yes," Cooper snapped.

"I sorry. I only meant..."

"I know. It's all right. Just hush now." He slid his Dickert out of the loop behind his saddle horn and held it muzzle skyward, curved butt on his thigh. And waited. He watched as three Crow warriors rode arrogantly across the prairie heading for the stream, though they would enter the woods a quarter of a mile to the east if they kept on their course. Which they did, much to Cooper's relief.

The mountain man sat there for a few minutes, then shook his head. "Reckon we ought to head back."

"Is not all right?"

"Reckon it is, but there might be some other Crows about. No need to test our medicine. We got enough food?"

"Some pemmican, yes. And jerky. Maybe we go to see Pale Thunder and maybe get meat?" she asked hopefully.

Cooper nodded.

They waited a while longer before moving out in the opposite direction the Crows had gone. A couple hours later they rode into the Nez Percé village a few miles from their own camp. They let others tend their animals, then Goes Far went to spend time with her mother and sister; Cooper went and paid his respects to Pale Thunder. With the day's temperature beginning to fade a little, they sat outside the war chief's lodge.

Cooper gratefully accepted the gourd bowl of broth with small chunks of buffalo floating in it, realizing he was ravenous.

"Why aren't you with friends raisin' hell?" Pale Thunder asked while Cooper ate.

"Ain't much joy in it nowadays, I found," the mountain man answered with a shrug.

"You fight with friends?"

"No. It's just that I..." He shrugged again. "It ain't your concern, Thunder."

The Nez Percé nodded. "Not my concern, yes. But I am your friend too, yes?" When Cooper nodded, he added, "Friends listen, maybe can help when a friend is troubled. And you seem much troubled, Hawley."

"Reckon I am," he said sourly, "but I doubt talkin' about it'll do any good. It's my problem to wrestle with."

Pale Thunder nodded again. "Dark comes soon. You stay night here, you and Goes Far?"

"I don't think that'd be..." He paused, thinking. "Yes, Thunder, I believe we will."

"Good." Pale Thunder was silent for a little bit while Cooper ate, then said, "Tell of big fight with Blackfeet in winter."

Cooper stopped with a spoonful of stew halfway to his mouth. He was about to ask how the Nez Percé had heard of it but then realized the mountain men had been at the rendezvous site for a week and with several of the men having Nez Percé wives, some men would've visited and likely said something. He wondered, though, why no one had said anything about Sits Down. "Ain't much to tell," he finally offered lamely.

"I think you not tell the truth," Pale Thunder said, casting a baleful eye on Cooper.

"We were in a big valley mindin' our own business when a passel of Bug's Boys come ridin' in half froze for hair. We killed a heap and sent the others packin'."

"That many Blackfeet against a dozen mountain men maybe?" Pale Thunder asked skeptically.

Cooper put down the bowl and swiped a shirtsleeve across his mouth. "You got something to say, Thunder, spit it out."

"Most warriors like to boast of victories."

"I ain't like most, I guess. So, like I said, Thunder, you got something to say, say it."

"There is more you not say. You..."

Cooper rose, cutting off the Indian's words. "I'm obliged for your hospitality, Thunder. I reckon, though, that it's best me and Goes Far head back to our own camp 'stead of spendin' the night here."

"Sit, my friend." It was a request, not an order.

Cooper hesitated, then sat back down.

"Tell me," Pale Thunder said after a few moments, "how you and...others defeated Blackfeet."

"We saw the Blackfeet comin' and hunkered down in the cabins we built. They..."

"That not true, Hawley." He saw Cooper's face darken with anger. He took a deep breath, then said, "You and my daughter's husband and one other defeated the Blackfeet, just you three."

"Where'd you hear that?"

"Daughter tells me."

"Then you know who the third person was."

"She tell me. I want you to say to see if she tells truth. I want to hear it from warrior."

Cooper hesitated, then, "He does not want to be seen by the People as other than he has been. So I don't need to name him."

Pale Thunder nodded. "I am only one who knows among the People. As his father, I not tell unless I have to. Tell me of fight."

Once more Cooper hesitated, then he shrugged. He could see no harm in describing the battle, though it could lead Pale Thunder to change his mind about not saying anything. "Sittin' out in the open ain't the best idea for what we're discussin'," he said.

Pale Thunder nodded and rose, "Come, we go in lodge."

Inside, they sat. Pale Thunder spoke briefly to his three wives, one of whom served the two men coffee, then all three left. "Squaws maybe don't pay much heed to warriors most times. But at others...no need to take chance. Now, tell me of fight."

SIX

"AIN'T MUCH TO SAY, really. Heaps of Blackfeet come down into the valley where we were winterin'. Outnumbered us four, maybe five, to one. Things didn't look good. Your son said he knew a way to get up the mountain, around, then down behind the Blackfeet. Him and me and Zeke went that way and got there a little before dark. We figured Bug's Boys were plannin' to attack the cabin where everyone else was just before dark. We attacked stealthily from behind, kept 'em too busy tryin' to fight the army they thought was behind 'em to attack the cabin." Cooper shrugged. "That's about it."

"More to it, I think."

"Well, it weren't a fun time like rendezvous, I can tell you."

"How did Zeke die?"

"Took a Blackfoot arrow in the throat," Cooper said, fighting back a wave of anger mixed with loss.

"He was scalped?"

"Nope. I made sure of that."

"He was taken care of properly?"

"Yep. Made sure of that, too."

"You?"

"Took an arrow in the leg, but that wasn't so bad. Got thumped pretty well, though. Seems like every Blackfoot in the mountains managed to count coup on me with some sort of weapon. But I was all right in a couple weeks."

"And Sits Down? How did he acquit himself?"

"Best damn warrior I ever seen of any tribe. It was like there were a dozen warriors instead of just him. Saved my bacon several times. Did the same with Zeke too. Weren't for him, me, Zeke and all the other men would've been made wolf bait of, had our hair lifted, and all the women, children, and horses took. You had a dozen just like him, you could wipe the Blackfeet off the land entirely."

"He does not say this. Acts like always."

"I asked him about that. He says he wants it that way." Cooper hesitated. "There was more to him before than folks knew."

"Oh?"

"He told me an uncle taught him how to fight, how to make bow, arrows, how to be a warrior. He said he would follow your other warriors and attack Blackfeet when the others had moved on. Sometimes went off on his own to fight Blackfeet."

Pale Thunder offered a rueful smile. "We wondered where he went on those times. Each time, we thought he left us forever, but he kept coming back. I was ashamed of my son."

Cooper nodded. "He wants to keep his life the way it was."

"But we can use..."

"He knows that. I figure that if the Blackfeet ever came against the village, he would show what he can do. But I reckon he's still hurtin' inside from the ridicule he took as a boy, and he deserves to be left to his own ways."

Cooper watched Pale Thunder mull that over for some moments, then said, "I got a heap of respect for Sits Down, and I think he respects me. If he learns that I told you all this—though he's sure you know already— he'd like as not consider it a betrayal, even if you did know. And that"—he paused for a long, deep breath— "would cost me the loss of a...another...friend."

"You won't betray him. I won't either. We smoke on it."

Cooper nodded.

As they puffed away, Pale Thunder said, "You say you maybe lose another friend. You put Zeke to rest already." At Cooper's grimace, he asked, "You lost one besides him?"

Cooper hesitated. then nodded. "Lost a father and sister too."

"Killed by Blackfeet?"

"No. They just cast me out of their lives."

"Your family sends you away? Would be wrong for Nez Percé. Maybe not so for white families?"

"Not white. Shoshoni." At Pale Thunder's surprised look, he smiled wanly. "A white trapper I hired on with some years ago, and I had a fallin' out, I reckon you could say. He thumped me on the head, stole all my possibles and left me in the dead of winter with nothin'."

"Bad man, that one."

"Yep, that he was. I wandered 'round for a spell just tryin' to keep alive. I was fightin' off a pack of wolves when I went down, thinkin' I was gone under. But I woke up in a Shoshoni lodge. Cheyenne Killer, who became my father, had saved me. His daughter, Pony Woman, cared for me. He adopted me. I married a gal named Black Moon Woman; Pony Woman married a feller named Cuts Throat, who became my friend."

"And those are the ones who throw you away?"

Cooper nodded.

"Why? You good man, Hawley."

"I ain't so sure about that. They did it because of a decision I made that, lookin' back on, was foolish. But I thought it right at the time, not havin' any time to think on it then."

"What you do?"

"Took a war chief of another band of Shoshonis hostage..." He smiled and explained what a hostage was, then continued, "One of our men had killed a girl, and some warriors were fixin' to kill him. I couldn't let them do that even as much as I hated the feller. Considerin' what happened some months later, I should've let the Shoshoni's have him. But I didn't."

"You killed this chief?"

Cooper's head jerked up in surprise. "No. Wasn't no need to. I didn't want to either. Just wanted to get me and the rest of the boys out of that village alive. After a couple hours' ride, I let him go."

"And he told your family of this?"

"I saw him the other day. He says he didn't, and I believe him. But other warriors likely did so."

The two men fell silent, puffing their pipes, sipping a little coffee.

Finally, Pale Thunder said quietly, tentatively, "None will replace Shoshoni family, even though they were wrong. But you have new family." When Cooper looked quizzically at him, he added. "You have Nez Percé wife. I say before, I am friend, but maybe I be more. Maybe I be your Nez Percé father. And Sits Down is friend, even if he won't show it most times."

Cooper sat, his mind awhirl. He loved Goes Far and was glad she was his wife. But he had never considered other Nez Percé as family even though he had always enjoyed talking with Pale Thunder and he had come to like, even admire, Sits Down. The idea of those Nez Percé being his family was a strange thought, though as he pondered it, he could not figure out why that would be.

"Like I say, we not replace Shoshoni family, but maybe we help ease loss? You find joy in new?"

Cooper considered that some more. Goes Far had just said he had a new family, with her and their anticipated child. Adding a father and a friend would make his new family complete, he thought. He nodded slowly. "Never thought of it, but it makes sense. Be different from Cheyenne Killer and Cuts Throat, but that don't mean it can't be a pleasin' thing."

"Always good to have family and friends," Pale Thunder said.

Cooper smiled wanly again. "Ol' Zeke said a similar thing to me a few years ago, not long after we first met."

"Zeke was wild but had good heart and was wise beyond years."

"All true." He worked the idea around in his mind and could see no fault with it really. It would not change the ways things were, at least not substantially.

And, it was true that it would not replace his loss, but it might lessen the pain of that loss somewhat. He nodded. "You might regret havin' such a feller as me as your son," he grunted.

"Other son is trouble. New white one won't make worse for me." The Nez Percé laughed.

"Well, seein' as how we're now family," Cooper said after some hesitation, "I reckon you got a right to know. Our family will be growin'. Goes Far is with child."

Pale Thunder's eyes lit up. "That is good. Maybe have son. The People need warriors."

"Well, it might be a girl baby, and either way, it'd be half white."

"No matter. Baby will be Nez Percé." Pale Thunder sounded definite.

Cooper decided it was not worth arguing over, at least not yet. He rose. "I best go get Goes Far and try to figure out where we're gonna spend the night."

"You stay here."

"You sure? Might get crowded what with you, your three wives, and that youngest daughter of yours."

"With family not too crowded," Pale Thunder said with a grin.

"Don't you go gettin' carried away with this family thing, Thunder. It don't become you."

"You speak true, Hawley. But to have new son and daughter is good for an old man like me."

"You ain't that old."

"Old enough."

Cooper's melancholy lifted a trifle, and he managed a smile. "Reckon you may be right, old man. I think I hear your bones creakin' every time you move."

"You hurt old man's feelin's."

Cooper laughed. "Doubt it, you crusty ol' buzzard." He paused. "You got enough meat to feed everyone?"

"Yes. Some of us found buff'lo not far. Bring back much meat for all."

"Good. Well, I'll go fetch Goes Far, though it might be a little while before we're here. She and I need to do some talkin'."

"White man talks too much to women." But Pale Thunder grinned.

COOPER FOUND GOES FAR STILL WORKING on scraping a buffalo hide with her mother and other women outside her mother's lodge. He had worried for some time about how Bright Eyes would keep her lodge after her husband, Hawk Flies, had died at the hands of the Blackfeet in Pierre's Hole. But some warriors, respecting Hawk Flies, had made sure she was fed and had shelter and skins for clothing and other necessities. More than a year ago, she had married Bull Head, a noted warrior among the People.

"We go?" Goes Far asked sadly.

"No, we'll stay the night here."

"You stay in my lodge?" her mother asked.

Cooper shook his head. "Nope, we'll be stayin' with Pale Thunder."

Bright Eyes looked disappointed but nodded.

"We go there now?"

"Soon. First you and me talk."

Goes Far looked surprised and a little worried. Cooper saw it. "No need to fret, woman. I have news. I'm thinkin' maybe good news."

The woman smiled and rose, wiping her hands on a piece of old cloth. They strolled to a grassy spot along the stream, where the water ran, cool and slow.

They sat next to each other and Goes Far waited patiently as Cooper hesitated. Finally he said, "I wound up tellin' Pale Thunder about the Shoshonis," he started. "Didn't mean to, but he was askin' about some things, and I decided it best to talk to him. So I did."

"And he say...?"

"He was sympathetic that I had lost a family. But then he said mostly the same thing you said to me this afternoon—I have a new family."

"You told him I carry your child?"

Cooper shook his head and offered up a small smile. "Not then. He said I have a Nez Percé wife, a good woman." He grinned for real. "I had to tell him that you were no such thing. That you were a naggin', foofaraw-desirin' squaw with a sharp tongue and a poor disposition."

Goes Far laughed. "It's true."

"If it was, you'd not be my woman."

"I know."

"Anyway, he said I have a Nez Percé wife, a Nez Percé friend who would be like a father..."

"Pale Thunder?"

"Yep. And a good Nez Percé friend."

The woman looked puzzled for a moment, then nodded. "Sits Down."

"Yep. Then I told him you were with child."

"All makes good family."

"Reckon so." Sadness drifted across his face, but he fought to shed it. "'Course, I won't forget my Shoshoni family, nor will the pain of their loss go away, but a new Nez Percé family will be a good thing."

"Yes, it is a good thing." he rested her cheek against his shoulder. "I say before, Shoshonis are fools. Nez Percé make better family."

Cooper thought that over for some moments, then said softly, "That might be, Sally, that just might be."

They sat for a little longer before Cooper rose, tugging Goes Far up with him. "We best hurry," he said with a grin. "Pale Thunder says he has fresh meat, and I don't want those naggin' wives of his to eat it all."

Goes Far giggled.

SEVEN

FOR THE FIRST time in a number of years, Hawley Cooper was not hungover as he rode out of the rendezvous, unlike all the others in his group. He watched with a mixture of humor and sadness. It was amusing to see the suffering of his friends, knowing with embarrassment that until today he had been in the same wretched shape as the others at such times. But there was sadness, too. While he did not miss the roiling stomach and pounding head that came with a hangover, he did miss the camaraderie. For some reason, he did not feel as close to these men as he had over the years they had traveled, trapped, and fought alongside each other. Elson Brooks was part of the cause.

Cooper could not fathom why the leader of the group had been testy toward Cooper for the past month and a half or two months.

But he also missed Zeke Potts. The younger mountain man had been his boon companion and usual trapping partner since they had joined up five, maybe six years ago. Cooper was still amazed that the two had become such close friends, considering the way they had met.

It was Potts' first season in the mountains and Brooks had brought his band of free trappers into a winter encampment of a large group of Rocky Mountain Company men. Cooper had met Brooks before and had even been invited to join the group but had declined. Taking an unwelcome though necessary break from his search for the Crows who had killed his Shoshoni wife, Black Moon Woman, he also was at the same wintering spot, though by himself. While there, Potts had conspired with a man with whom Cooper had had a feud. They wrecked his small, sparse camp and stole his animals. Cooper found out that Potts was responsible to a large degree and aimed to kill the young man for it. But Brooks had intervened. Even though Brooks' men were free trappers and owned all the plews they trapped, Brooks, who had been elected captain of the group, gave Potts' furs to Cooper. Cooper had tracked down the actual thief, killed him, and recovered his animals. Potts spent the next year or so trying to make up for his perfidy. Along the way, they became close friends, much to Cooper's surprise, though it seemed like a natural course of events when he thought about it, considering that Potts helped him dispatch the Crows who had killed Black Moon.

Cooper shook his head now, in sadness as he usually did when thinking of Potts, who had died during a hellacious battle with the Blackfeet this past winter.

Herding the huge remuda of horses and mules with the help of Two-Faces Beaubien's wives, Dancing Water, a Nez Percé, and Little Fox, a Flathead, Cooper looked over the group through the haze of dust kicked up by the animals. Some, like Beaubien, Duncan MacTavish, Bill White, Paddy Murphy, Alistair Wentworth, and Brooks—were old-timers with the group and had become good friends of Cooper's, though not as close as Potts. A few others, who had been enemies not so long ago, like Dan Anderson and Dave Wheeler, could not be considered friends, as animosity lingered. He barely knew the three new men who had joined the group at rendezvous—Colin Leary, Angus Farley, and Sam Berryman.

As usual, the group made little progress this day, and after a few hours called for a stop. Aided by still-suffering Bill White and Dan Anderson, Cooper and the two women got the animals hooked up to several hastily thrown-up picket lines.

They had started the day riding off to the side of the band of Nez Percé that had been at rendezvous, but the Indians kept moving on when the mountain men and their families stopped.

"Can't help but wish we'd kept on with the People," Cooper said as he plunked himself on a log and watched as Goes Far cut him off a piece of deer that Beaubien had jumped the day before and brought it to him. He nodded his thanks. "Feels queersome even though we've not done so every year."

"You not suffering like others, so would like to keep going." She took some meat for herself and sat next to him. "Every other year, you are like those." She nodded toward Brooks and the others.

"Reckon that's it. It, too, feels queersome."

They ate in silence for a bit before Cooper asked, "How's Mornin' Song doin'?"

Goes Far hesitated, then said, "All right."

"I don't think you're tellin' me the truth. Elson treatin' her well?"

"I think so."

"You don't sound so sure."

"She misses the one who was her husband much."

"Makes sense. They were together a long time, and she ain't really had enough time to grieve properly. That why she seems so melancholy?"

"Yes."

"Not because Elson mistreats her?"

Goes Far hesitated. "He treated her all right I think."

"She went to his lodge because she needs a man, but she misses her dead husband still."

"I reckon that means she ain't bein' as attentive to him as a wife should be. And that means he's got a reason to be testy. Seems like he got tetchy not long after the time she moved in with him."

Goes Far said nothing. She felt bad about having put Brooks and Morning Song together before the woman was ready. But now it was the way things were and she could not change it. She was fortunate, she knew, in having Cooper as her husband. He treated her well, and so *she* treated *him* well.

THEY PUSHED ON MUCH FASTER the next day. Now that the men had recovered for the most part, Anderson, Murphy, and one of the new men, Angus Farley, had taken over the animal handling, allowing Cooper to ride up near the front, out of the choking dust kicked up by the hooves of more than forty horses and mules. He pulled up alongside Brooks, who was, as usual, leading the way.

"Mornin', El," he said casually.

Brooks looked at him and just grunted what Cooper decided to take as a greeting.

"I do something to earn you enmity, El?" Cooper asked after a few minutes.

"What makes ye think that?" Brooks responded after an equally long spell.

"You ain't exactly acted neighborly toward me these past couple months. I ain't said anything before, but after the other day, I've been wonderin' more and more."

"Just my mind is preoccupied, I guess ye could say." Brooks kicked his horse into a slightly faster motion and moved ahead.

Cooper stopped and sat on his horse, watching Brooks' back with a combination of anger and bafflement.

"T'ings are not good, 'Awley," Two-Faces Beaubien said as he stopped next to Cooper.

"You heard?" Cooper asked, surprised.

Beaubien shook his head. "*Non*. But just watching, it's obvious t'ings ain't right. "

"I think it's because of Mornin' Song."

"Maybe she's not attentive enough? Misses Zeke too much still, maybe. Doesn't act like wife should?"

"That's my thinkin'. And I fear it might be getting' worse."

"Could be. And he's not showing any signs of changing back to the Elson we know." Beaubien paused. "Maybe it is time to leave, eh?" the half-breed said hesitantly.

Cooper looked at him for a few moments, then shook his head. "No, not yet anyway," he said thoughtfully. "I'd like to figure out if that's what's really gnawin' on El's innards and see if it'll change if Mornin' Song gets more attentive. No reason to really think so, but we can hope." He shrugged. "That don't happen after a spell, then it might be time to move on."

"Some of ze other 'ommes, they don' like ze way he's been acting either. 'E just 'asn't been ze same ol' Elson lately."

"That's a fact." Cooper sighed. "Let's let it simmer for a spell, see if things get better."

"*Oui.*"

As Beaubien turned to leave, Cooper said, "And if you and some of the others decide to leave, I'll like as not go with you."

"Good t'ing, *m'sieur,*" the half-breed said with a grin. "We will need a *capitaine.*"

"That ain't me, dammit," Cooper called after a laughing Beaubien.

———

TWO NIGHTS LATER, as the usual group of Brooks, Cooper, Beaubien, MacTavish and White sat around the fire, White said, "We seem to be driftin' northeast, away from the trail we usually take to Nez Percé country, El."

"Yep. Figured we've spent enough time with the Nez Percé, and it'd be a good idea to mosey on a different way, head straight to Blackfoot country where the trappin' is the best."

"Y'all did so without seekin' our opinions?"

"Ye elected me captain. I've been makin' such decisions all along. Can't see any reason to change now. 'Sides, I reckon none of ye would protest."

"Likely would nae have," MacTavish said, "but it would've been better to consult with us lads before just springin' it on us."

Brooks shrugged. "Don't like the way I been doin' things, pick someone else as captain."

"Y'all been pretty tetchy lately, El," White said. "I've noticed that you and Mor..." He clapped his mouth shut when Beaubien shot him a warning look.

Brooks glared for a few moments, then rose and stalked off.

"Damn fool, lad," MacTavish snapped.

"Can't argue with that, Duncan. It's just that I've never seen El like this befo' in all the time we've been ridin' together."

"Neither have the rest of us. Some of us are thinkin' that maybe Mornin' Song's not been attentive enough. She's been mighty gloomy of late. If that's true, mayhap he'll get back to bein' his own grumpy self soon if she changes her way a little."

The others nodded acceptance. After a bit, MacTavish asked, "What about Slow Calf? We said just after Jacques went under that we'd figure out something, She did nae go wi' the People and it seems odd that she has no man now not to head back to their country with them."

"So?" White said.

"So, now that Jacques has gone under, she's got no

one to care for her. I'm some surprised she didn't pack up their two young lads and head north with Red Leggings' band."

"Does seem odd. Maybe in her grief she ain't thinkin' straight."

"Ye know, she did nae think much of Jacques as a husband or a father. He bought her and she had no say in the matter. I don't expect he was carin' for her the way a man should care for a woman in the robes. Maybe other ways too."

"'E also said at least two times," Beaubien threw in, "that 'e would rather save 'is own 'air than that of his woman and children. I'm not sayin' 'e was a bad fellow. Maybe it was just 'is age. 'E was not a young man anymore."

There was silence as the men puffed on their pipes and sipped coffee, then Cooper asked, "Why don't you take 'em in, Duncan?"

"Me? Why would I...?"

"You've given her some favorable looks at times, I've seen."

"I..."

"And since you're an honorable man..."

"'Onorable?" Beaubien said with a laugh, "'e doesn't know what ze word means. I t'ink 'e t'inks it means we should kneel before 'is *magnifique* self."

The others joined in.

"'Tis true, my *caraid*—friend. Ye should all do so. I am from royal blood."

The laughter grew.

"Royal my ass, ya Scottish bumpkin," Cooper chuckled. "You're from the slums of Glasgow."

"Well, 'tis true, but I was king of that slum."

The laughter lasted a few minutes. Finally Cooper said soberly, "Like I was sayin', I've seen you givin' that gal some favorable looks." He held up his hand to forestall any protest. "Also as I was sayin', since you're an honorable man, you've never done anything untoward about her. I've also seen her givin' you some encouragin' looks, as if she were wishin' she could be with you and was sad because she was stuck with that old fart."

"She might have," MacTavish said almost defensively.

"If she had no interest in another man here, she would have left off with her people and found herself a warrior as a husband. Instead, she's stuck with us, and I've seen her lookin' at you and it seems when she did so, she had a yearnin' look in her eyes."

"Don't she need time for grievin'?"

"Reckon there wasn't much real affection in that union, so I doubt she'll do much grievin', if any at all."

"All ye boys think the same?" MacTavish asked after a few moments' thought.

"*Bien sûr*—of course," Beaubien said as the others nodded in agreement.

MacTavish looked over to where Slow Calf sat talking with Goes Far. A smile spread across his weather-beaten face.

"Y'all best be sure, though, Duncan," White said. "She comes with a pair of young'uns."

"A couple wee *bairn* would make for a good family, I think," MacTavish said solemnly.

EIGHT

WITH SUMMER still laying its hand heavily on the land, there was no trapping to speak of, so the men moved quickly but without rushing.

A week out from rendezvous, Cooper and Beaubien rode up alongside Brooks, one to each side. "Need to start t'inking of making meat, El," the latter said.

"You're right, Two-Faces, and I've been thinkin' on it."

"And?" Cooper asked.

Brooks ignored him. "Ye recall that place along the Judith River, Two-Faces?" When Beaubien nodded, he said, "I think that'll do well—if the buffler are still there."

"Far piece to ride before startin' to make meat," Cooper said. Again he was ignored.

"'E is right, El," Beaubien said, trying to smooth things over. "Maybe better near Antelope Creek or another place near ze Musselshell."

"I still think up on the Judith'll be better, but the

Musselshell's along the way, so we can see if there's enough buffalo there."

"*Bon*."

"Either way, I'll be ready," Cooper said, agitated at being ignored.

Brooks nodded diffidently, then said, "Angus'll help ye with the shootin', then ye and he can join in the butcherin'."

"I don't need..." Cooper shook his head at Brooks, turned his horse and rode off a little way.

A few minutes later, Beaubien rode up alongside him.

They rode in silence for a bit before Cooper said, "I'm thinkin' more and more of movin' on, Two-Faces. I know I said a few days ago that we should keep on for a spell, give it time for things with El to settle down. Now I ain't so sure."

"'E still 'as 'is 'eart blackened against you, 'Awley."

"That's why I'm considerin' goin' my own way."

"Now I ask you to stay longer, 'Awley. Maybe once we start makin' meat, or at least when we start trappin', he'll come 'round and be his old self again."

"Gonna be tough. I ain't used to takin' such abuse from him or anyone else."

"No man should, especially one who 'as done so much for me and the rest of us."

Cooper shrugged. "I ain't done nothin' more than anyone else here would've done if called upon."

"That is not true, *mon ami*."

"Don't matter. It just ain't like him. We've been friends, him and I, since I joined up with you boys, and he's always treated me with respect and friendship. But where he came up with this idea about me, especially since we never saw anyone but that one group of fellers, and we didn't spend enough time with 'em for me to do much braggin' even if I was of a mind to."

"True. I t'ink 'e did too much t'inking on ze ride to rendezvous and worried that it was you, not 'im, who pulled our asses out of the pits of 'ell we were facin', and it began to eat at 'im. 'E is used to being ze leader, 'aving men follow 'im, instead of looking to someone else, especially when he made you 'is second in command. I t'ink maybe he is worried that you are becomin' ze leader instead of 'im."

"I got no such thoughts."

"I know that. But maybe 'e thinks different. Maybe 'e feels like 'e is losing power. He t'inks that, maybe, on our trip to rendezvous. Then, when we get there, 'e 'ad it fixed in 'is mind that you were crowin' about what you did."

"I never did such a thing, and he ought to know it. I spent the first few days with Pale Thunder and the other Nez Percé or with Goes Far. Wasn't no one to brag to 'cept maybe Pale Thunder, and all I told him was that we had a big battle with the Blackfeet. Well, I told him that me and Zeke and Sits Down got behind the enemy and caused 'em some trouble., But I didn't give myself a great role in it. Just that me and the other two caused them damned Bug's Boys sufferin'. I gave Sits Down the biggest part in it, which he deserved."

"You told Pale Thunder about Sits Down?" Beaubien asked in surprise.

"He already knew. He just wanted me to tell him it was true."

"So 'ow is Sits Down takin' 'is newfound status as a big warrior?"

"He ain't. He's gone back to bein' his old self." Seeing Beaubien's look of surprise, he added, "Sits Down wants it that way. He explained it to me, but it don't make sense to me." He shrugged. "But if that's where his stick floats, I ain't about to argue. And I ain't about to give him grief about it, like El's doin' with me."

"I t'ink 'is pride tells 'im 'e should have been the one to do what you and ze others did, and now he is feelin' low. I t'ink 'e t'inks the men don't respect him as much anymore."

"Doesn't seem to me to be the case. You ain't given him a hard time. Neither have the other boys. And he seems to favor those new fellers considerably, so he's got some support."

It seems that way, *oui*. But like I say, give it time, maybe making meat and trapping will restore 'is feeling's toward 'imself."

"You were the one ready to cut out just the other day."

"*Oui*," the half-breed said with a grin. "But you make sense in telling me to stay. Now I do ze same for you."

FIVE DAYS LATER, they made camp in a pleasant, grassy hill-surrounded valley with a decent-sized herd of buffalo. There was a stand of trees at the base of one of the hills and other trees scattered over the hills. A stream rushed through the welcoming valley nearby.

"Reckon this is a good place to start makin' meat," Brooks said, as if everyone didn't know.

The next morning, Cooper and Angus Farley headed out to make a stand. As usual, the others followed and took seats on the grass some yards behind the hunters to watch.

Cooper stretched out and sucked in a deep breath. This was the first time in several years he was without Zeke Potts by his side in this situation. Instead, he was lying next to a man he barely knew and didn't particularly like. He shoved the annoyance out of his mind and made sure powder, balls, and caps were handy. With a deep breath, he took aim. Just as he pulled the trigger, Farley coughed. Cooper's shot went wide.

"Reckon you ain't as good a shot as you like to pretend," Farley said in a scoffing voice.

While Cooper fought back his rage, Beaubien stalked up and slammed a foot down on the new man's neck, shoving his face into the short grass. "Do not do that again, m'sieur."

"Do what?" Farley asked, trying to keep his mouth and nose out of the dirt under the grass, which was difficult with Beaubien's foot pressing down on his neck.

"M'sieur Coopair is ze best shot 'ere, and 'e don't miss unless some damn fool 'causes a disruption just as 'e fires."

"I had to cough."

"If you are sick, *mon ami*, you had perhaps go back to ze camp with ze women."

"I ain't..."

"That's enough, Two-Faces," Brooks said. "A cough is..."

"*Pardonez-moi*, Elson, but 'e did not cough because

'e 'ad to cough. 'E did it to throw 'Awley's aim off. It was a childish t'ing to do."

"I just said..."

"It was also a damn fool t'ing to do, Elson, and you should know it. There's every chance a poor shot could send the 'erd running off, and maybe they not come back for days or we 'ave to chase them. And you, m'sieur," he added, pressing a little harder on Farley's neck. "If you do that again, you will pay for it. I will see to that."

"Shut up, you half-breed idiot," Colin Leary said, rising. He took a step forward only to come face to face with Duncan MacTavish.

"Sit down, lad, and watch yer tongue."

"Or what, old man?" Leary said with a sneer.

MacTavish slammed a forearm across the face, knocking Leary down. "That is what, lad."

"Let him be now, Duncan," Brooks said harshly.

The Scot turned an angry face toward the group's captain. "I dunna ken what ye're thinking these days, El, but it nae sits well with some of us, men who've been your partners for many a year. Ye brought these three shit piles into our group, so ye be responsible for 'em. Put a chain on 'em or they'll not be our partners for long."

"You son of a bitch," Leary said, scrambling up. "I'll..."

He suddenly found himself on his rump again courtesy of another MacTavish forearm. The Scot loomed over him. "Dunna cross me again, lad." He turned, walked a few yards, and retook his seat.

Leary, looking both angry and scared sat up.

"'Awley," Beaubien said, "you may shoot now, m'sieur. I don' t'ink this fellow will disturb you again."

"You don't get your foot off my neck, I'll cause even more of a ruckus."

"Let him up, Two-Faces," Brooks said. When the half-breed stared at him, he added, "That's enough from ye, Angus. Now come on back here and join the rest of us and quietly watch Mr. Cooper do his work."

Beaubien lifted his foot and stepped back.

Farley rose. "Don't you ever touch me again, you damned half-breed." A moment later *he* found himself on his rear in the dirt.

"You 'ad better teach these *jeunes insensés*—foolish youngsters—'ow to behave around their betters." He looked down at Farley. "Go back with ze others, m'sieur, and keep your mouth closed." When the young man did so, his face a mask of anger, Beaubien said, "Proceed, 'Awley."

Cooper downed six cows in less than fifteen minutes. He fired one last time, nicking a bull, sending the herd lumbering off. He rose and gathered up his gear.

"All right, boys, time to go to work." Brooks paused, then, "Good shootin', Hawl. Why don't ye go off and clean your rifle."

Cooper looked at him in surprise, then nodded and wandered off. The other men grabbed mules and headed toward the dead buffalo, following the women.

IT WAS a blood-drenched group of men and women except for Cooper, who sat to their fires that night, but all the meat had been butchered out. It and the hides were waiting to be processed. All were piled in a tent ringed with several fires. And men would stand guard through the night. Raw meat and untanned hides would be an attractive draw for wolves and other scavengers.

"Nice work, Hawley," Brooks said. "Reckon two or three tomorrow ought to be enough."

Cooper nodded.

"What about me?" Farley asked angrily from the fire nearby that he shared with his two friends.

Everyone ignored him.

"I asked what about me? I'm a better shot than that old fart."

"Shut yer hole, lad," MacTavish snapped. "I dunna ken where such lads who have no manners come from. His mam must be a wretched creature."

"Don't you talk about my ma that way, you son of a bitch. I'll..."

"Sit down!" Brooks roared.

A stunned and angry Angus Farley did as he was told. "You and your two friends need to learn some manners. These boys've gone through more dangers and hardships than ye could even imagine in your worst dreams. They deserve your respect because they've earned it. Now watch your manners. And, Duncan, don't refer to his ma like that. She's my sister after all."

"*Tha mise duilich*—I am sorry, El."

Brooks nodded.

The men were quiet, sipping coffee, some of them smoking their pipes. Finally Cooper rose. "Robe time for this chil'." He headed off.

A few minutes later, Brooks stopped in front of the

lean-to Cooper and Goes Far used. Though it was open, as a courtesy Brooks called for entrance.

"Come ahead, El," Cooper said a little tensely. "What can I do for you?"

"Just listen, mostly."

Cooper nodded.

After a deep sigh, Brooks said, "Apologizin' ain't easy..."

"Never is for a prideful man."

"But I got to do so for the way those young fellers behaved today."

"Why'd you bring 'em along anyway?"

"My sister's husband sent Angus and the others out here with a note sayin' the boys—Colin and Sam are cousins of Angus'—were causin' trouble and maybe some time out here gettin' their asses run ragged by beaver and Blackfeet would make decent men out of 'em." Brooks grinned crookedly. "I can't say that any of us are decent men but we ain't troublemakers either. 'Least most of the time. So I reckon we're stuck with 'em now."

"They're gonna get their hair raised by Blackfeet." Cooper paused. "Or one of us."

Brooks nodded. "And I..." He paused. "Well, I best be gettin' on to the robes myself." He rose. "Night, Hawl, Goes Far."

"He had more to say," Goes Far said with Brooks had left.

"I know. Wish I knew what it was."

"Maybe to apologize for way he's been treatin' you."

"Could be, but I doubt it. Reckon whatever it was will come out sooner or later." He smiled at her. "You look tired, Sally."

"I'm all right. Much work, though." She grinned. "You don't do any of the hard work."

He laughed. "Shootin's hard."

"Then you need sleep more than me."

They both laughed as they settled in for the night. Goes Far's blood-caked clothes notwithstanding.

NINE

THEY SPENT MORE than a week at the spot, making jerky and pemmican and tanning the buffalo hides. It was hard, exhausting work, and the men grumbled at their fires in the evening.

But Brooks grew less testy as the days passed, though he still was not his old self. Cooper mostly kept out of Brooks' way, not wanting to cause trouble with his friend, and he was grateful that Brooks left him alone for the most part.

But Brooks was also troubled by the three young relations whom he had brought along. All three, but especially his nephew, Angus Farley, spent far more time not doing work than doing it. Cooper kept his mouth shut mostly, but the other men, especially Beaubien and MacTavish, were not so reticent.

"Those t'ree together do less work than Sits Down did," the half-breed said one night.

"Well," MacTavish added, with a not-so-pleasant laugh, "at least they don't eat nearly so much."

"Y'all need to do somethin' about this, El," Bill White said.

"Ain't much I can really do, I suppose," Brooks said with an annoyed sigh. "Reckon maybe I could hogtie 'em, but then they'd do even less work than they're doin' now."

"They can't do less," MacTavish groused. "They are nae doon any."

"Ah, leave 'em alone, fellers," Paddy Murphy said from a fire nearby that he shared with Alistair Wentworth, Dan Anderson and Dave Wheeler. "Ain't a one of us wasn't a troublemaker when we first got out here."

"Aye, 'tis true, lad," MacTavish said. "But we dinna shirk our duties. These boys want to howl at the moon, they can do it at rendezvous. Otherwise, they can do their share of the work."

"We're free trappers, ain't we?" demanded Sam Berryman, the third of the newcomers, who had been mostly silent in the few weeks they had been with the group.

"Aye. 'Least we are, lad. Canna say the same about ye and yer two friends there."

"Well, we are. And as such, we only need to do what we need to for ourselves."

"That right, boy?" Beaubien snapped. "You may come to regret that."

"Ain't likely. And we sure as hell ain't takin' orders from a half-breed and especially that Black boy there."

The silence from the men at Brooks' fire was sudden and deafening. After several uncomfortable minutes, Cooper said, "Now you listen here, you..."

"I'll handle this, Hawley," Brooks snapped.

Cooper looked at him with raised eyebrows but then nodded.

"Now you listen to me here, boys," Brooks growled, staring from Berryman to Leary to Farley. "If it weren't for this half-breed and this Black boy, as you call 'em, my scalp would've been hangin' from Blackfoot's lodge-pole years ago. These two men—and all the rest of these fellers—have proved themselves in battles that'd have ye boys shittin' in yer britches and callin' for your mamas. I'd trust all these men here—hell, I have many a time—with my life. Now, Angus is kin, but ye and Colin ain't, not really, so I've got no reason to treat ye with any respect or care. Maybe I do with Angus, since he's my sister's boy, but even that ain't a certainty. Now, I'll warn ye three to watch yer manners around these men. *All* of these men."

"Or what, Uncle El," Farley said with a sneer. "You ain't gonna do anything to me or the others. Just think what my ma'd say to you."

"Your ma wouldn't know you've been made wolf bait of. At least not by me. I'll just tell her, if I even ever see her, that you were a goddamn fool and challenged Bug's Boys without knowin' what ye were doin' and ye was put under."

Farley laughed a little. "You' don't scare..." He shut up in a hurry when a tomahawk landed in the log on which he was sitting less than half a foot from his leg.

"Next one takes a hunk of flesh out, lad," MacTavish said. He rose and pulled the tomahawk free and slid it back into his belt before retaking his seat.

The three young men were rather subdued for a few days, but some of their rambunctiousness returned

within a week, a few days after they had left the valley
with mules loaded down with meat.

Brooks, however, seemed to have descended back
into moroseness, worrying some of the others.

"CACHE!" Brooks bellowed as he darted into the
woods.

Cooper and Murphy dashed to help Dave Wheeler
and Dan Anderson push the cavvyard into the trees.
Cooper was glad to see that Goes Far and Beaubien's
two wives were herding the other women and the children toward safety. Over his shoulder he saw Farley,
Leary, and Berryman sitting on horseback, frozen. He
whirled around and charged toward the three young
men. MacTavish raced toward the three from the other
side, Arrows flew by, and though none of the men was
hit, Berryman's horse went down with two arrows in its
chest. The young man managed to get his feet out of the
stirrups so he didn't get trapped under the animal.

MacTavish slapped Farley's and Leary's horses'
rumps, getting the nervous animals moving toward the
trees off the trail. "Come on," Cooper snapped, holding
out his hand. It took a moment before Berryman
grabbed it and with his aid, swung up on the mare
behind Cooper.

They darted into the woods and slammed to a halt.
"Get down," Cooper ordered, elbowing Berryman off
his horse. Farley and Leary almost fell off their animals
and looked around in a daze.

Leaving their rifles in the loop behind their saddle
horns, Cooper and MacTavish slid off their mounts.

The Scot shoved Leary out of the way as a Blackfoot came charging forward knife in hand. The young man fell to the side. MacTavish ducked and blocked a thrust of the Blackfoot's knife and rammed a shoulder into the Indian's chest. The warrior staggered back. MacTavish kicked him in the crotch, grabbed the warrior's knife as the Blackfoot sank to his knees, and thrust the blade deep into the Indian's vitals.

Farley ran behind a tree.

Cooper kicked the legs out from under Berryman as a Blackfoot burst out from behind a tree. Being off balance, Cooper was unable to fully avoid the Indian's charge. The warrior stumbled over Farley but managed to slide a knife across Cooper's side as he fell forward.

Hissing with the sudden sharp pain, Cooper clubbed the back of the Blackfoot's head, sending him to his knees. Cooper grabbed the Indian's hair, yanked his head back, and slit the warrior's throat.

"Slow Calf!" MacTavish suddenly shouted. "And the children!"

"Go," Cooper ordered.

With a nod, the Scot crashed through the trees on foot, his horse and the others having scattered, toward the other side of the trail.

"Get your ass up, boy," Cooper snarled at Berryman, kicking him in the side. "Go join your pals there cowerin' in the bushes and keep quiet. If you don't make noise, maybe Bug's Boys won't see you."

"Where're you goin'?" Leary asked, voice quavering.

"Take care of business." Cooper darted off, eyes wary, watching for Blackfeet as he searched for all their horses, which had bolted at the sudden activity and violence. He quickly found his mare nervously shuffling under a tree not far away. He tied the animal to a huckleberry bush. He found Leary's next, then Farley's. As he stalked quietly through the woods, another Blackfoot popped out from behind a tree, aiming to smash Cooper's head with a stone warclub.

The weapon missed, and Cooper swiftly slammed the sole of a moccasined foot onto the side of the warrior's knee. His leg gave out, and he listed to the side. It was enough for Cooper to avoid a feeble swing of the war club and instead slam the heel of his hand into the man's forehead. Then he proceeded to pound the Indian's face into a mask of bloody mush, punctuating his blows with, "I'm sick of you sons a bitches comin' after me, dammit."

He finally regained control of himself and stood breathing heavily. He scalped the Blackfoot, then wandered off to find the MacTavish's horse. It didn't take too long to do so, and once he had all the animals, he gathered them, mounted the mare, and towed the others to where the three greenhorns still cowered. He smiled a little when he saw a couple puddles of vomit. He dismounted and taking deliberate care to make sure the young men saw him, scalped the other two Blackfeet. Berryman and Farley renewed their vomiting, though it appeared they had nothing left inside them.

"You're hurt," Leary suddenly said, pointing to where blood was drying on Cooper's shirt.

Cooper shrugged. "I've had a heap worse, boy, a heap worse. This ain't but a scratch."

"'Awley!" Beaubien yelled from deep in the woods on the other side of the trail. "Are you all right, *mon ami?*"

"Yep."

"Did ye see Angus and the others?" Brooks called.

"All of 'em are right here, lookin' mighty pasty but all of 'em are alive and unharmed."

"Do ye have my steed, lad?" MacTavish called.

"Yep. I do. Slow Calf and the children all right?"

"Aye. All the other women and *bairn*, too."

"All right, boys," Cooper said to the three young men, "Angus, you and Colin get mounted and head on up the trail a bit to where the others'll be. Sam, kill your horse if it's sufferin' then drag the saddle off and walk on up the trail."

"Carryin' it?"

"Yep."

"Can't I use MacTavish's horse?"

"No."

When everyone finally gathered, Paddy Murphy said, "Camp here, Cap'n, or move on? I don't know this area well, so maybe there ain't a good place to rest up."

"I think we'll press on," Brooks said. "Let the wolves and coyotes have their fill of Blackfeet meat without us disturbin' them or them disturbin' us."

The others nodded their agreement.

"Sam, get yourself another horse. Then ye, Angus, and Colin help Dan and Dave with the horses." He mounted his horse. "Two-Faces, ride on up ahead and see if ye can find us a decent place to bed down for the night."

"*Oui, mon capitaine.*"

"All right, boys, let's move."

Minutes after getting on the move, Goes Far rode up alongside Cooper. "You all right?"

"Yep."

"I heard one of those boys say you were hurt."

"Ain't much. A Blackfoot caught me a little across the side with his knife. Won't be a bother."

"I look."

"Not now. It can wait."

"You can wait. I can't."

He grinned as she rode around to his other side. She lifted up the bottom of his shirt and gave the wound the once over. The blood had already crusted. She let the shirt fall back into place. "You right. Only a scratch. I fix tonight."

The mountain man nodded. He nodded to her stomach. "Are *you* all right?"

"Yes. We saw no danger. Dan and Dave handled horses and mules well, helped soon by Paddy and Alistair. All kept good watch over us and the animals. We safe."

"SO HOW DID Angus and his friends do?" Brooks asked, looking from Cooper to MacTavish. His voice was filled with concern.

"I canna say, El," the Scot said. "I killed one devil, then hurried to help protect the women."

Brooks nodded. "Hawl?"

"Depends on what you expected, El. If you expected 'em to put up a good fight and rid the world of a couple more Blackfeet, well, they didn't do so well. If you expected 'em to hide behind some trees and bushes and puke their guts up, well, they succeeded pretty well."

"They ain't the only ones got sick at the first sight of

bloody death and scalpin'," Brooks said almost defensively.

"That's true, but most of us waited 'til after we took care of the business at hand before we gave way to sickness."

Beaubien, MacTavish, and White murmured acknowledgment.

Brooks nodded somewhat sadly, then sighed. "Well, Lord willin' they take care of business next time."

"I wouldn't count on it, El. They looked mighty squeamish, but I hope I'm wrong. They may be wrong-headed fools, but I'd not like to see them gone under with a Blackfoot lance in 'em. And I'd like it a heap less to have one of us go under from a Blackfoot lance because those boys couldn't stand up to what needed doin'."

Brooks nodded gloomily, but Cooper caught a glint in the man's eye indicating that Brooks still harbored some ill will against him and that his comments about how the three young men had acquitted themselves had made it worse.

TEN

THE THREE YOUNG men were rather subdued for some time. They did not complain about sharing group duties and even helped in the hunting for fresh meat for the group, though one at a time and always accompanied by one of the old-timers. All complained, though rather quietly, at times.

Brooks and the others began teaching the three the ways of the mountains—how to read sign, both of animals and men, what broken twigs might mean, the differences between moccasin tracks left by Blackfeet or Crow or Flathead or the many others, signs that bears were around or that wolves were threatening their food supply, what the flight of birds might mean, and the score of other things that if missed could mean their scalps hanging from a warrior's belt or they could face starving times.

Berryman seemed to take to it all more easily than Farley or Leary, showing interest and even talent.

After a couple of weeks, however, Farley and Leary

began slackening off. More than once, one of the older men had gotten up in the middle of the night to relieve himself and found the former dozing or sitting with his back to a tree, devouring some fresh buffalo or elk that someone else had brought in.

At times, one of the old-timers with the group would complain, telling Brooks he needed to do something about the situation. To which the group's leader would shake his head and say, "Ain't much I can do."

"Cut the son of a bitch loose," White said one evening at their fire, referring to Farley. "Give him his horses, both of which I reckon you paid for, and a mule with enough supplies to last him a couple days.

"Boy'd be dead in days," Brooks snapped.

"Serve him right, I'd say," Paddy Murphy offered. "Bastard ain't no use to any of us."

"Leary ain't much better," Alistair Wentworth threw in. "Probably ought to send him packin', too. Like Paddy said, give 'em a horse and some supplies, and point 'em toward that big adobe place down on the Arkansas."

"Bent's place?" White asked.

"That's the one, yes. It's about the only place those two bloody fools'd be able to make, maybe, without gettin' their hair took by some young buck lookin' for honors."

"Can't do that, boys. He's my kin, my sister's boy as you all know, so I just can't send him out into the wilderness on his own."

"Bein' kin don't give him leave to endanger the rest of us," Murphy said.

"Quiet down, Paddy," Brooks snarled. "The boy can hear you."

"Damn right," Farley hollered. "And I don't take kindly to such talk."

"It don't matter if you take it kindly or not, m'sieur," Beaubien said. "You should listen to what is said 'ere and change ze way you look at ze way t'ings are out 'ere. If you don't, you won't last long."

"I can handle myself, Frenchie."

"That's good because with ze attitude you 'ave, no one 'ere will be looking out for you."

"I don't need no help from the likes of you, you damn half..." He stopped when Berryman whacked him on the arm with his slouch hat.

Farley did not change his ways, nor did Leary, and the other men rebuffed them at every turn they could. Brooks grew more and more morose. It made for a tense camp.

They moved on slowly, starting to set their traps as fall eased its way into the mountains. The first plews were of good enough quality, but soon, they were thick and plush.

As soon as trapping started for real, the men partnered up. The old-timers, for the most part, worked in teams that were used to each other. It looked for a while as if Bill White was going to be on his own until, to everyone's surprise, Sam Berryman approached him one night.

"A word with you, Bill?" When White nodded, Berryman said, "I'm thinkin' that since Elson and Duncan, and Hawley and Two-Faces, Dan and Dave, and Paddy and Al are all partnered up, it seems that you might be the odd man out."

"What's that to y'all?" White said peevishly. He wasn't entirely upset about being on his own hook as far as trapping when he knew there was an odd number of men, but he didn't like having rubbed it in his face.

"Well, I was thinkin'," Berryman said hesitatingly, "that maybe you'd take me on as your partner for trappin'." Seeing everyone's surprised look, he added, "I know I ain't really learned yet what I need to, but I reckon you're as good at trappin' as all the others, so you could teach me."

"Y'all really want to work with a Black boy as one of you called me not so long ago?"

"I'm powerful sorry I said them things about you and Mr. Beaubien. It wasn't right, and I regret havin' said any of it. Y'all don't want to work with a dumb-ass white feller from back in the States, from one that don't favor people of your color, maybe, just say so. Or if you don't want to work with a feller don't know his ass from a hickory tree about trappin', that's fine too."

White stared up at him from his seat on a log for some seconds. "Y'all're serious about this, ain't y'all?"

"Yes, sir."

"Hey, Sam," Farley yelled from his fire, "don't you go callin' that Black boy 'sir.' What'n hell's wrong with you?"

"If you ain't got anything useful to say, Angus, just shut your trap." As Farley began to say something else, Berryman snapped, "I said shut it, Angus." He turned back to White. "Well, Mr. White, what do you say?"

"Y'all sure about this, hoss? Y'all will be takin' a heap of grief from your two friends over there."

"Can't rightly say they're friends. Not anymore, anyway. Might be kin but ain't anything I can do about that."

"You'll heed my words?"

"Yessir."

After a short hesitation, White nodded. "Well, I reckon I can take a risk and let y'all join me."

"Obliged." He turned to head back to his fire.

"You ain't comin' back here, boy," Colin Leary said. "Me and Angus ain't about to have some nigra-lovin' son of a bitch sharin' our fire and food."

Berryman sighed.

"Come join us, Sam," Murphy said. "Be best for you. You stay with those blokes, you'll like as not get lice crawlin' all over you."

THEY LINGERED where they were for a couple of weeks, until the supply of beaver had been exhausted. Most of the men did well.

"How's Sam workin' out, Bill?" Cooper asked one night a week into their stay.

White saw Berrymen's ears perk up and the nearby fire he still shared with Wentworth and Murphy. He grinned. "Best damn trapper I ever saw. 'Cept myself, of course."

"Sounds like booshwa to me," Cooper said.

"Aye, lad. But if he's thinkin' that way, I canna see anything to do but have us a wee contest." MacTavish said.

"You'll lose again," Cooper said with a grin.

MacTavish sucked in a deep breath and let it out slowly, not sure how what he was about to say would be taken. "Now ye dunna have ol' Zeke wit' ye, ye be in trouble, lad. He was the better half of your trappin' duo." He waited with bated breath.

Cooper's jaw tightened and anger and loss flooded over him. Then he sighed. It was, he thought, time to put Zeke Potts to rest. Not to ever forget him, but let him rest in peace, occupying a spot in Cooper's heart but not living in his mind every minute. It was a freeing thought. He grinned. "That's maybe true, you Scottish reprobate, but that degenerate half-breed I'm stuck with'll take up the slack. He was the one kept you in furs the past few years."

"*Mais oui!*" Beaubien said. "We—well, mostly me *bien sûr*—will teach these 'ommes 'ow to be master trappers."

"You're on," White said with a laugh. "Y'all hear that, Sam? We're gonna be rollin' in shiny possibles soon."

"Nae, lad," MacTavish said. "'Tis me and the captain here will be stackin' up the goods." He was not nearly as confident as he sounded. Brooks had been reasonably personable though still morose and given over to snappish comments while the two worked together.

Brooks sat quietly. There was the smallest smile on his face but it seemed more angry and sad than joyful.

It was no surprise that Cooper and Beaubien ended each day with the best catch. The two kept their women busy curing the furs. The others good-naturedly handed over some prize—a bear-claw necklace, a Green River knife, otter-fur hair ties, and other small items.

The first time that payment came due, Berryman was horror stricken. "I got nothin' to put up, Bill," he said, looking almost desperate.

White laughed. "Don't worry about it, hoss. I can cover things. One day maybe y'all will win some bet at rendezvous and share with me. 'Sides, I'll like as not win most of it back from these fellers before long."

Angus Farley and Colin Leary had nothing to wager either, but they did not take part in the gamble. Not that anyone asked them to join in the contest. They did complain, though, loudly and abused Berryman most of all.

"How's it feel to be beholden to a Black boy?" Farley shouted one night. "First time I've ever heard a white man in debt to a nigra."

Berryman had taken it for several days, but this time he rose and stalked to Farley's fire.

"What're you gonna do, boy?" Farley asked with a sneer. "You ain't got the stones to stand up to blackie over there, you ain't got the stones to come against me. Now you just back and sit down at..."

Without warning, Berryman slammed Farley's forehead with the heel of his hand. Farley fell over backward, dazed.

Leary jumped up and charged at Berryman. The latter was caught a little by surprise but managed to duck the fist the former threw at his head. He skipped out of the way.

The two of them stared at each other waiting for the other make a move.

Brooks rose, muttering something about stopping the fight, but both Cooper and Beaubien stepped in front of him. "Sit back down, *Capitaine*," the half-breed said.

"But one of 'em might get hurt."

"And that is suddenly a problem? Others 'ave

fought without you interfering. Like usual, let them test themselves. If it looks like one will be bad hurt, then we step in. But not before, eh."

Brooks stewed for a few moments, then plopped down, anger showing on his face. Berryman and Leary pounded each other, wrestling, kicking and swinging wildly for some minutes before Cooper nodded at Murphy and Wentworth, who rose and got between the two combatants. The young men were too worn out to protest when they pushed Leary down alongside the still-stunned Farley and led Berryman back to their fire.

In the morning, Berryman and Leary were colorful and hobbling around a little; Farley still looked rather dazed, but he and Leary cast angry, hateful eyes on Berryman, who carried himself a little straighter despite the soreness.

Over the next several days, when they were tending their traps, Cooper and Beaubien went back and forth about leaving the group. First one would suggest riding off, the next the other would. But always they decided to give it a little more time. Part of the reason was that Brooks was sometimes morose and testy, at others he was closer to his normal self, though never quite all the way.

Cooper continued to avoid him as much as reasonably possible, though it was difficult when the two shared a fire with the others. But with the others' presence, Brooks could ignore him, which allowed Cooper to manage.

Two weeks later, they pulled out, having emptied the streams of beaver. They rode northeast, moving slowly, trapping as they went in any stream or river that showed beaver sign, heading through Crow land toward the Three Forks area—the heart of Blackfoot country. They were concerned, though not worried. Either the Blackfeet had been tamed by the battle the previous winter or would be seeking vengeance. Either way would not keep the men from prime hunting grounds

ELEVEN

THE FIRST INDICATION they had that Indians were about was a war whoop, a few gunshots, and the sound of almost three dozen horses and a like number of mules galloping away through the trees being pushed by several Crow warriors.

"Dammit to hell," Brooks bellowed as he and the others rolled out of their robes and ran for the horses in a vain effort to stop them from being driven off. Each man halted for a moment to fire a shot. Three slugs connected and Crows fell to the ground dead.

The men spread out but managed to catch only three mules.

"Dammit, who the hell was supposed to be watchin' over the animals, El?" Cooper demanded as they all gathered in the middle of their camp.

"Angus," Brooks said, voice torn between anger and almost despair.

"Kin of yours or not, I'm gonna go kill that son of a bitch," Cooper growled. He reloaded his rifle and stepped off after Angus Farley, who was trying to make himself scarce behind a tree.

Duncan MacTavish fell in alongside him. "I'll help, lad."

"Stop, both of ye. The rest too," Brooks snapped. "We ain't got time for such things now. We'll deal with Angus later. Ye hear me, boys? Right now we've got to try to get those horses back. We don't, we are in a heap of trouble." He glanced at where Farley was trying to make himself invisible.

Cooper glared at him for a few moments, then snapped, "I don't know if those mules have ever been ridden, but they're gonna be ridden now." He grabbed his apishemore and saddle.

"Ye ain't goin' alone," Murphy said. He grabbed his tack.

"I come too," Two-Faces Beaubien proclaimed. "Ze rest, you watch ze camp, eh. Maybe stop them Crows from comin' back and stealin' the plews and maybe your teeth, too, eh."

Cooper nodded. He liked the half-breed, who had had a tough life, caught between two worlds. But he made out the best he could. There was no better tracker in their small company than Two-Faces, and no one as good on a horse.

"Are ye nae gonna stop 'em, lad?" MacTavish asked Brooks.

"Hell, no. If anyone can get those damn horses back it's those three. The rest of ye make sure there're no more of those red devils around. And scalp the ones we got. Might not teach the others a lesson but these boys'll rot here on earth 'stead of goin' to the Happy Huntin' Grounds."

"Too bad Red Leggings and his village weren't around," Bill White said. "Might not've lost them horses if some of his warriors were about." He glanced menacingly at Farley.

"Well, they ain't here." Brooks looked at the three men saddling the mules. "Ye boys need anything?"

"No," Cooper said flatly.

Minutes later the three men rode recalcitrant mules out of the camp.

IT WAS NOT difficult to follow the trail of almost three dozen shod horses, several unshod ponies and more than thirty mules. But the Crows were moving fast and had almost a half-hour head start.

"Why'd they take the mules?" Murphy asked at a time when he and Cooper could ride by side where the trees had thinned out some.

"Mules just came along when the horses bolted, I reckon. They were tied to the picket lines."

The men came upon one mule, then another. They roped 'em and towed them along. In another hour, they had found five. They stopped.

"We don't need these mules with us slowin' us down," Cooper said. "Two-Faces, take 'em back to camp."

"*Mais non*, m'sieur. My 'orses were taken, too, and I will get them back. I stay."

Cooper sat thinking for a few moments, then nodded. "All right, boys, let's hobble 'em, but do it fast. We'll grab 'em on the way back." He grinned grimly. "After we take back the horses."

Within the next hour, they came across most of the other mules that had been taken. They took a few minutes to hobble each one before rushing back onto the trail again.

"Dammit, Hawley, this is takin' a heap of time," Murphy said when they found the sixteenth mule. "We don't need the damn mules. The ones we're ridin' are slow enough that we're fallin' farther and farther behind. Takin' time to deal with the ones we find—even just hobblin' 'em—ain't helpin'. If we don't get the horses back, we ain't goin' nowhere."

"Like hell. We can move on foot if we have to, but we can't do it and each carry a couple packs of plews on our shoulders."

"We can cache the plews and ride the mules."

"Then what do we do when we get to rendezvous? We'd have no plews to trade for horses. And mules ain't likely to bring the same price as horses. The mules may be cantankerous at times, but we need 'em."

"Well, these three seem to be gettin' stubborn, and that don't shine. We'll never catch up to them Crows at this pace."

"They're gettin' stubborn because we're pushin' em harder than they're used to. They don't move as fast as horses and will get willful when pushed too hard I reckon, lookin' out for themselves."

"But those Crows are puttin' more distance between us every second."

"And they're runnin' the horses hard. They'll stop soon, partly to give the horses a rest, but partly because they'll figure since they got all the horses we can't catch up. That's when we will catch up."

They kept up a steady though slow pace and by midafternoon, Cooper thought they were getting close.

"Two-Faces, you go on ahead on foot and see if those bastards are nearby," Cooper said. "Don't cause no trouble though."

"You mean I can't shoot them?" Beaubien said in sarcasm.

"Sorry, Two-Faces. I'm a little testy after all the ridin' on this damn mule."

"*Moi aussi*." The half-breed slipped off into the trees. He was back in what had been a tense fifteen minutes for his two companions.

"They are there, oui. Five of them. Lazing 'round ze fire. Horses tied to a line strung from a few trees. Can't run if we let them be."

"Boys, I think it's time to go get our horses back."

The three tied their mules to trees and began filtering between pines, hoping the animals didn't announce their presence by braying.

But just as the three took their positions, one of the mules let loose with a loud honking bray. The five Crows started moving without even looking up. Three rifle shots brought down a trio of them. The three mountain men burst out of the trees. Beaubien and Murphy headed for one Crow, while Cooper went chasing after the other, who had fled into the forest.

Empty rifle in hand, Cooper went crashing through the brush, leaping over logs and deadwood, closing in on the Crow. He dropped the rifle, pulled a pistol, and fired, to no effect. He dropped that, too, drew his other pistol and fired, but missed again.

"Damn," Cooper muttered through breath that was getting a little ragged. He put on a burst of speed and threw himself at the Crow. They both landed in the dirt, the latter face first. The mountain man landed on the Crow's back. Bending backward, he yanked out his knife, pulled back the Indian's head by his hair and slid the knife blade across the warrior's throat.

"Steal my horses, will you, you son of a bitch? That don't shine, and now you've paid." He sliced off the warrior's scalp, wiped his blade off on the warrior's shirt, then headed back toward the Crow camp, picking up his weapons as he did.

"About time ye got back, hoss," Murphy said. "We were beginnin' to think maybe ye, bein' so old as ye are, had to stop and rest a bit while ye was chasin' that Crow."

"Nah. Just lettin' that ol' chil' think he was gettin' away. I see, though, that it took two of you to bring down that last one here."

"That's because this useless *'omme* needed 'elp," Beaubien said with a laugh.

Cooper grinned and squatted by the fire and reloaded his rifle and two pistols. "Nice for those boys to leave us some supper," he said as he worked.

"Deer is not ze best, but better than some t'ings I eat, eh?" Beaubien said.

The others laughed.

"There's still a heap of daylight left, but these horses have been run hard, and there's a good camp here," Cooper said. "I say we stay right where we are and head back come daybreak."

"Shines with this *'omme*," Beaubien said.

"And me," Murphy added. "I ain't lookin' forward to herdin' these damn horses all the way back to our camp."

"And all the mules."

"Forgot about them. Reckon we should bring in the three we were ridin'. No need to leave the poor critters out there, even as tetchy as they are."

In the morning they left riding their own horses and herding the three mules in with the other steeds and several Crow ponies. Along the way, they picked up the hobbled mules, one here a couple there, until almost all of them had been accounted for. In preparing to leave, they counted only twenty-nine horses but did not know whose animals were missing. They moved slowly, wanting to rest the animals some, and arrived not long before dusk.

They were greeted with great enthusiasm and thanks after which the men sorted out the animals. Wheeler had lost one, as had Bill White and Berryman; Murphy lost two. All quickly laid claim to one of the Crow ponies.

Afterward, they gathered around a central fire.

"Ye boys've elected me your captain," Brooks said unhappily. "And because of that, I should make the decision that needs to be made here. But I reckon this is important enough and involves all of ye—and it's personal—that I figure to put things to a vote. We need to figure out what to do about Angus. If it weren't for Hawley, Two-Faces and Paddy, we'd all be afoot. And that ain't a good thing out here as ye boys know full well."

The men sat in the dirt, surrounding Farley, whose weapons had been removed. Brooks paced before them, looking stricken.

"We got two choices far as I can see," Brooks said, voice offering a glimpse of the turmoil roiling his insides. "We turn him loose on his own hook here and now or we cut him loose when we get to rendezvous."

"There's a third choice," Murphy said. "The obvious one. We shoot the son of a bitch."

There was a rumble of agreement from some of the men.

"We could, yep. But I don't favor that. He's my kin as ye know, so I ain't about to let ye boys make wolf bait out of that young feller." His face had turned hard and his voice harsh.

"Dammit, El," Murphy snapped, "Me and Two-Faces and Hawley went through a heap of trouble to get them animals back. I lost two of 'em. Others lost some too."

"I know that. And it pains me to know Angus is the one responsible. But wasn't a one of ye got put under."

"Ain't my fault," Farley said, voice almost a wail of despair. "Damn Injins snuck up on those horses. Wasn't nothin' I could do."

"If you 'ad been awake, m'sieur," Beaubien said in a tight, angry voice. "We would've 'ad some notice before those savages run off with our animals and we could 've prevented all this trouble maybe."

"And this ain't the first time ye've been found to be nappin' on duty, lad," MacTavish added. "Ye've been warned before."

Angry grumbling rumbled through the group.

Brooks held up his hand asking for silence. When he mostly got it, he said, "Ye boys elected me captain a heap of years ago, and I reckon ye've been pleased enough with my service in that capacity since ye've not seen fit to choose someone else." He paused and paced a little more before continuing. "But if killin' Angus is where you boys' stick floats, then I aim to unelect myself as your captain and fight my damnedest to stop ye—all of ye—from doin' it." Brooks surveyed the faces in front of him. Many were hostile.

"It don't shine with this chil' to turn out a feller all on his own here with winter comin' on," he continued. "And maybe I feel that way because he is kin. But turnin' out a boy who don't know his ass from a gopher hole ain't right, either." He sighed. "But I reckon he can't be one of us regular, like before. If he stays with us, none of ye will trust him to watch over the animals agin. I won't either. But it ain't right that he doesn't take his turn spendin' part of the night bein' awake.

"What do ye suggest, lad?" MacTavish asked.

"He accompanies whoever is on night guard duty four times a week."

"Ain't good enough, El," Wentworth said.

"I won't be so lax again," Farley pleaded. "You boys taught me that those horse-thievin' Crows can sneak up on a feller and steal his toenails and you wouldn't know it 'til you went to put on your moccasins in the morning."

"Might be, Angus," Wheeler said. "But losin' my animals 'cause you let some damn Crows take 'em don't shine with this bloke whatsoever."

"We'll figure something out," Brooks said over the grumbling. He paused, then, "It's early in the season yet, but I propose that if he stays with us 'til rendezvous, we keep all his plews among us."

"He ain't got that many," Anderson said. "Like you said, it's mighty early in the season."

Brooks nodded. "I mean all of 'em, what few he has now and whatever he takes 'til we get to rendezvous."

"We hang the son of a bitch, Murphy said, "And we get whatever plews he has anyway and don't have to worry about what to do with him keepin' us company while we're on watch."

Murmurs of agreement circled the fire.

"That'd have him pay for his perfidy, but again, it's early in the season and he don't have many. And it'd cost us a man."

"So?"

"So, if those Crows come back or the Blackfeet decide to pay us a visit like last year, we can use as many guns as we can come up with."

"We handled those Blackfeet just fine last winter," MacTavish said, "and we did it while missin' a few guns." He ignored the enraged look that spread briefly across Brooks' face.

Seeing how Brooks was steaming, Cooper jumped in. "Don't matter. We might not be as lucky as that time." Another glance at Brooks showed him his effort to smooth things over a bit had not worked.

"What do we do about guard duty?" Wentworth asked. "We can't trust him, but it ain't fair to the rest of us that he doesn't have to do so."

Brooks thought for a bit, then nodded. "Ye boys remember a few years ago when we tracked down those fellers who stole horse and beaver from us? Remember what we did to the one feller to try to get him to talk?"

"Looped a rope around 'is neck so 'e couldn't sit or sleep or anyt'ing," Beaubien said.

Brooks nodded. "I suggest we do the same with Angus," he said despite the pain of doing so. "That should keep him awake for the night. He falls asleep he'll choke. But we won't leave him there for the wolves like we did that other feller."

"Oh, no you don't, Uncle El," Farley shouted. "I ain't..."

"Shut up, Angus. Just be lucky these boys didn't raise your hair like they wanted to."

The men mumbled among themselves. Finally, Two-Faces Beaubien said, "We do like you say, *mon capitaine*. But if 'e causes more trouble..."

TWELVE

"SOMETHING'S BOTHERIN' you, Sally," Cooper said one night in their lodge. "You ailin' with the baby or something?"

"No, baby good inside."

"Then what is it?"

"Nothing."

"Don't give me that nonsense, Goes Far. Something's eatin' at you and I need to know what it is so I can help overcome whatever it is that's troublin' you."

The Nez Percé woman hesitated, then said softly, "I worry about Mornin' Song."

"More than before?"

"Yes."

"Has Elson taken to beatin' her?" Cooper asked tightly.

"I don't think so, no. But I think he may start. El is angry all the time. Mornin' Song is becoming afraid. And she is sad all the time. She never has any joy."

"Damn." Cooper sat in thought for a while, then nodded. "I'll talk to Elson first chance I get."

"Say nothing about my worry about him beating her maybe."

"I won't. Maybe I can get him to talk about whatever's tormentin' him. I do that, maybe he can defeat it."

COOPER RODE UP ALONGSIDE BROOKS. "It ain't like me to stick my nose in other men's business, El," he said without preliminary. "You know that. But you seem to be treatin' Mornin' Song less favorably than you used to."

"That ain't your concern, Cooper."

"Yes, it is, El. Zeke left Mornin' Song in your care. You pledged to look after her the way he did. Maybe she ain't been the wife you expected or wanted, but she's still grievin'."

"You were right, Cooper, ye shouldn't stick your nose into my business. How I treat Mornin' Song ain't your concern, like I said. And don't ever mention Zeke Potts to me again. Now leave me be." He started to ride off, but Cooper grabbed his arm, stopping him. He turned furious eyes on Cooper.

"Get your hand off me, boy."

"I'll do so when I finish what needs sayin'."

"Ye aimin' to go agin me, boy?"

"Ain't plannin' to, but I damned well will if you keep actin' like this. And you know damn well I can put you down in any fight."

Rage crossed Brooks' face. "Spit it out," he said through tight lips.

"You've been actin' mighty strange these last few months, El. I don't know what's got stuck in your craw, but it doesn't sit well with me and most of the others. Might be best for all of us if you was to figure out what troubles are plaguin' you—not just made up ones like you're been spoutin' about me and others—and let 'em out into the light of day where they can burn off. Or freeze off with the weather changin'."

"Ye through?" Brooks hissed.

Cooper stared at him for some seconds, then said sadly, "I reckon I am, El. But the boys ain't gonna go easy on you the way they've been."

"I don't give a good goddamn, Cooper. I'm tellin' ye now, leave me the hell alone and keep out of my concerns. And ye can tell the rest of those boys the same." He paused. "And ye can tell 'em to find themselves a new captain, likely ye since ye're such a hero to 'em all."

Cooper felt as if he had been slapped in the face. "Might be best if you rode on out."

"Reckon not. Mayhap it's ye who should be ridin' on."

Cooper started to respond, then clapped his mouth shut. He simply pulled away and rode back to ride alongside Beaubien as he usually did.

"You do not look 'appy, *mon ami*."

"I ain't."

"It didn't look like your talk with Elson went well."

"It didn't," Cooper said sourly.

"You talked of t'ings we discussed, eh? 'Is melancholy and anger, Mornin' Song?"

Cooper nodded. "He didn't take kindly to my talkin' to him about any of it. And he said something strange."

"*Qu'a t'il dit*—What did he say?"

"He told me never to mention Zeke again."

"*Mon Dieu*, that is strange. "E must have gone *en fou*—crazy. 'E must be touched in ze 'ead."

"I'm beginnin' to think so."

"Then it is time for us to leave."

"No, not yet."

"We 'ave put it off many times already," Beaubien with a quizzical look.

"I know," Cooper said. "But I'm worried about Mornin' Song."

"'E is abusing 'er?"

"Don't think so. Not physically. 'Least not yet. Goes Far is worried he might, though. Way he's been actin', that might change any day."

"You know it's a man's right to keep his women in line, eh? Even if that means lodgepolin' them at times."

"I've never seen you touch one of your women in a way I might consider wrong."

The half-breed smiled. "Ah, that is true, *mon ami*. But I 'ave ze right to do if I choose."

"You try whompin' on Dancin' Water and she'll have your hair."

"You are right, *mon ami*," Beaubien said with a faux sigh of resignation.

They rode in silence for a bit before Beaubien asked, "So we wait some more, eh? 'Ow long?"

"I don't know," Cooper said a shake of the head. "I got to see that Mornin' Song is all right."

"She should 'ave gone with 'er people when we left rendezvous."

"Can't say that ain't true. But she didn't, and now we have to deal with things the way they are."

COOPER AVOIDED Brooks as much as possible. It was easy for the most part as Brooks kept to himself, sitting at a fire with only Morning Song with him, and she only for serving him. He was sullen and difficult. The men didn't exactly unelect Brooks as captain, but they generally ignored him and looked to Cooper and Beaubien for any such things that the leader would order.

Brooks was alone, too, on his trap lines. He seemed to want it that way and was cantankerous enough that MacTavish had enough after a week of such a situation.

"I canna ken what that lad is thinkin'," the Scot said one night at the fire he shared with Cooper, Beaubien, and White. "But I dunna like it. Och! Not one damn bit, and I've had enough of trappin' with him."

"You'll be on your own too, then," Cooper said.

"Aye. But it'll be better than dealin' with that *mac na galla*—son of a bitch."

"I'll help out when I can, Duncan," Cooper said.

"*Moi aussi*," Beaubien threw in.

"And me," White offered.

"We'll take turns helpin'," Cooper said. "One of us'll run our traps lines together with you. Next day another of us'll do so. You boys agree?"

Beaubien and White nodded.

"Ye lads sure? 'Twould be a lot of work."

"Well, then, you Scottish devil, that lets me out," White said. "I'm against work of all kinds and never do any, 'less eatin' or fornicatin' is considered work."

"I've noticed that, lad."

They all laughed, then Beaubien said seriously, "I

say again, 'Awley, I t'ink it is time for us to go. I know you want to wait, but 'e is becoming an unbearable bastard."

"I agree, lad," MacTavish.

"I'm ready if that's what y'all decide." White added.

Cooper shook his head. "You boys can go on ahead, but I can't leave "til I figure out something to do about Mornin' Song. I just can't ride away and leave her here with Brooks. I never thought I'd see the day when he'd become such a troublesome, belligerent son of a bitch. It baffles me, boys. It purely does."

"Well, I don' mind staying a little longer," the half-breed said, "but I can't wait forever, 'Awl."

MacTavish and White nodded in agreement.

"I understand, and I won't try to stop you if all of you want to bug out. You're your own men, and all of you are too proud, too long in the mountains, too seasoned to put up with the buffler shit El's been throwin' on us. I won't blame you if you ride off."

"We do, ye'll be on your own against several fellows," MacTavish said. "Ye don't get along with Wheeler and Anderson, understandably so. And those new lads El brought in will be trouble for ye. And, of course, there's El himself."

Cooper drew in a long breath and blew it out with some force. "I reckon I can handle 'em. I doubt Wheeler and Anderson will come against me. Of the new men, Sam has shown he's a decent feller by workin' with Bill. The other two? Greenhorns who don't worry me at all. As for El, I think I can take him with no trouble as long as he doesn't get help from his nephew and that other boy." He drew another long breath. "So, like I said, I just can't leave Mornin' Song.

The way El's been, there's no tellin' what he might do."

"Lodgepolin' a woman is a man's right," White said.

"Someone else said that to me not so long ago," Cooper said, looking at Beaubien, who smiled just a bit. "But do you think Mornin' Song's the kind of woman who'd ever do anything to provoke any man—well, any decent man—to lodgepole her?"

"Reckon not. She has the sweetest temperament, though she's certainly been hangdog these past months."

"Yes, she has. And it's what's been troublin' me more and more. Every time I see her, it seems, she looks sadder."

"She still misses Zeke," MacTavish said. "We should ne'er have let El take her to his robes when he did. It was much too early. She had no time to mourn."

"You took in Slow Calf right off," White said.

"Aye, and ye know she had no love for that cranky old fart Dubois. Does she seem unhappy to ye?"

"Reckon she does," White said with a grin. "Any woman'd be unhappy if she had to share the robes with y'all, ya festerin' stinkpot."

They all chuckled.

"Ye do realize, don't ye, Hawl, that winter'll be on us soon?" MacTavish asked when they had settled back down.

"I do."

"And with it comes makin' a winter camp. And that means we'll be livin' close together without hsvin' any time to spend some time away from each other. And that means..."

"I know what that means, Duncan, but I'll tell you

again, I ain't leavin' 'til I can figure out how to keep Mornin' Song safe. She was Zeke's woman, so she means a lot to me. It also means I feel responsible for her."

"El was supposed to be responsible for 'er," Beaubien said. "That's why 'e said what 'e did in his will."

"True. But he don't seem to be livin' up to that agreement."

"There's that, but ain't he still angry at y'all?" White asked. "That'd make things even worse."

"Yep," Cooper said with a sigh. "I reckon he has a right to. After all, I've been crowin' about my great deeds to any man who'll listen. Especially all the fellers we've met on the trail before and since rendezvous," he said sarcastically, sourly. "I still don't know how or where he got that damn fool notion."

"And you said 'e told you not to speak of Zeke again," Beaubien said. "That is strange, very strange as you said to me. It's another thing in ze great mystery that Elson Brooks 'as become."

"I dunna ken, but I think maybe he's had too many battles, too many run-ins with the Blackfoot, too many mountain winters and starvin' times, too much Lightning at rendezvous and it's all twisting his mind. It might be best if we could talk him into leavin' the mountains, go back to civilization, marry some fine town woman and regain his reason."

"Might be good for him all right," Cooper said. "But do you want to be the feller who tries to tell him that? Tries to make him do that?"

"Och, not me, lad. Nae. I'm nae that foolish."

"So we all stay and put up with his crossness for another stretch of, what, days? Weeks?" White asked.

"Yep."

"I still don't like it, lad," MacTavish said, "but aye, I'll stay. I'll say this, though, Hawl, if he gets much worse, me and these other two lads just might raise his hair."

It was followed by affirmatives from White and Beaubien.

THIRTEEN

"MORNIN' Song wants to go back to our people, Hawley," Goes Far said as they sat in their lean-to one night.

"Kind of late now that we've been on the trail for a few months or so goin' our own way. She should've left rendezvous with her people."

"She was afraid that her new husband would be angry."

"Hell, he's angry now with her here. If she had left rendezvous with her people, he likely would have been angry then, too. At least for a spell, but I reckon he would've gotten over it. And if she was gone maybe he'd settle back into the old Elson. If he didn't, he couldn't be any worse than what he's been."

"I'm afraid for her. You see her. She is pale, looks sickly, no life in face, no joy in heart."

"I don't know, Sally. I suppose I could give her one of my horses and some supplies. But really, it'd be too dangerous for her out there alone."

"You can take her."

"You're crazy, woman. That'd cause no end of trouble."

"You were Zeke's best friend."

"So?"

"So, she still grieves for him. To make her stay with Elson is bad."

"You wanted them to get together."

"So did you."

"Only because Zeke wanted it and said so in his will."

"I was wrong to want them to be together so soon," Goes Far said, hanging her head. "Now is bad for them."

"That's certain."

"Then take her away."

"I can't do what you're askin', Sally. El is my friend, too, and to take his woman away and bring her back to her people will certainly worsen the troubles we've had between us."

"He's not a friend anymore. Treats you bad, treats everyone bad."

"Can't argue with that. But doin' what you ask would only make it worse."

Goes Far shook her head in annoyance at Cooper's reluctance and her own shame at having caused this problem by suggesting Morning Song join Brooks too soon. "You should do this. I ask. You can't say no. If you do...I be angry."

Cooper's eyes narrowed in anger. He rose, grabbed his rifle and a buffalo robe and walked out.

"Where you go?" Goes Far asked, fighting back tears.

"None of your business, woman. You don't want me around, I ain't about to stay where I ain't wanted."

All the other men stared. They had never seen Cooper and Goes Far have a fracture between them, and it was shocking. But no one said or did anything. It was not their place to interfere in business between a man and his woman.

Cooper tossed down the buffalo hide not far away, laid down his rifle, and then lay on the robe. He was furious but also saddened. They had had occasional spats before, but this one seemed far deeper than those few other times. He lay with his hands behind his head, trying to will himself to sleep for some time with no luck. His anger and melancholy occupied his mind so much that he was not aware that Goes Far was there until she was stretched out beside him. Cooper froze.

"I sorry," Goes Far said quietly.

Cooper just grunted.

Goes Far pushed up on an elbow so she could look into his face. "I not mad. I worry about Mornin' Song. Want to do something to help her. I'm afraid she'll die soon, fade away to nothing if I don't help. If we don't help."

"There ain't anything I can do. Sally," he said. "I can't just give her a horse and send her on her way. And I can't pick up and take her. It wouldn't be right to take another man's woman away because she ain't happy. I know you don't think the same way in this matter, but a man just doesn't do something like that to a friend."

The woman laid her cheek on Cooper's chest. When he heard her soft sobs, he placed an arm around her shoulders. They lay there for a while. Then Goes

Far raised her head a little. "We go back now?" she asked anxiously.

"You done scoldin' me?"

She managed a weak smile. "For now."

He glanced at her in surprise, then smiled a little himself. "Reckon a hard-headed man can't ask for much more."

COOPER WAS WALKING along with Beaubien, heading for their horses, when he froze. The half-breed got two steps, then stopped and looked back. "*Qu'est-ce que ç'est*—What is it?"

Cooper jerked his chin under to the side.

Beaubien looked, then shrugged. "It's Mornin' Star gettin' water. She does it every day, just like ze other women."

"Look at her," Cooper said through clenched teeth. "Not at what she's doin'."

Beaubien stared a bit as Morning Song walked across their path a few feet away, ignoring them.

"I don' know what you see, *mon ami*. I..." He stopped. "'Er face. It is bruise."

"Yep." He stood in anger a few more moments, then muttered, "I got to go find that son of a bitch."

But Beaubien grabbed his arm. "Don't do anything rash, 'Awley. It's none of your business."

"Like hell it ain't."

"Would I come after you if you hit Goes Far?"

"I'd never..."

"I know that. But pretend you did. Would you want

me to interfere in a quarrel between a man and his woman?"

"I'd consider it."

"Perhaps you would. You are that kind of man, 'Awley. But you would talk to me first, try to explain why you think it's wrong and that I should too."

"Maybe. But this is different. She's Zeke's woman."

"She *was* Zeke's woman. Now she is Elson's, and you 'ave no right to interfere."

"But..."

"*Non, mon ami*. You must stay out of this. I know it is 'ard, but you should keep away."

Cooper looked over at Beaubien with rage flickering in his eyes. He finally nodded tightly.

"Come, we check out traps like we were heading to do."

Another curt nod accompanied by a raspy breath in and out, and he stepped off alongside Beaubien.

"YOU ARE STILL angry with me, husband?" Goes Far asked nervously as she handed him a hunk of roasted beaver tail.

"No." He tore a chunk off with his teeth and chewed.

"Then you are troubled."

"Yes." He swallowed and took another bite.

"Tell me what it is."

"Not now."

"But if..." She clamped her mouth shut when she saw his face. It wore a look that told her that more talking would be a very bad thing for her to do. She had her own news to tell but would hide it from him for now. So she sat near him, but not too close, and desultorily ate her own portion of beaver tail.

Finished eating and done with another cup of coffee, he said quietly, "I'll take Mornin' Song back to your people."

"It is good," Goes Far said, trying to tamp down her joy. "Why you change mind?"

"I saw her today. She had a bruise on her face. I figured El put it there. I was gonna confront him, but Two-Faces convinced me it'd not be a good thing, so I told him I'd let it be because it was a matter between a man and his woman. But she was Zeke's woman, and if he's watchin' us from up in the Spirit World and he saw what Brooks did and that I didn't do anything to stop it, he'd raise hair on both of us, spirit or not."

"I'm glad. I knew he hurt her but was afraid to tell you."

Cooper nodded in the darkness.

"When we leave?"

"You ain't goin'."

"I am goin', yes. No argue. Do you want to leave me here alone with the others, especially El, who'll know, or figure, you've taken his woman."

"That would be damn foolish on my part," Cooper admitted. "But what about the baby?"

"Me and baby will be fine. Better with you than left alone here. So, when we go?"

"Tomorrow night, maybe the next. I have things to figure out. We can't let anyone know. Can't tell Mornin' Song either until the last minute. So you keep quiet about this."

"All right."

Cooper heard the disappointment in her voice. "I know it'll be hard for you not to say anything, but if you do, there'll be big trouble, and she'll be in more danger than she already is."

"I can do. But might have trouble tellin' her when time comes."

"Why?"

"That man, he don't let me talk to her when he around. Will be hard to tell her of plan unless he not around, and if we wait 'til almost time to go, will be hard to get her alone to tell."

"You'll manage it. Get enough meat for three of us for several days and have it handy, though don't let anyone see what you're doin'. You got extra coffeepot and such for cookin'?"

"Yes."

"Good, set that aside too. We'll leave the ones we use here so it'll maybe take a little while for others to figure out we're gone."

"All right."

"Mornin' Song might have to ride bareback. I don't think there's any way to get her saddle out from the lean-to she and Brooks are usin', and I ain't about to find out by tryin'. She might have to use one of my ponies, too, since I don't know if we can cull hers out from the others without raisin' a ruckus."

"Yes. Good. I'll be ready, and no one will know."

"Now, get some sleep."

"Might be hard. I excited. Maybe a little scared too."

AS HE GLIDED SILENTLY ALONG through the scattered trees, a pannier on each shoulder, Cooper began to think this was a fool's errand. The more he thought about it, the less convinced he became that this would end well. As quietly as he could, he cinched the pack saddle onto a mule and hung a pannier, one with foodstuffs, one with cooking utensils and more, everything packed tightly with cloth or buckskin so as to make no noise, on each side of the forked saddle. He took a few minutes to stand and listen for sign that anyone was checking on what he was doing. Dan Anderson, who was on horse guard duty, had just woken Dave Wheeler who would be taking over his duty, and the two men were off a little way having coffee and a bite to eat. Satisfied that he had not been noticed, he saddled his horse, then Goes Far's pony. He attached a rope rein around another pony's lower jaw. Holding the reins to the four animals, he walked slowly away from the camp. A quarter mile away, Goes Far and Morning Song were waiting for him. The former looked excited, the latter scared but hopeful.

They walked on another quarter mile before they stopped and mounted. They rode off slowly, Cooper in the lead, followed by Morning Song, then Goes Far, who had the mule in tow. A mile or two farther, and they picked up speed, riding at a comfortable trot.

They traveled through the night and all the next day, stopping occasionally but only briefly to let the animals rest and drink, before finally making a camp an hour after dark. While Cooper tended the animals, the two women got a fire going and food cooking. By the time he was done, so was the food. He sat and gratefully took the piece of pemmican on a piece of bark.

As he ate, he realized that the women were exhausted. He cursed himself silently for having pushed them so long. But, he reasoned to himself, to not put as much distance as they could between them and Brooks could be dangerous. He was certain Brooks would come after them. Whether he would have help with him Cooper could not know. Beaubien, White or MacTavish would not join Brooks. Nor would Murphy and Wentworth, whom Cooper also considered friends. And even though Wheeler and Anderson were still not exactly on the best of terms with him, they had not been fond of Brooks' behavior lately either. That left the newcomers. Sam Berryman had become rather estranged from Angus Farley and Colin Leary and might not be inclined to get involved. The other two, however, especially Farley, he being kin, could very well join Brooks, though they had shown little stomach for any real difficulty.

"I know it's hard for you ladies," he said between bites, "but we'll have to press on hard and fast tomorrow, startin' just before dawn. Another day or two of hard ridin', and we should be able to ease up some."

If Brooks doesn't catch up to us first, he thought. He dreaded a confrontation with Brooks. Not that he was afraid of his old friend but because the bad blood between them offered little hope for a peaceable ending.

FOURTEEN

"WHERE THE HELL IS COOPER?" Brooks demanded of Beaubien, who sat at a fire playing with two of his young children.

The half-breed looked up eyes wide not only at Brooks' tone but also his demand. "I don't know. 'E is not 'ere?"

"No, he ain't here, dammit, and ye damn well know it."

Beaubien nodded at Dancing Water and Little Fox, who took the children away as he stood. "You 'ave looked all around? Maybe 'e is 'unting?"

"Yea, I've checked, and no he ain't huntin'. Mornin' Song is also gone. Now tell me where they've gone off to."

Once more, Beaubien was shocked at the news. "I 'ave no idea. I t'ought 'e was 'ere just like always. I was waitin' for 'im to come by to go check our traps."

"Ye lyin' son of as bitch. I..."

"That is enough, m'sieur! I will not 'ave you make accusations that are not real, eh. I do not know where 'es is, I don't know where 'e went, I don't know where 'e is going."

The other men began to gather around.

"Maybe 'e…" He stopped. "I t'ink maybe 'e wants 'er to be safe for a while."

"Safe from what?"

"From you. 'E saw the other day that you 'ad 'it 'er."

"That's my business," Brooks said, still steaming.

"*Oui*. That is what I tell him to keep 'im from going against you."

"Good thing he didn't."

"Good t'ing for you, El. You would have lost your 'air."

"I could take him easy. I…"

"*Mais non*, you couldn't."

Brooks steamed some more, then said, "I should've known it. That son of a bitch has gotten arrogant since that fight…since he was such a hero, at least in his mind. And stickin' his nose in my business, tellin' me how I should treat that melancholy bitch he and Potts stuck me with."

"If you feel at way, let 'er go. Let 'er be with one of ze others 'ere. Or maybe stay with 'Awley."

"That's what he wants, ain't it? To have that woman for his own. It'd be like him to…"

"'E does not want 'er. 'E just wants 'er to be safe, and 'appy like she was with Zeke."

"I told ye before, I don't ever want to hear that damn man's name again, dammit. I wish to hell he never left that woman in my care."

"I say again, El, that you should let 'er be free."

"Not now, I won't. She was left in my care, and she was sharin' the robes with me. Not that she served me well, but she was mine. And I treated her the way she was supposed to be treated. She disobeyed me more than once, and she had to pay for it like any woman who goes against her man."

Beaubien shook his head. "She is gone, m'sieur. That is enough for you to know. She is no longer your woman."

"I ain't lettin' that son of a bitch, or any other, steal my woman. Now, ye and the others get packed up. We're headin' out after 'em."

"*Non, mon ami.* If you want to go after 'im, go. I won't follow."

"Do what I say, ye bastard. I'm still the captain of this outfit."

"No, El, you ain't."

"I..."

"He's right, El," MacTavish said from a few feet behind Brooks. "Ye've given up that right with the way ye've been actin' these past many months. We've put up wi' it because no one was interested in bein' the leader. But now..." The Scot shrugged. "I canna be sure, but maybe the men will be without a captain or maybe we will choose another. It will nae be ye."

Brooks turned, eyes red with rage, and looked from one man to the other. He saw no sympathy from most.

"I'll go with you, Uncle El," Angus Farley suddenly piped up.

"Finally someone with the balls to stand up for a man's rights," Brooks snapped.

All he got in return were stony looks, ones that told him that if he insulted them again, he would be unable to chase Cooper and Morning Song—he would be dead.

He turned and headed for his lean-to, snapping, "Come on, then, boy."

———

THEY WERE DESCENDING another one of the interminable, sage-covered rises and hills when Cooper suddenly stopped. Surprised, the two women jerked to a halt too.

Cooper was tense, watching intently as a group of warriors was descending the next hill. He hoped they were peaceful; there was nowhere for him and the women to run, nowhere to hide, nowhere to use as a fortification. He slid his Dickert out from the loop behind the saddle horn and held it loosely across his thighs, waiting.

The Indians spotted him and picked up their pace. Cooper stood in his stirrups so the oncoming warriors could see that he had a beard. He also told Goes Far and Morning Song to pull up alongside him. Unless the oncoming Indians were Blackfoot, they would see that he was a white man and that he had women with him, which meant he was not looking to go to war.

The warriors slowed, and with relief, Cooper sank back into the saddle, shoving his rifle through the loop again.

"Flatheads?" Goes Far asked.

"Yep."

"They friendly."

"Yep."

They met at the bottom of the hill. The men sat, the Flatheads letting their ponies graze freely, the two women watching over their and Cooper's animals.

Cooper handed out some jerky and the men gnawed at the leathery meat.

"Where're you boys headed?" Cooper asked.

"Look for Blackfeet."

"You'll find plenty of 'em the direction you're headed."

"It's why we go this way," one of the men said with a grin.

"Where you go?" one of the others asked.

"Bringin' these women back to their people." He saw no reason to try to explain why he was taking one back to the Nez Percé and not the other.

"She have baby soon," the first warrior said.

Cooper nodded. "If we move fast enough, we'll get there in time to have friends help her."

"It is good."

"Well, reckon if that's gonna happen, it's best we were back on the trail." He went to his packs and pulled out three knives and handed one to each of the warriors. The Indians nodded thanks, grabbed their ponies, leaped on, and rode off.

Cooper watched them for a moment, then he climbed on the mare. The two women also mounted and moments later they were moving.

———

"YOU THINK SOMEONE FOLLOWIN'," Goes Far said more than asked, riding up alongside Cooper.

"What makes you think that?"

The Nez Percé smiled in her knowledge. "I watch. You act different. Look behind more. You tense."

"You're pretty smart for a woman," Cooper said with a small smile.

"Yes." She grinned widely. "You say it before, so you know for long time."

"I also know you're a sassy, troublemakin' woman who annoys me all the time."

"Shows I care."

Cooper laughed. "That's a funny way of showin' it." He grew serious. He glanced over at Morning Song, who rode a few yards off to the side. "How's she doin'?" he asked, nodding toward the other woman.

"Better. She needs more food. She too skinny. But spirits better a little. Each day, she feels a little safer maybe." He paused. "But if someone comes after her, she will not feel so good."

"I know." He shrugged. "Just because I think there's someone behind us—and I ain't sure of that, I just have a suspicion—doesn't mean it's someone intent to do us harm. If there's somebody there, it could be an Indian or even a lone mountaineer makin' his way somewhere by himself."

"You don't think that?"

He glanced at her and shook his head. "No. I think it's Elson. And he might not be alone."

"What we do?"

"Push on a little harder. I don't think we can outrun him if they're determined, but maybe I can find some-place where I can put up some kind of defense."

"You know of place?"

"No. I've been in this area before, but I ain't real familiar with it. But we ain't far from yonder mountain, which is covered with trees and might have a cave or two where we can fort up. Big Hole River ain't far either, which may give us some cover if the mountain doesn't."

"We make short camps," Goes Far said with determination.

"That'll help, yep."

THREE DAYS later they had not found anything that Cooper thought would do for defense. He was growing more tense but tried not to show it that night as he wolfed down some deer meat. He had shot the animal that afternoon, hoping the strong wind would either hide the sound of the shot or at least diffuse it so anyone following would not be able to determine where it came from. He should have known, however, that he could not hide his worry from Goes Far.

"We find place," she said. "Soon. Then we wait, raise hair of whoever foolish enough to chase us."

"Got a lot of faith in me, do you?"

"Yep. You great warrior. No one can kill you. You fought whole Blackfoot Nation last winter and still live."

"I had some help." A dose of sadness rushed through him at the thought of Potts' death.

"Maybe, but all the Blackfoot on Mother Earth counted coup on you and could not kill you."

"There weren't that many."

"I hear the men talk, say how many Blackfeet bodies were in woods. You mighty warrior. Not argue. You will find a place. Even if you find no good place, you still protect us. I am sure of this, husband."

Cooper was still amazed that he had found two

women such as this one in his life. He had laid Black
Moon Woman to rest in his mind a year or two ago,
though she still lived in his heart. She and Goes Far
were much the same—strong both of body and will,
filled with conviction of his abilities, loving, smart. He
wasn't sure he deserved either of them, but both had
become his and showed their love for him in many
ways. He smiled inwardly. Of course, both were feisty
as the devil and had a way of cutting him down to size
with a sharp tongue when she thought it necessary.

Goes Far leaned her head on his shoulder, content.
He enjoyed it for a few moments, then said quietly,
"Move away, Sally."

She looked up at him in surprise.

He nodded toward Morning Song, who sat a little
back from the fire, staring at them. Her eyes were sad in
the firelight, and her shoulders were slumped. "Such a
thing reminds her of Zeke and what she's lost. It ain't
fair to her. I should've thought of it before."

"No, I am her friend. I should've thought of it
before now. It will be hard for me, but I keep away a
little."

"Won't be as hard for you as it will be for her." He
smiled wanly. "Or for me."

HE SAT LOOKING at the cave and its surroundings.
It was fairly large and likely would accommodate both
the people and the animals. A patch of open space, its
grass browning in the November chill, stretched out for
maybe twenty yards in front of the shelter, but it was
ringed with trees. That worried Cooper. Someone

could hide behind one of the trunks and calmly blast him into oblivion, then take Morning Song, and likely Goes Far too. But he had found little else that would offer any protection, and his instincts told him that whoever was following them was getting close.

"This'll do," he announced. "It'll have to."

The women went about gathering firewood and starting a blaze. They had some elk left over from two days ago when Cooper had shot it amid a thundering rainstorm. Cooper tended the animals, hobbled them, and let them graze. They ate, and then Cooper said, "Cover the fire with dirt after a little while."

"So he not smell fire or food."

"Yep. And you two stay in the cave as much as possible. Only go out when you really need to. I'm going to take a look around."

He found a spot above and to the right of the cave mouth where he could sit fairly hidden and keep a watch on the woods across from the shelter. He was there a day and a half later when he heard a horse from in the trees and caught some movement. Rifle ready, he waited.

FIFTEEN

"TURN around and ride back the way you came, El," Cooper called. He was greeted by silence. "I know you're there, El, and as soon as you move, I can drop you. I don't want to do that, but I can't have you doggin' our trail causin' trouble."

More silence ensued. Cooper waited, annoyed. He really did not want to shoot Brooks, but he was not about to let his former friend come in and take Morning Song. There were still three or four hours of sunlight left, and Cooper figured that Brooks was thinking he'd wait Cooper out, sneak to the cave in the dark, kill him and take Morning Song. Cooper vowed silently that he would not let that happen. He considered a warning shot or two, but he did not want to give his position away, so he sat.

An hour later, Cooper yelled, "You need to regain your reason, El. You've been actin' like a crazy man for months now, and it ain't becoming of you. You're a better man than that, El."

"Uncle El's just fine, as good a man as ever there

was one," a voice floated out of the trees. "It's you who've lost your reason, stealin' another man's woman. That ain't right, and not something a man would do to another."

"So, you brought that chicken fart of a nephew with you, El. Ain't gonna help. Likely make it harder on you. I'm reluctant to shoot you, El, because you're a friend, or used to be a friend. But Farley ain't a donkey's turd to me, and I'll drop him without a second thought."

"You just wait 'til dark..."

"Shut up, Angus," Brooks snapped.

"You have any family feelin's for that shit bucket of a nephew, you'd best turn around and get him out of here along with yourself."

"You're a dead man, Cooper," Farley shouted.

"And I'll make sure of it," Brooks added. "Ye made a big mistake when ye stole my woman, Cooper. Like Angus said, a man doesn't do that to another."

"Reckon that's true. But it don't shine with me for a man to go smackin' his woman around just because she ain't pleasin' him enough because she's still grievin' for her man."

"Potts has been gone what, nine months now? Plenty of time for her to have gotten over her grief. She's just a cantankerous bitch who needs lodgepolin' now and again."

"Maybe you're right, but you took her to your robes too soon."

"Your woman encouraged it."

"That's true too. And it was a damn fool thing for her to do. She knows it and she's sorry she did it, but it can't be changed now. What can be changed is gettin' her somewhere she'll be safe and finish her grievin'. You turn around and head back to the others, I'll make sure she gets to such a place. She stops mournin' in a few months, maybe she'll consent to rollin' in the robes with you again."

"I don't need her consent. Nor any other woman's. Once a man's decided what woman he wants to be with, she's got no say in the matter."

"Some do."

"Sure, folks like ye. Men who ain't got the balls to control their women like they should. Let some bitch of a squaw walk all over him."

"You've become a bitter man, El, and it's a sad thing to see. Not only moonin' over a woman you didn't want in the first place and treated mostly poorly since you took her in, but spreadin' lies about me and others. I never would've thought you capable of such things, El. You were always a prideful, upstandin' feller, a rough bastard like the rest of us, but fair and welcomin' to others. But not now." Cooper shook his head, sad at what Brooks had become in his eyes.

"It's ye who've changed, Cooper. Ye've become a weak-willed feller who lets his squaw rule him. It's a shameful thing, and I'm saddened to see it and determined to not let such softness rub off on me."

Cooper sat silent for a spell, He was troubled at what Brooks had become. His once close friend had lost all his sense between the spring when they left the valley where the battle had taken place and when they reached rendezvous a few months later. Cooper wished he knew what had really brought on the change. If he did, maybe he could fix it. He would much prefer that than possibly having to kill his old friend. He just could not fathom how a man's mind could turn to mush in so short a time with no reason it seemed.

Though he doubted it would do any good, Cooper decided to try one last time to convince Brooks to leave. "I say again, El, that it'd be best for everyone if you were to just turn around and head back to the others. Or maybe back to the States seein' as how your mind has gone astray."

"And I'll tell ye again, Cooper, that I aim to get my woman back. And," he added after a pause, "raise hair on ye in the doin'."

Cooper sighed. There would be no good ending to all this. Blood would be spilled here and while Cooper did not want to kill Brooks, he would not allow his former friend to attack the women.

"I might even let ye watch when I cut that bastard out of your woman's belly," Brooks added with a maniacal laugh.

A shiver went through Cooper as he knew for certain now that he would have to kill Brooks.

"And after that, if you're still livin'," Farley said, "I might even geld you, make sure you don't produce more little bastards,"

Cooper took a deep breath and let it out slowly in an attempt to ease his rage. It was only a partial success. He shifted, and while he kept a peripheral eye on where he knew Brooks was, he watched where he thought Farley was. The young man was impetuous—and stupid.

"You think he's still up there, Uncle El?"

"Yep."

"I don't. I think he's a coward and is runnin' off to save his hide."

"Don't be a fool, boy," Brooks warned.

"Don't be a yellow belly like Cooper." He poked his head around the trunk of a tree. "See, he ain't the..." He stopped when his head exploded from a .54-caliber ball fired from Cooper's Dickert.

As soon as he fired, Cooper dashed off a few feet. He was sure Brooks would be able to see the small, lingering cloud of powder smoke. He was right. Brooks fired, and the ball whizzed through the bushes behind which Cooper had sat moments before.

"Ye shouldn't have done that, Cooper," Brooks said, voice filled with rage and insanity.

"He was a blight, and takin' him out was relievin' the world of a festerin' shit pile."

"You're a dead man now, Cooper. I might've given thought to lettin' ye live—after raisin' your hair, but that don't hold now."

"Go home, El," Cooper said with a sigh. "This ain't gonna end well for you."

"I ain't the one this'll end poorly for."

Cooper was moving across the hill above the cave, easing his way across the steep slope, when Brooks darted out from the trees.

"Shit," Cooper muttered. He could not bring his rifle to bear from where he was, so he dropped it and headed down, half running, half sliding on the grass and stones.

Brooks skidded to a stop when he saw Cooper coming and fired a pistol. He missed. He grabbed his other pistol and fired just as Cooper landed and slammed into him, knocking him to the ground. The shot ricocheted off the cave wall and hit Goes Far in the shoulder. She screeched.

Cooper's eyes blazed as he pulled a pistol and pointed at the sprawled Brooks' chest. Then he shook his head. "No, shootin' you's too good for you, dammit, even after all we've been through together." He slid the weapon back onto his belt.

As Brooks started to push himself up, Cooper kicked him in the jaw, knocking him back down. "Cut my baby out of his ma's womb, will you?" he screamed as he stomped on Brooks' shin, cracking at least one of the bones. He glanced at Goes Far, who was pale but seemed all right. "Geld me, you putrid pile of buffalo shit?" He stomped on Brooks' ribcage, snapping several.

Brooks moaned but still tried to rise.

"No you don't, dammit," Cooper said, as he stamped on the other side breaking a few more ribs.

Breathing heavily, Cooper stood there looking down at his old friend.

"Not do more," Goes Far said quietly moving a bit out of the cave. When Brooks turned angry eyes on her, she added, "He's not same man who was your friend. Bad spirits take away his reason. Make crazy. So no more punish. He was good man."

"Might be, but he needs killin'."

"Yes. But do so fast."

Cooper nodded and pulled out the pistol again and aimed it at Brooks' forehead. He hesitated. There was light—an old light, one of reason and friendship—in the man's eyes.

"Go on and do it," Brooks said, not as a dare but as an acknowledgment that it would be best.

"I don't know, El," Cooper said uneasily. "I don't…"

"I know I ain't been a sane man for a spell now.

Don't know how my mind got twisted, but it sure as hell did."

"But now you're, I don't know, more like your old self."

"Might be, but there's no tellin' how long it'll last. I can feel the strange spirits tryin' to crawl back in my head." He managed a weak smile. "And if there's anybody in this world who I'd want to put that devilish man I've become into the Spirit World, it's ye, Hawley Cooper." He drew in a shuddering breath and let it out. "Now do it before the demons take over again."

With a desolate heart, he ended his old friend's suffering. "I hope God and the Great Spirit take you in and make you comfortable, Elson Brooks. And may they forgive you the troubles you've had and caused these past few months."

He stood for a few moments, fighting back the sadness that threatened to overwhelm him. He wondered why the Great Spirit had let him live those years ago when he was lost and struggling through the wilderness with nothing to help him. It made no sense when in the past nine or ten months, he had lost his Shoshoni best friend and his two best friends among the mountain men. None of it made sense to him.

Then he looked at Goes Far. *Well, there's one reason*, he thought. He went to her and looked at her wound. It was little more than a scratch.

"I all right," she said, taking one of his hard, callused hands and holding it against her cheek for a few moments.

He glanced at Morning Song. "And how are you?"

She hesitated, then slowly and quietly said, "I'm all right too."

"You certain?"

"Yes. I miss Zeke. I don't like Elson, not the way he was lately. Now he's gone too. Not good to see an old friend die, but I feel better now. Some. That makes me bad person, I think."

"No, it don't. He mistreated you. He mistreated others too, but men are able to take such slights maybe better than women. We could always pack up our plunder and move on, but you couldn't do that. It's all right to hate the man who abused you. But that's over now.

"Yes. I glad."

"Now, I best get to buryin' Elson. Not sure I should do the same with Farley."

"You do. Your god would want it."

"Yes' ma'am, reckon he would." He climbed back up the slope and retrieved his rifle, made sure it was not damaged, then reloaded it and leaned it against the cave wall just inside the opening. He reloaded his pistol, then grabbed a shovel. He found a good spot under a small but sturdy oak and began digging.

SIXTEEN

COOPER, Goes Far, and Morning Song rode into the Nez Percé village along the South Fork of the Salmon River on a cold, drizzly, wind-whipped day in late November much to the surprise of the residents, though guards had reported the imminent arrival of the three.

People came out from the warm lodges to stare as the visitors briefly stopped at Red Leggings' lodge and paid their welcoming respects to the old civil chief. Then they rode to Pale Thunder's tipi. The older warrior was surprised, and it showed on his face. But the expression quickly changed to a smile. "Welcome, my friend, no, son," he said. "Come. Let us go inside, get warm, share food."

"Sounds welcomin' to me, Thunder."

He and the two women dismounted and handed the reins of their horses—and the pack mule—to some teenagers not yet ready to go on the hunt or warpath to be taken care of.

Goes Far turned and embraced her mother, who had rushed over at the first sign of her daughter.

Morning Song's mother, Walking Bird, one of Pale Thunder's wives, pushed past her husband, much to his amusement, grabbed her daughter and dragged her into the lodge.

"She misses her mother," Cooper said with a grin.

"I think maybe you right," the Nez Percé said with a laugh.

They sat against willow backrests at the fire. Pale Thunder's two other wives served the men coffee and fresh roasted elk.

"Fresh?" Cooper asked.

"I was lucky. Saw small doe yesterday."

"No wolves, though?" Cooper grinned.

"One or two maybe, but none was foaming." He smiled and nodded. "I still owe you my life, Hawley."

"It was a long time ago, Thunder. You don't owe me anything."

They were silent for a spell as they ate. Walking Bird fussed over her daughter, whose shoulders shook as she let her emotions out. She and her mother talked quietly.

Finally, Pale Thunder said, "So why have you brought daughter back?"

Cooper took a deep breath. "Brooks wasn't treatin' her well."

"And you interfered?" The Nez Percé was surprised.

Cooper nodded. "I know it's an unusual thing for one man to stick his nose in another man's affairs, but I just couldn't stand by and see her mistreated."

"That is not right, my friend."

"Maybe not. But I wouldn't be able to live with

myself had I let such a thing continue." He held up a hand to forestall any protests. "I owed it to my friend."

"You took his woman away from Brooks because he was your friend?" Pale Thunder was confused.

Cooper shook his head and took another sip of coffee. "No, I did it because Zeke was my friend."

"But he is dead."

"Yep. But Mornin' Song didn't really have enough time to grieve his passin'. Goes Far was foolish and suggested your daughter share a lodge and robes with Elson before she should have. She shouldn't have done that, and she knows it now, but it can't be changed. Mornin' Song tried, best I can tell, to be a good wife to Elson, but it wasn't workin' well."

"Still none of your concern."

"Normally, I'd agree though I'd not like it then either. But there was more to it."

"Oh?" The Indian took another bite of elk and chewed.

"Bad spirits got into Elson's head. He just wasn't the same man anymore. He was treatin' everyone disre-spectful, made accusations against me..."

"What kind?"

"Said I was crowin' about my part in the fight with the Blackfeet last winter, tryin' to make everyone see me as a hero and great fighter."

"If what I heard of the battle—and Sits Down and I have had some talks in secret—you were. You deserve to boast about your deeds there."

"Ain't my way, Thunder. You should know I ain't such a man."

The Nez Percé nodded.

"He also wasn't bein' very hospitable to the men, fellers he had ridden with for years. It wasn't like him at all." Cooper shook his head sadly. "It was like his mind went astray, wanderin' around in dark places haunted by evil spirits."

"Is not good."

"No," Cooper said with a sigh. "So I thought I needed to interfere. I figured if I could get Mornin' Song back here to her people, she could have the time and place to grieve properly for her lost husband, then go back to Elson at the next rendezvous if she wanted."

"What did he say about it?"

"He didn't know we were leavin'. We rode off in the middle of the night."

"Not like you to hide from trouble."

Cooper suddenly felt uncomfortable. He had been so intent on getting Morning Song away that he had never really considered running away in the dark. But he shrugged. "It was either that or fightin' El over takin' her, and that wouldn't..."

"I understand. Not run off in dark because afraid but to avoid fight with friend."

"Yeah. Didn't do much good though."

"Oh?"

"He followed us. Him and a nephew."

"One of those who Two-Faces said joined at rendezvous?"

"Yep. A steamin' shit pile of a feller."

Pale Thunder looked confused for a moment, then grinned and nodded. "I don't know the meaning of what you say, but I understand. Two-Faces didn't think much of him either. You sent them away?"

"No," Cooper said flatly. He chewed a piece of elk for a bit, then said sadly, "Had to put him under."

"Nephew too?"

"Yep. Weren't no trouble with him. He didn't mean a duck fart to me. A ball in the brainpan made wolf bait out of him right off. Killin' El was something different though. The way things went, where we were and all, I couldn't just shoot him, though we did end up fightin' it out. But it came to a time when I had him down and had a pistol on him."

"And?"

"And, he regained his senses. At least for a spell."

Pale Thunder raised his eyebrows in question.

"Asked me to put him under. He knew he'd been a troublesome feller for some time and that his mind had gone askew. Still, staring into his eyes when his sense had returned and thinkin' of putting a bullet in his head was some difficult I tell you."

"But you did."

"Yep." Cooper sighed.

"It was good, my friend. You saved the man much misery and did the same for many others. You sent him to Spirit World when mind was clear and he was at peace."

"Reckon so, but it still wasn't easy."

"Such things never are."

They ate and drank in silence for a while, the sound and warmth of the fire welcome on such a raw day, and the soft sounds of Morning Song and her mother talking were comforting.

"Your woman is well?" Pale Thunder finally asked. "She looked ready for baby to come soon."

"That's a fact. I wasn't sure we were gonna make it here before she produced."

"It's good you did. On trail not so good for a man, though Morning Song would have taken care of it."

"Still, not easy for a feller sittin' there tryin' to pretend nothin' unusual's goin' on."

"I go huntin' when time comes for one of my women to have a child. I come back when over. All is good."

Cooper grinned, working to put the gloomy talk of a few minutes ago behind him. "Maybe you and I can go huntin' when Goes Far's time comes."

"Always good, my friend."

"Well, old man," Cooper said with another grin, I best go find us a place to stay the next few days."

"You stay here."

"Be kind of crowded."

"Not So." Pale Thunder laughed. "Well, maybe so but we all are family here now."

"Reckon it's fine with me. Ain't so sure about Goes Far. She might want to stay with her ma."

"Not her choice," the Nez Percé said with the slightest edge to his voice.

It was Cooper's turn to laugh. "Seems you never had yourself a feisty woman, one who ain't afraid to speak her mind."

"Never. My women know place."

"Next time I need to find a woman, I'll consider such a one. Still, though, she might be more comfortable with her ma considerin' her condition."

"Mornin' Song and my wives will be here to give care."

"But what're we gonna do when the time comes?

Where are we gonna go if it happens soon and the weather is like this?"

"Make sense."

"Me and her stay with her ma, when the times comes I can come here, send your wives and Mornin' Song over there, and you and I can spend the days here in comfort."

"You pretty smart for a white man."

"Reckon that's a fact. Smarter than any red man anyway."

Both laughed, then Pale Thunder said, "Wait. Is wrong for a man to stay with wife's mother."

"Ain't no taboo among my people. I ain't concerned."

"You're a brave man to tempt spirits," Pale Thunder said with a grin.

"Not brave, my friend, just foolish. I figure I've done enough foolish things in my life that the spirits ain't gonna take one more as too many."

———

COOPER BEGAN to fret after a few days when Goes Far had not gone into labor. Not that he minded the time there or that he was worried about the birth. But winter was coming fast and if he was going to make any kind of fall hunt, he needed to get back to trapping. And since much of his gear was with the group—he had not had the time or chance to carry everything with the quick, quiet way he had left their camp—he was hampered with what he could do.

Goes Far sensed his anxiety and figured she knew

what was causing it. "I have baby soon," she said one day. "Very soon. You see."

"I know."

Pale Thunder also could sense his worry. "I give you traps and things. You go take beaver near here. Plenty sign."

Cooper nodded.

"I come with you," Goes Far said when he told her.

"No."

"I help. Cure furs, make good."

"You need to be here. The baby hasn't come yet, but you know it'll be soon. You can't be out there with me and no one to help you when the time comes."

She was not happy about it and she bid him a sad farewell when, with a half dozen traps, some small wood vials of castoreum, and a few supplies, he headed out. Several miles from the village, he found a spot where there indeed was plenty of beaver sign. He made his camp and set his traps.

When he returned to his camp the next day after having emptied his traps, he found Sits Down sitting there eating from a haunch of deer hanging over the fire.

"Save some of that for me, Sits Down."

"I do." He grinned. "Maybe."

Cooper dropped down the half dozen bloody hides, sat, whacked off a hunk of meat, and sank his teeth hungrily into it. "What're you doin' here, Sits Down?" he asked around chewing.

"Visit old friend. Well, he may be friend, maybe not, but he old," the Nez Percé responded with a twinkle in his eye.

"You must be in the wrong place, boy. I ain't old."

He let loose a laugh. "Glad you come by, Sits Down. I was wonderin' if I was gonna see you while I was in the village. You were kind of scarce there, though Lord only knows how a feller your size can be scarce."

"Good medicine makes me disappear."

Cooper chuckled. "After seein' the way you so easily went through that little cut in the mountain that me and Zeke had trouble gettin' through, I can believe that." He took another bite. "How are you?"

"I good. Same as always. Fought Blackfoot twice."

"Take scalps?"

"Yes."

"What do you do with 'em if you aren't showin' yourself to be the great warrior you are?"

"Hidden cave far up mountain. Hang 'em there. I take you someday, show you."

"I'd like that."

"What about ponies? Where do you keep them?"

"With the others." The big Nez Percé grins. "There are so many in the herd, they don't notice my few."

"You're one sneaky ol' feller."

Sits Down grinned again, then grew sober and asked, "I overheard that Brooks treated Mornin' Song bad. You tell me where he is. I put him under," he said bluntly.

"No need, Sits Down. He's been taken care of."

"You do?"

"Yes. It was hard, him bein' an old friend and all, but it had to be done, so I did it."

The Nez Percé stared at him for a few moments. "You good man, Hairy Face. Special, like greatest Nez Percé."

"No, nothin' special, Sits Down. Just a man who

does what he needs to do or thinks is right at the time. It ain't always right and sometimes it makes a bigger mess, but I try to do good by folks." He fought off the sadness at the loss of his Shoshoni family and friend.

"I say you special. I not lie. Now let's care for the beaver hides so you don't have time to argue with me."

SEVENTEEN

COOPER HAD STILL NOT HEARD anything about the birth two days later, so he packed up and headed back to the village with a couple dozen plews on his pack mule. He took care of the animals, then carried his furs to the tipi he and his wife were sharing with Goes Far's mother.

The two women were sitting near the rear of the lodge working on things he neither could see in the dimness nor care about. His wife smiled at him, then went back to her work.

"I'm leavin' tomorrow," he announced. He had made his decision on the ride back that if she had not gone into labor by that night, he would head on.

"I'll be ready." She sounded tired but determined.

"No, daughter," her mother said. "You must stay, have baby."

"She's right. I can't have you droppin' the baby along the trail with no one to help you."

"I must be with husband."

"No, it ain't practical now."

Goes Far seemed torn between anger and tears. "You're brave man. If you not want me anymore, say so."

"Where'd you get that notion?"

"You say you're leavin', and I ain't goin' with you. That's where."

"Reckon that's true," Cooper said thoughtfully. "But it ain't. I'll be back for you in a few months when the spring hunt is done and we're headin' to rendezvous. If I can, I'll be here before you and the People leave. If not, I'll meet you at rendezvous."

"Why you want to do this? Leave me, not be here for child."

"Ah, hell, Goes Far, men don't take part in such things."

"Yes. But after, you not see baby first day."

"I'll miss that. Surely I will." He sighed. "But I ain't had much of a hunt so far, and winter's gettin' mighty close. If I'm gonna have any success and have enough plews to trade in for next year's supplies"—he grinned— "and foofaraw for you and the baby, I need to get back to work." He did not want to say that while he wanted to be with her and looked forward to being a father, he felt lost without trapping—especially with the men he had spent so many years with. And he did not want to take another woman—this one with a newborn—into the wilderness, alone, with winter coming on fast. He had done that before, and it had almost turned fatal. He did not want to risk his new son or daughter in such a manner.

"You trap here, like last few days."

"Some of the possibles I need are back with the

others. I also need to tell them about Elson and Mornin'
Song."

"You wait. I have baby soon. Then we all go."

"You thought you were gonna calve a few days ago,
and you don't look any closer to it now than you did
then. At least to a man's eyes."

"Only one day, two, maybe three more days."

"If it starts to happen tonight or in the early
mornin', I'll stay, if not, I'm leavin'."

Bull Head, Goes Far's stepfather, had entered some
minutes earlier. He was listening intently as he sipped at
the coffee his wife had provided as soon as he came in.

"Who'll take care of me?"

"Your father."

"No," Bull Head grunted. "Not do. She yours. You
keep. Take."

Cooper still standing, looked down and glared at
him. "You that cheap or dishonorable that you'd let your
wife's child starve to death?"

"Not my daughter."

"When you marry someone who has children, they
become your responsibility."

"No," He sliced the air horizontally with an open
palm.

Cooper glared for a few moments more, then
turned his attention to Bright Eyes. "You need to shed
this feller. He's lower'n a snake's belly. Nay, he ain't
even really a man."

Bull Head started to rise but Cooper turned an
angry face to him. "You get up, boy, and I'll knock you
down and drag your ass out into the cold so everyone
can see what a wretched excuse for a man you are. You

may think you're a great warrior, but I think you're shit pile."

Scowling, furious, Bull Head sat back down.

"I'm goin' over to talk to Pale Thunder and likely Red Leggin's too. I'll be back shortly." Once more he turned to the warrior, face enraged. "Listen to me good, boy, you harm either of these women now or any time in the future and I will have your hair." He stalked out.

A few minutes later, he was explaining the situation to Pale Thunder. The war chief nodded as he listened, then said, "We must talk to Red Leggings."

"Thought we might."

Minutes later they were calling for entrance to the old civil chief's lodge. When they were seated and the formalities were over, Cooper once again explained the situation. A suddenly alert Morning Song, working in the rear with her mother, perked up her ears.

"She's his wife's daughter, so he can do—or not do— as he pleases about her," Red Leggings said. Cooper was about to argue but the chief waved him off. "But it's not the *Nimiipuu* way to treat a friend so poorly as he is treating you."

"So what do you propose?"

"I have no answer. Yet." He called to one of his wives. "Bring Bull Head to us here."

It was not long before an enraged Bull Head stepped in, followed by a waddling Goes Far and her mother. All sat.

"You won't care for daughter while her husband is away?" Red Leggings asked.

"She's not my daughter."

"Maybe you're not a real *Nimiipuu*," Red Leggings said harshly. "*Nimiipuu* men help friends when asked.

This man"—he nodded toward Cooper—"has been a friend for long time. Good friend to the People. You won't help?"

"He's not my friend."

The old chief's eyes widened in surprise.

"I ever did anything to anger you?" Cooper asked, also surprised.

"No. Just not like you or your kind."

Cooper sucked in a breath and eased it out, trying to control his anger.

Before he could speak, Pale Thunder said, "I will care for her." He turned a stern face to Bull Head. The latter cringed at the look of loathing Pale Thunder gave him.

As he rose, Bright Eyes turned to her husband. "Lodge is mine. You take your things. Go. We no longer married. Be gone by the time me and daughter get back."

Scowling, angry, Bull Head left.

There was silence for a few minutes before Cooper asked, "You mean what you said, Thunder?"

"About takin' care of Goes Far? Of course. I wouldn't have said it if I didn't mean it. I'm a man of honor. You know that, old friend. And, as I consider you my son now, I consider her as my daughter."

"That I do. Sorry I questioned you. I just had to be sure I was leavin' Goes Far in good hands."

"You can't wait a little longer?"

"No, Thunder. I've spent way too many days away from trappin', and if I don't get back to it, I'll never have enough to supply myself for next season."

Pale Thunder nodded. As did Red Leggings.

All the visitors rose, paid their respects to the old

chief and left. Pale Thunder headed back to his own lodge while Cooper and the two women went to Bright Eyes'.

The warrior, with some help, was angrily carrying his belongings from the lodge. He glared at the three arrivals but said nothing. The three entered the lodge and sat, ignoring the furious Bull Head as he hurriedly worked.

Finally, Bull Head said bitterly, turning his face from Cooper to the two women, "I go now. Not come back."

As the man turned to leave, Cooper said, "Remember what I said, boy. Hurt either of these women and I'll have your hair hangin' from my rifle."

When he was sure Bull Head was gone, Cooper left and headed toward Pale Thunder's lodge. Sits Down fell in beside him, The mountain man was a little surprised, "Do you want to be seen with me?" he asked. "People might talk."

"They always talk," the warrior said with a grin. "They see, they think crazy Sits Down talks with white man foolish enough to take him on last trip, they think I ask to go again."

Cooper chuckled.

"I heard talk in the chief's lodge." Seeing Cooper's new look of surprise, he added, "I see you and Pale Thunder go to Red Leggin's. Not usual. So I go listen around side where few can see, if any are out on cold day."

"And?"

"And I don't like shit piles, as I hear you say, like Bull Head not helping friend. Or any of the People."

"I'm not one of the..."

"Yes you are. Pale Thunder said…"

"You talk to your father?"

"Yes. Not often but at times, places where no one can see. He told me you are his son now, along with me, though he can't say that part to anyone. And Goes Far is my sister now. You are family."

Cooper acknowledged it with a nod, then shook his head. "That means I'm married to my sister. That ain't right. Not among my people or yours."

"Is different this way. We not blood family."

Cooper nodded again.

"I hear my father say he will take care of Goes Far and Bright Eyes. Is good. I help."

"How can you do that?"

"Like I have done for many years. Hunt, bring meat, leave it at lodge for those who don't have enough. Always at night, when no one around to see. Especially in cold."

"Thank you."

"And I follow when you go back to Bright Eyes' lodge. I hear your warning to Bull Head."

"I meant it."

"I know you well enough to know you not say such things if you don't mean them. But you plan to leave. You will be back—unless you get rubbed out by Blackfeet—soon," he said with a grin. "If he is as foolish as I think, he maybe is foolish enough to not heed your words."

"I was afraid that might happen. Nothing I can do about it other than take care of it when I return."

"No need to worry, brother. I'll handle him if he tries to harm the women."

"You are a wonder, Sits Down," Cooper said with

an amused shake of the head. "A pure, certain mystery. Every time I talk to you, it seems, you say or do something new to me."

"I good at that," he said, laughing as he walked away.

GOES FAR WAS both sad and angry as Cooper prepared to leave in the morning. But she did as much as she could in her condition to help him, all the while holding back her tears.

The longer it took, the worse Cooper felt, but he could not change his mind now. To him, this had to be done—for Goes Far's and the child's safety and for his own sanity.

Finally the small amount of packing that needed doing was done. Cooper embraced the woman and held her tightly. "Pale Thunder will take care of you and your ma well. You know that. I'll come back. I promise. Either on the trail to rendezvous or at it." He paused, then grinned. "Unless the Blackfeet get me."

She pulled back a little and looked up at his face in horror. "Not say that. No. Never."

"All right. *When* I get back, my son or daughter..."

"Son," Goes Far said firmly with her cheek again pressed against his broad chest.

"My son'll only be a few months old then, so he won't have missed me, though I will him, I reckon. I'll be thinkin' about you both while I'm trappin' with Two-Faces and the others."

"You should still wait, take me when baby is born."

"It wouldn't be wise takin' a few-days-old baby into

the winter for several weeks while I search for my friends and trap. Too dangerous, and I ain't puttin' my son into so much danger when he's just come into the world."

"It will be a long time 'til I see you."

"It'll seem a long time to me, too. But it won't be long. Six months maybe." He gave her a strong squeeze, kissed her, and mounted his horse. "You just take good care of that baby when he comes, woman," he said gruffly, tying to mask his own sadness.

"I will." Goes Far finally let the tears flow as her mother came up to try to console her.

Cooper turned his head away gloomily and rode off.

EIGHTEEN

COOPER WAS LESS than a week out from the Nez Percé village when he sensed coming up behind him. He was on a short grass hill plain between two barren hills with no trees or anything else he might use for cover. So he dismounted, quickly drove two picket stakes into the ground, and hooked the horse and mule to them. Then he moved a few yards away, knelt, rifle leaning against the cook of his neck, and waited.

Before long, a large horse rider crested the previous hill. In moments, Cooper smiled. And only minutes later, Sits Down pulled up to where Cooper stood waiting.

"You got to stop followin' me around like a sick puppy, Sits Down," Cooper said with a laugh.

"Need to make sure you don't get lost."

Cooper pointed. "I see you have a nice young deer on the back of your saddle there. You fixin' to share?"

"Might. Might not if I'm hungry."

"I might starve to death ridin' with you despite all the meat at hand."

"I save you some. Little. Maybe." He laughed his great rumbling laugh. "Come, we fill bellies. There's a place just over next hill. Plenty wood, good grass, good water."

Cooper nodded, pulled up and stowed the picket pins, then mounted up. He and Sits Down rode easily on. Half a dozen miles away, they came to the spot, which was indeed a good one, the mountain man thought.

Each man took care of his horse, then, while Cooper tended his mule, Sits Down gathered wood. Soon they were sitting at a fire with the full coffeepot resting near the flames and with a large hunk of deer meat sizzling over the fire, juices dripping into the flames, making them dance a little.

"So what brings you out here chasin' me, Sits Down?" Cooper asked with a combination of hope and worry in his voice.

The Nez Percé's face broke into a smile. "You are father now. You have son. Goes Far named him Strong Bow."

"They both all right?" Worry was overriding joy for the moment.

"When I left, yes."

Cooper breathed a sigh of relief. "A papa. I wasn't sure it'd ever happen." He let the news settle in before finally asking, "What about you, Sits Down. You ever thought of becoming a father?"

Sadness shoved the jovialness off his face. "At times, yes. But it never will happen."

"Why not?"

"What woman would agree to have child with the fat, lazy village fool?"

"Not many, if any, I reckon, that's true. But you and I both know how great a warrior you really are. You live like the great warrior you are and any eligible woman—hell, *any* woman—in the village would consent to it or to anything else you might want."

"You're wrong. Even if I was to pretend to be a real warrior..."

"Wouldn't be no pretendin' about it, Sits Down. You have to quit thinkin' you're the same feller you was when you were a boy."

Sits Down shrugged. "Even if they see I'm good, what woman would want to lay with a big fat man like me." A smile began to creep back across his lips. "I would crush any woman foolish enough to lay with me."

"Hell, boy, there are ways around that. You'd find a way."

The grin spread. "I'll consider it, brother. Now it's time to eat."

They dug in, wolfing down baits of deer meat and swallowing hot coffee. As they did, Cooper said, "Thank you for bringin' me news of my son, Sits Down. I appreciate it."

Sits Down nodded, swallowed, then said, "There is another reason." He was somber now.

Cooper looked at him in question, a bite of meat halfway to his mouth.

"As we thought, Bull Head was a fool."

Cooper shoved the meat into his mouth and chewed. "He do something?"

"Yep."

"With Goes Far?" An icy feeling snuck into Cooper's stomach.

"No. With her mother. I watch lodge. She comes out, heads toward bushes. Bull Head sees, runs over, hits her. He pulls knife ready to...well, he didn't reach her."

"You stopped the son of a bitch."

Another grin crossed the big man's face as he nodded. The grin fell. "His hair is hangin' in my cave."

"And no one saw you?"

"It was late, dark. No one around."

"What about Bright Eyes? She had to know who saved her."

"Maybe. Not many—well no one—as big as me in the tribe, but she was dazed from being hit. I grabbed Bull Head's body, slung him over my shoulder and go. I think she think it was a spirit who helped her."

"Likely. Well, that's good, Sits Down. Now Goes Far and her ma can live in peace. I'm obliged."

The Nez Percé shrugged, uncomfortable about the thanks.

They ate in silence for a spell before Cooper asked, "You headin' back when we finish here? There's still plenty of daylight, so I figure to be movin' on bit more today."

"I ride a day or so with you maybe."

"Shines with me. Move on now as I was plannin'? Or stay the night here? Good place, like you said."

Sits Down laughed. "Everyone knows I am fat and lazy. Live up to name. So we stay."

"Sound reasonable to me."

THREE DAYS LATER, when Cooper woke, Sits Down was gone. The mountain man shook his head. "Can't tell when he'll show up, can't tell when he's leavin'. Ah well, at least he left me a couple days' worth of meat."

He relieved himself, splashed some icy water from the stream on his face and sat down to warmed over coffee and a few big slices of deer meat. He took his time, not seeing any reason to hurry, but it was soon time to leave.

As he rode, his mind returned to Goes Far—and the baby. It still seemed unreal to him and likely would continue to be so until he actually saw the child and was able to hold the boy. It was a strange feeling and not one he was sure he could get used to very soon.

But he also wondered about Sits Down. While the Nez Percé had explained his feelings about why he remained the way he had always been, Cooper could not understand it. The warrior was giving up all hope of real joy, of having the respect of all the men—and women—in his band, and likely the entire Nez Percé Nation. And not only would he have the respect of the women, he would also have the favors at any time of anyone he asked. It was a very strange man who would give that all up for a life of ridicule when he was so much more. He didn't know any other man—red or white—who would consent to such a life. He figured he would never understand and soon realized it was not his business anyway, and he would be better off leaving it lie without him keep suggesting that Sits Down take the due that he had earned.

RELIEVED AT KNOWING of the birth of his son and that his wife and mother-in-law were safe and cared for, he pushed on hard. He stopped for a day or two every few days to trap. His catch was plentiful and plush, but he could not afford to spend too much time in any one spot if he wanted to find his friends before they entered winter camp.

He made good time despite several days now and again of sleet, snow, or rain. He nearly lost the mule—and the plews he had taken plus what supplies he had—once when crossing a fast-rushing, rain-swollen river but managed to come through with himself, animals, and plews unscathed.

It was well into December when he neared the camp he had left a couple of months ago. The weather had taken a decided turn to winter, and trapping was getting more difficult as many of the smaller streams were beginning to freeze over.

He estimated that it was just after the new year when he found the old camp. Following the trail of the men as they moved was not difficult mostly though there were days of snow or rain that made tracking tough. But three weeks later, he found the men he was looking for.

"Hallo the camp," he hollered under the cover of a light snowfall.

"'Awley, *mon ami?*" Two-Faces Beaubien said, staring through the soft white curtain.

"One and the same."

"I think it's a ghost," Duncan MacTavish said with a laugh. "A fellow we knew as Hawley Cooper was killed by the damned Blackfeet and has come back to us to warn us that we'll all lose our hair to those red devils soon."

"Likely ain't got no hair himself now," Bill White threw in.

"You boys are just worried 'cause now that I'm back, you ain't gonna catch no more beaver. I'll do all the catchin'," Cooper said with a laugh as he dismounted.

There were handshakes and greetings all around—except for Colin Leary, who was still not a member of the group really. Sam Berryman was shy but had been accepted by the old-timers and was among them greeting Cooper.

"Come, m'sieur," Beaubien said, "we eat, get warm in my lodge." He pointed to a tipi nearby.

"You winterin' here?" Cooper asked, surprised. It did not seem like a good place for such a thing.

"*Mais non*. With the weather 'aving been bad lately, me and Duncan's women put up lodges. We need to keep the children safe and warm, eh."

"Makes sense."

They took a few steps toward Beaubien's lodge when the half-breed stopped and moved in front of Cooper. "Where is Mam'selle Goes Far?" he asked almost urgently.

"Back with her people."

"She threw ye over, lad?" MacTavish asked, surprised.

"No," Cooper said with a shake of the head. "I left her there. She hadn't birthed the child and time for trappin' was runnin' short, so I set off without her."

"'Ow will she get back to you?"

"She won't." It was said sadly. "We'll meet up again on the way to rendezvous, or there."

"But you don' know about ze baby."

"It's a boy child. She named him Strong Bow."

"I'm confused, lad. If she hadn't had the child before ye left, how do ye know about the wee lad?"

Cooper grinned. "Sits Down caught up to me some days later and told me."

"Is 'e still pretendin' to be the old fat, lazy Sits Down?" Beaubien asked.

"Yep. I've tried talkin' some sense into him, but he ain't havin' any of it."

They started walking again and soon were in Beaubien's lodge. It was crowded with the half-breed, Cooper, MacTavish, White, and Paddy Murphy, plus Beaubien's two wives and three children. But no one minded. The rest of the men and the other women and children were off in MacTavish's lodge nearby, which was also crowded with five men, two women, and three children.

Food and coffee were passed around, and they ate for a bit, then relaxed with coffee and pipes.

"So," Beaubien said, "did you ever encounter Elson and 'is nephew?"

Cooper nodded and sighed. "They caught up with us week or so after we left. I knew they were comin' and found us a cave for protection. There was a mostly open spot in front of it but not far off were trees they could—and did—use for cover."

"So y'all chased 'em off?" White asked.

"Chased 'em to the Spirit World," Cooper said with a sad shake of his head. "That pissant Farley was a fool, and a ball in his brainpan put an end to his nonsense. Elson, though..." Cooper shook his head again at the remembrance. "The damned fool was so crazy by then that he rushed the cave. I was in the trees above the cave. If I had stayed where I had been when I shot Farley, I would've been able to drop El before he got too far. But I had moved off after firin' so Elson couldn't get a bead on my position. Because of it, I wasn't in any position to fire, so I headed down, half slidin' in the grass and rocks, and landed on Elson. He fired a pistol just as I hit him, and the ball creased Mornin' Song. Nothin' serious, little more than a nick."

He paused for a sip of coffee, reliving the event in his mind. "He was down and helpless, and I was ready to put a ball in him, But his reason returned right then, givin' me pause."

"Would've me too, lad," MacTavish said.

The other three men agreed.

"He knew he'd been an evil man over the past several months and feared he'd go back to that. Said he could feel the bad spirits tryin' to get inside his head again. Damn." Cooper paused.

The others waited expectantly though patiently.

"He asked me to put him under, make sure the demons never took over his mind again. So..."

"You did ze right t'ing, *mon ami*," Beaubien said. "Now 'e is a peace and roaming ze Spirit World."

"Reckon so, but it sure as hell wasn't easy lookin' him in the face as he lay there askin' me to kill him."

"'Twould nae been easy for any of us, lad," MacTavish said quietly. "I dunna ken if I'd have had the strength to do it."

The others murmured their agreement.

Beaubien rose and rummaged under some buffalo

robes at the rear of the lodge, pushing two of his children out of the way. He returned to the fire with a jug. "We will 'ave a toast to our old *ami*, rest 'is soul."

NINETEEN

"SO WHERE DO we go now, *mon ami*?" Beaubien asked as they sat around the fire in the chill afternoon. Everyone had checked his traps and it was time to relax with some roasted meat and coffee.

"Why'n hell're you askin' me?" Cooper retorted, looking at Two-Faces Beaubien more in annoyance than in surprise. He had been suspecting what he figured was going to happen now in the few days since he had been back.

"You lead ze 'ommes now."

"*Mais non*, as you say. I ain't havin' no part of such doin's, Two-Faces. You been doin' the job, just keep on doin' it."

"I did so waitin' for you to come back and take ze lead."

"Don't know why you'd be so foolish. I told you before, more'n once, that I ain't interested."

"But you were El's second in command."

Cooper stared at him for a few moments, then shook his head. He rose stiffly and walked the short distance to his lean-to, where he grabbed a pack saddle. He strolled to the herd of horses and mules, picked out one of his mules, and tossed the saddle on it.

"Where you go, *mon ami?*" Beaubien asked, having followed Cooper. The others were only a few feet behind.

Cooper ignored them.

"Ye canna leave, lad," Duncan MacTavish said, moving up to stand next to Beaubien. "'Tis nae safe for ye alone out there."

Cooper still did not react.

"Why you do this, 'Awley?" the half-breed asked, both annoyed and puzzled.

With a sigh, Cooper turned. "Like I just told you, Two-Faces, and like I've told you many a time, I don't want no part of leadin' this group or any others. Since you boys don't seem to understand it—or don't think I mean what I say—I'll just mosey on. Once I'm gone, you can figure out who's gonna be in charge." His eyes moved from one man to the next.

Beaubien and MacTavish looked at each other, then at the crowd. Most of the men nodded. The half-breed turned his gaze back to Cooper. "You win, 'Awley."

Cooper stood, hard gaze on the men, then he nodded. "I'll say this, though, fellers, you best understand that if you ask this of me again, there won't be any stoppin' me from leavin' and goin' my own way." He undid the one strap of the pack saddle he had already tightened. He turned and dropped the saddle off at his lean-to, then retook his seat at the fire with Beaubien, MacTavish, Bill White, and Paddy Murphy. His face was still stony, and the others looked uneasy. Finally the half-breed said, "You and I still trap together again, eh, *mon ami*? Like we did yesterday?"

"You gonna badger me about bein' booshway of this motley group of fellers?"

"*Non.*" Beaubien grinned a little. "Maybe."

Cooper glared at him, then chuckled. "You're worse than any woman when it comes to naggin', hoss."

"I practice."

There was a small ripple of laughter as everyone relaxed.

They ate and drank in silence for a few minutes before Beaubien rose and called to the men at the two other fires. "Come, *mes amis*, we need to talk of t'ings we 'ave been puttin' off."

The other five men sat in a semicircle behind Cooper and the others.

"As I say, we 'ave put this discussion off since 'Awley came back, but now is ze time to finish this business. We must decide what to do with Elson's possibles." He waited out the short rumble of interest. "I suggest that all of Elson's plews go to 'Awley. 'Is 'orses and mules too."

"Why'n hell should he get everything?" Dave Wheeler called.

"Why the 'ell not, m'sieur?" the half-breed countered. "You 'ave done not'ing to earn them."

"Aye," MacTavish added from where he sat. "He had to kill a good friend who had lost his reason at great peril to his life as well as those of the two women."

"He killed my friend, too," Colin Leary said. "Wasn't no reason to kill Cousin Angus far as I can see."

"'E says there was, and I believe 'im," Beaubien said.

"I reckon he's lyin'. I figure he just wants Angus' plunder too."

Eyes blazing, Cooper started to rise.

"Sit, *mon ami*," Beaubien said quietly.

Cooper glared at him for a moment, then nodded and retook his seat.

"I 'ave ridden, trapped, starved, feasted, drank and fought alongside this man." He pointed to Cooper. "So 'ave all these others. Neither of you 'as. And none of these men would be 'ere if it weren't for M'sieur Coopair. Our 'air would be 'anging from some Blackfoot's war shirt. 'E would not lie to us. *Non, non, non.* There is no reason for 'im to lie to us. Any of these men would put 'is life in 'Awley's 'ands. In fact, we all 'ave. More than once."

"That don't mean..."

"Shut yer trap, lad," MacTavish snapped, rising to stand beside Beaubien. "To call him a liar is to call all of us liars, lad, and none of us will countenance such an insult."

"You do that agin, y'all," Bill White said, rising to stand on Beaubien's other side, "and you'll join your cousin in the grave."

Leary stood. "I ain't about to take such a threat from some damn nigra."

He stopped as a collective gasp, followed by a profound silence suddenly descended. He looked around and swallowed, realizing how much danger he was in. Worried, he sat.

After a few moments more of silence, Beaubien said, "I say 'e gets Farley's plews and animals too."

"No," Cooper said. "No, Two-Faces. It's too much."

"Than what do we do with them?"

"Well, that festerin' shit pile wasn't much of a trapper, so I don't reckon he has all that many plews."

"Half a pack, maybe a bit more," MacTavish interjected.

"So divide 'em up, as little as they are, among all you fellers."

"You deserve them, too, *mon ami*. You lost much trappin' time when you took Mornin' Song back to 'er people."

"You thought I was interferin' in a man's right to control his woman."

"*Oui*," Beaubien said with a nod. "But I learn that 'e 'ad lost all 'is reason and 'ad stopped bein' ze Elson we knew and who was our partner in all that we did."

"Take 'em, Hawley," Alistair Wentworth said from the semicircle of men. "Like Two-Faces said, you deserve them. 'Sides there ain't enough to share among all of us."

Cooper rose and turned to face the men. "I'm obliged. It don't shine with me exactly to take all these plews, but seein' as how I lost so much trappin' time, they'll be appreciated. But I don't need all the animals. I'll take one of El's mules for the extra plews. You boys can argue over the rest." He grinned, then grew serious again. "Reckon a few of you boys've lost a horse or mule crossin' a river or fallin' off a cliff. You can replace 'em from El's stock. And Angus's, though he ain't got many. As for the rest of the possibles and such..."

"You can..."

"No, Two-Faces. Let the boys divvy it up among themselves as they can decide. All those plews are enough for me. The rest of the boys, who've been with El as long as I have, or even longer, like you, Two-Faces, should share in whatever largess there is."

Beaubien waited a few seconds but no one spoke. "Then it is settled, eh. We do the sharin' tomorrow after we run our traps." He headed for his lodge while MacTavish and White sat again.

Beaubien returned a few minutes later with a jug. "One cup each, *mes amis*. No more." He walked around, pouring a healthy dose of Taos Lightning into each man's cup. Done, he raised his own cup. "To our grand *capitaine* Elson Brooks as we remember our friend as 'e was in 'is good days and not ze bad ones when ze bad spirits stole 'is mind."

When the toast was done, Beaubien took the jug back to his lodge. At the fire, White said, "Y'all best watch yourself, Hawl. I don't trust that Leary feller."

"Me neither. I'll be watchful. You should be, too, considerin' how well he likes Black men."

White nodded.

"I dunna think Mr. Leary has a long future," MacTavish said. "I dunna see him lastin' through the winter."

"I do believe you're right, Duncan," Cooper said. He shook his head. "And there's a damn good chance I'll end up bein' the one who sends him off to the Afterworld."

White and MacTavish looked at each other, then the former said, "I can make sure that don't happen, Hawl."

Cooper stared at the Black man for a few moments, then shook his head. "Obliged, Bill. But I reckon not. Leastways not yet."

"You change your mind, hoss, let me know."

"And if Bill here is nae 'round," MacTavish threw in, "I can take care of the problem for ye."

"Thank you, boys. Don't know if I'm due such consideration and offers of help, though."

"Aye, ye are, lad. Despite El's dafty nonsense about ye crowin' of yer great deeds, we know ye nae did such a thing, though ye'd earned the right to do so. But like Two-Faces said, if it weren't for ye—and Zeke and Sits Down, of course—the hair of every man here would be decoratin' some heathen's war shirt. We owe ye our lives, Hawl, and I ain't a one to forget such a thing."

"Me neither," White added. "And I reckon the other boys feel the same."

"Thanks," Cooper said, embarrassed at the accolades.

"SO, where do we go now, 'Awley?" Beaubien asked with a grin. "We need a place to winter."

Cooper's eyes blazed in anger and he started to rise.

"Ah, sit doon, lad," MacTavish said. "Yon Frenchie is yankin' at yer trap chain."

"*Oui*. I jest, *mon ami*. I ask not to 'ave you make a decision but to advise this half-breed fool."

"You have a funny way of askin' for advice. I think you should go to hell, the rest of us can find us a good winterin' place that'll be warm but not so swelterin' as you'll be doin'.'"

The men laughed.

"Hell, I don't know, Two-Faces. None of us've been places north of here, though I hear the trappin's good near the Musselshell or even farther north on the Milk. Whether there's anyplace decent for winter camp..." He shrugged.

"I heard some fellers a few years ago down to rendezvous talkin' about an area up north of here," Paddy Murphy said. "They said there are some good places near the South Fork of the Musselshell."

"Any good places might be full up already," Alistair Wentworth said.

"Could be. Anyone else have any ideas?"

There was no answer to that.

"That's gettin' deeper into Blackfoot country," White said.

"Ye fearful, mate?" the Scot asked with a grin.

"Well, not with Hawley along," White said with a laugh. "We have any trouble with Bug's Boys, he'll take care of it while the rest of us sit and watch, maybe cheerin' him on."

"I just might send a few of 'em to come pay you a visit, you festerin' weasel humper," Cooper retorted, failing to keep the laughter from bubbling out.

The others joined in.

"Then that is where we will go, eh," Beaubien said. "Paddy, will you scout out a place when we get near?"

"Reckon I can do that. Ye mind goin' along, Hawl?"

"Rather not, Paddy. I'm still way behind on my trappin', and I need to make up some of that time."

"I'll go with ye, Paddy," Wentworth said. "We been partners on the trap lines, don't see why we can't be partners as explorers. Besides, you need someone to keep a faint-hearted fool like you out of the Blackfeet's clutches."

TWENTY

WINTER LAID its heavy hand on the mountain men's camp, slapping them hard and relentlessly. It pounded the men and animals with an almost unrelenting liturgy of snow, sleet, and rain all the while blasting the camp with icy, swirling winds that threatened to wipe away everything and everyone. There was little game, if any, their meat supplies were running low within a few weeks, forage was poor, and the animals were gaunting down. It made for a tense time, and the men grew testy.

"This was a damn foolish place to winter at," Dan Anderson said. "It don't shine at all."

The men had gathered in the one rickety cabin that served as home for all the men save Beaubien, MacTavish, White, and Cooper, who was staying with the half-breed.

"Damn right," Dave Wheeler snapped. "How could you choose such a place, Paddy? You been 'round long enough to know better."

"I..."

"Enough," Beaubien snapped. "It's done and there's not'ing we can do directly about it now."

"So we just sit here and watch all our animals freeze to death, and then watch each other fall prey to the weather?" Wheeler asked roughly.

"*Mais non, mes amis*," Beaubien said. "I will find us a new place."

"No," Cooper said. "You're needed here to keep a watch on these fractious fellers. I'll go."

"If you think you can find us a better place, you should've gone the first time," Colin Leary growled.

"Dammit," Murphy growled, "this place looked like a shinin' spot when I come here. There was no way to tell that winter had other plans for it."

"But you..."

"Waugh!" Cooper snapped. "Two-Faces said we'll find a new spot. And I will. You can count on it."

"You think you're that good a tracker?" Leary scoffed.

Cooper turned cold, hard eyes on the young man, who seemed to shrink under the gaze. "Yes," Cooper said simply.

"I'll go with ye, Hawley," Duncan MacTavish said.

"You certain? What about your women and young'uns?"

"Me and Two-Faces'll watch over 'em with our own," Bill White said firmly.

Beaubien nodded.

"When will ye boy-os leave?" Murphy asked, hope in his voice.

"No better time than the present," Cooper said. "It ain't much past dawn, though it's hard to tell with more damn snow comin' down."

"Your 'orses all right?"

Cooper nodded, as did MacTavish.

"You sure you want to use them? Might be better to take your extra 'orses."

"My mare's fine, and she's used to me. The gelding not as much. I'll be fine."

"And me," MacTavish said.

"Ye boys can take one of my mules," Murphy said. "Save yours for when we move on."

Cooper hesitated, then realized the Irishman was trying to make up for the disappointment and trouble caused by him recommending this place for wintering. He nodded.

"Take what meat you t'ink you need from our stores," Beaubien said. "You should 'ave what other supplies you 'ave need of in your own plunder."

HALF AN HOUR LATER, Cooper and MacTavish pulled out, the latter leading the pack mule. Within minutes they had disappeared into the white curtain of snow.

The Scot pulled up alongside Cooper. "Ye have any idea where ye're goin', lad?" he asked.

"Nope."

"Ye sounded mighty certain back there in camp."

"I was tryin' to keep the fellers from causin' too much of a ruckus, which could've led to a heap of trouble."

"We don't find a place, there'll be an even bigger free-for-all when we get back."

"Reckon there will be. So we best find a place soon."

"Might be hard without either of us knowin' much, if anything, about the area."

"True, but we'll do it."

"Ye ken that there's a difference between hope and cockiness, don't ye? Seems to me ye're confusin' the two."

"I ain't cocky," Cooper said flatly, "just optimistic."

"I'm nae sure about this, Hawley."

"Then why'd you come along?"

"Thought you might have some place in mind."

"Then turn back, Duncan. We ain't but a couple miles from the camp."

"What'll I tell the lads?"

"Cut your cinch and say you couldn't go on with a damaged saddle."

MacTavish was quiet for a while, then said, "We've rode together for some years now, Hawley, and in all that time, I ne'er known ye to lie about things. Especially about important things. I dunna ken how ye do it, lad, but ye always seem to find a way to do what ye say ye will, no matter the difficulty." He looked at his companion and grinned.

Cooper grinned back.

"So I believe ye, lad, and reckon I can ride along with ye 'til we find us a place. Or not, in which instance I'll be one disappointed critter." He laughed.

"Now I really gotta find us a place. Can't disappoint my ol' friend Duncan MacTavish." He, too, laughed.

Two days later they worked their way through a snow-choked pass, then along a forest trail until they came to a small meadow surrounded by low hills.

There was little snow on either the flatland or the hills.

Cooper sat on his mare looking the place over. There was a stream running through some cottonwoods at the far side of the meadow and more of the trees where the stream pooled. Large stands of cottonwoods and oaks stood at spots across the meadow. Cooper pointed, and MacTavish smiled as he saw a small herd of elk grazing on what vegetation could be found among the trees at the southern end of the field.

"I dunna ken how ye did it, lad, but damn if ye didn't find what looks to be the perfect place."

"Paddy thought so when he found the other."

"It hadn't been snowin' for two days or more. If it had been, the place would've been covered in snow like it is now. It's been snowin' regular all across the mountains, and there's hardly a couple inches here and little more on the hills. I swear there's a warm breeze comin' over that hill to the northwest."

"Does seem that way."

"Think ye can find it again when we bring the others?"

"I can. But can you?"

"If you can, I'm right beside ye."

Cooper shook his head. "You're headin' back to the others and bringin' 'em here."

"What'll ye be doon?"

"Sittin' on my ass takin' my ease."

MacTavish looked at him in annoyed surprise. "Ye aren't goin'?"

Cooper laughed at the Scot's look. "I'll be gettin' a start on cuttin' down some trees and doin' little huntin'. Give the boys a head start on makin' camp."

"But I can do that, too. Ye're better on the trail than I am."

"Nah, I ain't. Just mark your way if you're uncertain about the way. You'll be fine."

"But..."

"Go see to your women and children. Slow Calf's been made a widow once already. She don't need to be one again. Never can tell, there might be Blackfoot about."

"Might be Bug's Boys on the trail too. But I reckon it'll be nice to be with Slow Calf and the children as we head here."

The two men rode slowly down the hill, into the meadow, and stopped in a stand of trees. They dismounted.

"I'll leave first light," MacTavish said. "I'd leave now, but the animals need some rest and feed if we can gather some."

Cooper nodded.

A WEEK LATER, MacTavish led the group of mountain men into the vale. Cooper stopped hewing a log and watched as the men crossed the meadow.

"I t'ink when we go t'rough that pass," Beaubien said as he dismounted, "that *mon ami*, ze great pathfinder Duncan MacTavish, 'ad lost 'is way. And 'is reason. We almost turned back. I'm glad we didn't. This is paradise compared to ze other place. *Tres bien, m'sieurs.*"

Cooper nodded, not interested in the accolades. "Best put the men to work right off. I cut down enough trees, I think, to build a cabin, and there's fresh—well, freshly killed and frozen—meat under a tarp near that tree." He pointed.

"This is why you should be leadin' these men, 'Awley."

"Don't start that hogwash with me again, Two-Faces, or I'll ride off and find another nice place for winterin'."

"Bah." But he grinned and began issuing orders—or, rather, suggestions seeing as how this was not a company but a conglomeration of free trappers. The men—and women—were soon busy and the area filled with shouts, friendly insults, and curses as the work progressed smoothly and quickly.

About the middle of the next day, the camp was as put together as it could be. Lodges were set up for Beaubien and his family, with Cooper as a guest again; and another shared by MacTavish and White and their families. The cabin was unbalanced and looked like it might collapse at any time, but it was sturdy enough. Cooper had done more hunting and there was frozen meat to be had by all. Cottonwood bark has been stripped off and stored under a makeshift lean-to and fed to the animals regularly. Firewood was stacked against the cabin and the two lodges.

"It may not be as comfortable as ze Nez Percé village," Beaubien said as he and Cooper looked over the finished camp. "But it is good enough and much better than ze other place."

Cooper nodded. The half-breed started to say something, which Cooper figured was another thank you from his friend, but he cut him off. "It's time to fill our meatbags, Two-Faces. We've earned it."

"*Oui!*" Beaubien said with a grin as he led the way into his lodge. Minutes later, they were wolfing down baits of elk, juice running down into their beards and onto their shirts. They paid it no heed.

Paddy Murphy called for entrance and was soon sitting at the fire desultorily gnawing on some meat.

"This is good elk, Paddy," Beaubien said. "You insult my wives by not eatin' it with enthusiasm."

"Sorry, Two-Faces." He sighed. "I just wanted to apologize for my error in claimin' that other places would be a good one for winterin'. I..."

"Hush, boy," Cooper said quietly. "When we found this place, Duncan said that when you come across that other place, it hadn't been snowin' for days, the weather was warm for this country, and, I would guess, the wind wasn't howlin' around your ears. Hell, if I had seen it at the time, I likely would've thought it a fine spot for winterin' too. Turns out Mother Nature was playin' tricks on us. Could be that this place turned out to be poor, too, though it doesn't seem like it will."

"But..."

"Shut your trap, Paddy. It's over and done. It ain't like you was bein' evil when you picked that other place. It was just bad luck. Now, like I said, shut your trap." He grinned. "Except for fillin' it with this good ol' elk meat."

Murphy hesitated a few moments, then he, too, grinned and dug into the food.

THE CAMP FELL into a routine of mundane tasks and boredom broken up by minor skirmishes among the men. Beaubien and Cooper, who had somehow found himself the de facto second in command again, let the men roughhouse, stepping in only when it looked like someone would be seriously hurt.

"You notice, I'm sure, 'Awley," the half-breed said one day as they stood outside in the cold for a bit keeping an eye on things, "that young M'sieur Leary often starts ze rumpus?"

"Yep. Nothin' can be done about it, though I reckon, 'cept keep a watch on him to make sure he doesn't get too out of hand."

"You don't think we should talk to 'im?"

"Nope, that just might make him worse. He ain't done that much wrong, and he's gotten himself thumped by some of the boys. But we best keep a good eye on him. He's lost most of the fights he's started that I'm thinkin' he might go after someone with a knife or, worse, gun."

"That would be no good."

"No, it wouldn't. And at that point, I will put a stop to it however I need to."

TWENTY-ONE

THERE WAS NO REAL SIGN, no one thing that made nature's announcement, but the men just plain knew one day that spring was tearing a hole—a small one to be sure, but a definite one—in the winter's bitterness.

While this camp had been far less inhospitable than the last, it still was not winter-free. There was snow and sleet and bitter cold. The game drifted away after a few hunting excursions by the men. But relatively speaking, it was a pleasant place, or at least as pleasant as it could be under the circumstances.

With this intangible sign, the camp suddenly was bustling, with the men making sure their equipment was in good working order. And a week later, despite a snowstorm the day before, Beaubien announced that they would break camp the next morning and head to a spot Cooper had found a few miles away with plenty of beaver sign.

The mountain men spread out from their new, temporary camp the day after arriving, and soon were mighty pleased with the result. The furs were plush and thick with winter fur. Cooper, who had taken three of Brooks' traps, along with trapping partner Two-Faces Beaubien, brought in a few dozen plews.

But within days, the beaver in the area were no more and it was time to move on. The men worked their way north and east, then northwest through the Missouri Breaks, then to the great Missouri River, which they followed north traveling parallel to it though a few miles distance. They continued to pull in large catches of beaver. Everyone was happy—except Colin Leary, whose trapping had been dismal, which he let the others know often in a thin, whiny voice.

It was enough to propel Copper forward with his plan. As he, Beaubien, MacTavish and White sat at the fire outside the half-breed's tent, Cooper announced, "Reckon I'll be leavin' come mornin', boys."

"Where to?" White asked, though they all knew.

"Headin' for Nez Percé country or, rather, south-west from here, hopin' to catch the People on their way to the rendezvous.

"Y'all be all right alone, ya think?" White asked.

"Reckon so. Bug's Boys come after me, they'll regret it. After all, I took on the whole damned Blackfoot Nation last year and brought 'em to bay."

"We'll overlook yer small boast seeing as how it's just us lads here," MacTavish said with a grin.

"And it's almost true," Beaubien tossed in. "What're you plannin' to do with all your plews and such?"

"Take 'em along, I guess, Two-Faces. Ain't much else I can do."

"Be hard going with two, three horses and four mules," MacTavish said.

Cooper nodded. "Such is the way of things when one wants to get back to his woman after a winter away."

The others, each of whom had a wife and children, nodded solemnly.

Before long, MacTavish and White headed toward the tent they shared along with their families.

Cooper started to rise, too, but Beaubien said, "Sit, *s'il vous plaît*." When Cooper did so, giving the half-breed a quizzical look, the latter said, "I 'ave an idea to make t'ings easier for you. Some years ago, when you were 'unting for those Crows who killed your woman, El took your plews and such to rendezvous and sold them."

"He did that, yes."

"I propose ze same t'ing, *mon ami*. I will take your plews and your animals and bring them to rendezvous. If you are there, you can trade them. If not, I trade them for you and either get supplies for next season for you or take ze money and give to you when I see you to buy your own supplies."

"Might be troublesome carin' for everything."

"*Mais non*. My women can 'andle ze mules. Ze 'orses will be in ze remuda with ze others."

"What'll you charge me for such largess?"

Beaubien looked as if Cooper had just kicked him in the groin. "Get out, m'sieur," the half-breed said in a harsh voice, his face stony. "You are not welcome in my lodge ever again. Go. *Vite!*"

"I figured you'd react that way, Two-Faces, but I had to be certain. I've known you for some years now, and never had any reason to mistrust you." He shook his head. "But after Elson found himself with bad spirits rummaging around in his head, I've been spooked a little and had to make sure."

"You insult me, m'sieur," Beaubien said relaxing just a little.

"I know. Didn't mean to, really. But, like I said, since El's mind wandered off for good and left him without reason, I've been a little spooked. I'm sorry, Two-Faces, I should never have said what I did, nor have implied that you were dishonest." He stood. "I'll not bother you again in the short while before I leave tomorrow, and I won't bother you at rendezvous either. You're right to ban me from your lodge after what I said. Again, my apologies."

He started to leave but stopped when Beaubien said, "Sit."

Cooper did so.

"We 'ave known each other many years, *mon ami*. Fought together, faced starving times together, and more. I t'ink I know why you are worried that others 'ere might lose their reason. But I 'ave given you no reason to think that might've 'appened to me."

"You're right. Two-Faces. And I say again that I'll not bother you anymore."

"That is not necessary. I can forgive you after the years of our friendship. But do not challenge me this way ever again. *est-ce que tu comprends*."

"I ain't sure of the French, but I figure you're askin' me, no, tellin' me, that I had best understand."

"*Oui.*"

"I don't know as if you can ever forgive me for insultin' you, Two-Faces. Damn, that was a foolish thing to do, and makes my stomach knot up."

"We all make foolish mistakes, *mon ami*." He

smiled a little. "I once told El that he was the spawn of a *puta* and a sniveling coward, and that 'e 'ad stones the size of peas, that 'e was not qualified to lead a drunken man to ze latrine, let alone lead this group."

"You did?" Cooper said, eyes wide in surprise.

"*Oui*. We almost fought over it. But I apologize, and 'e forgive me. 'E treat me with respect ever since, at least 'til recently when his mind left him. And I treated 'im with respect. So I forgive you, *mon ami*. It is if it never 'appened."

"You're a strange feller, Two-Faces. A wise and decent man, though a little odd. Still, since Zeke went under, there's no one I'd rather have at my back in a battle against the Blackfeet than you."

"*Merci*."

Cooper took a deep breath. "Now, if you're offer is still open, I'll be glad to take you up on it."

"I'll get Duncan or one of ze others to write it down. I can't read or write."

"After our little chat here, I don't need a damn piece of paper promisin' anything. I have no doubt you'll do what you say and do it honestly."

"*Bon*." He said something in Flathead to Little Fox and she brought over a jug of whiskey. He poured some in Cooper's tin mug, then his own. "A toast, m'sieur, to seal this deal."

"Amen to that, Two-Faces."

———

THE NEXT MORNING, with a mule loaded with supplies, Cooper made ready to leave.

"*Avoir une bonne voyage, mon ami, et surveille tes*

cheveux—have a good trip, my friend, and watch your hair."

Cooper nodded, waved to his other friends, and rode out heading southwest. He soon reached the Missouri River and followed it southwest, paralleling the mighty river's course but staying a few miles away from it. A week or so later, he gave the roaring great falls a wide berth. He crossed the river in the Big Belt Mountains and turned west. A few days later, he swung southwest again. He hoped that the route would allow him to intercept the Nez Percé on their way to rendezvous. All he could do was travel as quickly as possible and hope it would not be too long. He was eager to see Goes Far—and Strong Bow.

As he rode, he wondered whether he should head out with the group come the next season. He enjoyed the company of Two-Faces Beaubien, Duncan MacTavish, and Bill White. They were good trappers and good companions, men he could—and had—stood shoulder to shoulder with against the Blackfeet on many occasions. But he was no longer sure of the others, even Paddy Murphy and Alistair Wentworth. The two men had been with Brooks for some time. Wentworth had always been amiable and faced the mountains and all their troubles with toughness and aplomb. But for some reason he had never really become close to either man. Then there were Dave Wheeler and Dan Anderson. He had not taken a liking to them right from the beginning. They were too close to Malachi Webster, backing the savage former riverman who had attacked Goes Far more than once. They had apologized shortly before Cooper had made wolf bait out of Webster, but he felt he could never trust them. Then there were the two new men—Sam Berryman and Colin Leary. Berryman had turned into a diligent, hardworking fellow who knew his place as a greenhorn among the old-timers. The same could not be said for Leary who, like his Cousin Angus had been, was a troublemaker without the real spine to back it up. He was a whiner and a slacker, and Cooper had no use for him.

So he began to seriously consider leaving the group and going his own way. It would be dangerous, just him and Goes Far and the infant, but he had faced danger before, and Goes Far was as sturdy of heart and will as anyone he ever knew. They would be fine he figured. Unless the Blackfeet came at him in numbers. He could consider trapping somewhere other than the heart of Blackfoot country, but the damned Bug's Boys were known to raid anywhere at any time. Going elsewhere might lessen the chance of attack but it would not eliminate it.

There were also changes in the wind. Talk at the last couple of rendezvous said hats made of silk instead of beaver were now the rage and that the beaver trade was dying. He wasn't sure he believed that. Felt made of beaver fur had been the best material for making top hats for long before Cooper was alive, and he could see no reason why it would be replaced by some slinky material that he thought might not stand up to the weather. Still, he had seen signs that maybe the beaver population was dwindling. A few areas he and the others had trapped seemed to empty out pretty quickly, and he wondered if that was an indication of things to come. If he were on his own, he could trap out a place by himself and make his money without having to spread the wealth of furs among the men. He did not begrudge them, but at the same time, seeing a dwindling supply of beaver would affect them all, and he had to protect himself and his woman.

He also began to wonder what he would do if the beaver trade did, indeed, die. It was something he really did not want to contemplate. What he would do if that happened was perplexing. He knew little other than trapping.

Such thoughts rummaged through his mind every day, though not so much that they cost him his vigilance. Still, it was a great surprise when an arrow punctured his chest near the clavicle and another thudded into his thigh, only inches from where he had been shot the winter before in the big battle with the Blackfeet.

"Damn, horse, let's move!" Dropping the rope to the mule, he kicked the mare into a run, heading for the tree- and boulder-studded hill rising to the west.

Another arrow skidded off the top of his shoulder and one sizzled its way through the side of his shirt. A glance over his shoulder told him that four warriors were racing toward him.

TWENTY-TWO

HE GRABBED his rifle and slid off his horse behind a jumble of boulders. He rested the Dickert on top of one boulder and fired. A Blackfoot went down.

The other three scattered.

"Waugh! This here's poor bull and no use denyin' it, ol' hoss," he muttered as he swiftly reloaded the rifle. He moved a few feet to his left just as two arrows screamed across the rock where he had been standing.

He took a moment to glance down. The arrow in his leg was not even the depth of the arrowhead. He grabbed it, yanked it out, and tossed it away.

He surveyed the area around him as best he could. He was well protected by the boulders, but there were trees all around providing the Indians some protection. The trees, though, were scattered and mostly a few yards away, so the Blackfeet would have to cover at least a little open ground to get to him. At that moment, they were well hidden, which concerned him. Some of them could be making their way through the trees to get around behind him. *How fitting*, he thought, *it would be to go under at the hands of Blackfeet who had gotten behind him much as he, Zeke Potts, and Sits Down had done to the Blackfeet last year.*

Well, there was nothing he could do about it except try to stay vigilant, which would become more difficult with his wound. The pain he could handle; it was less troublesome than other wounds he had had. But blood still oozed out around the arrow, dampening his shirt. He tugged gently at it but judged that it was too deeply embedded to try to remove. He wondered how long it would be before the loss of blood weakened him and clouded his mind. He sighed. There was nothing he could do about any of it. He set the rifle down for a moment and snapped the arrow's shaft to where only a few inches stuck out so it would not interfere with his shooting. And he waited, bleeding and sweating, head swiveling from side to side trying to catch any advance by the Indians.

A tense ten minutes or so later, he saw the smallest flicker of something in the trees to his left that was not natural. He turned that way and watched. It came again —the flash of branches in a way the wind would not cause. He lay his rifle atop another boulder and waited once more.

The movement came again, and though he could not see a warrior, he sighted on where the man should be judging by the movement. "Think you can sneak up on me, do you, you bastard," he muttered. He fired. There was a short screech and a crashing of bushes.

"That's two of you sons a bitches down. Your pals ain't gonna be far behind," he mumbled as he reloaded his Dickert.

Then he was waiting again.

As time ticked by, he began to feel his strength ebbing bit by bit. He figured he still had a couple of hours to go before it really incapacitated him. But he didn't like the idea of standing here bleeding while waiting for his end. "This don't shine at all," he muttered.

A few minutes later, he made up his mind. Leaving his nervous animals behind, he slid through a small opening between two boulders and darted into the trees. He moved deeper into the woods before making his way toward where the Blackfeet had first appeared. Fifteen careful minutes later, he stopped behind a tree and looked out at four Blackfoot ponies nibbling on bushes they were tied to.

Deciding the warriors were not close by, Cooper glided up and untied the four animals. Then he shouted once and slapped the animal facing the trail on the rump. The horse bolted, followed by the three others.

With a grim smile, Cooper dashed a little farther into the trees, barely making it out of the small clearing where the ponies had been before the remaining two warriors rushed up, trying to run down the animals.

Cooper shot both of them, then scalped them and the two others. He did not know what he would do with them considering the fact that he himself might not have long to tread the earth, but he figured it would at least leave their spirits wandering aimlessly in the afterlife.

He returned to the rough circle formed by the boulders and calmed his horse and mule. He grabbed a piece of jerky and plopped down, back against a rock, and gnawed at the leathery meat.

"Well, ol' hoss, what're you gonna do now?" he mumbled after a few minutes. But he had no answer.

He wiggled the arrow in his chest again to see if its grip had loosened any and hissed at the pain. He let his hand drop and he rested his head back on the rock and considered his options. They were few and unpleasant. He could try to get the arrow out, though he wasn't sure of the chances; he might pass out before he succeeded. While he had endured considerable pain at various times, especially in the battle with the Blackfeet the previous winter, this might prove to be too much. He liked to think he was tough enough to endure it but there was no way of telling unless he tried it. And if he managed, what would he do then? He had nothing to treat it with, no herbs that Goes Far would use as a poultice, nor did he have anything to bandage it with, though he likely had a muslin or calico shirt in his possibles sack. Of course, he could pull the damn thing out and then ride on.

Or he could ride on with the thing still stuck in his flesh and hope he could find some friendly Indians to help him. Considering where he was, that might be difficult since he was still in Blackfoot territory. On the other hand, almost anything west of the Missouri and north of the Platte might be considered Blackfoot country because they were known to raid throughout the land.

Or, he thought with a grim grin, he could just sit where he was and either bleed to death or starve to death over the next few days. Or maybe more Blackfeet would come along and raise his hair. But giving up like that was not his way.

So he sat, thinking.

Finally he sighed. He could not sit here any longer. He drew in a long breath and let it out slowly. He grabbed the short arrow shift, gritted his teeth, and yanked.

Pain tore through him and he slammed his back against the boulder, sucking in air through clenched teeth. Breathing heavily, he gingerly touched the thin, jagged piece of wood. It was still entrenched but jiggled a little more having been loosened a bit. "Damn," he growled. With another deep breath, he grabbed the shaft and yanked it one more time.

———

COOPER AWOKE SPRAWLED on the ground with fire in his upper chest. He was groggy and wasn't sure he actually heard voices. He pushed himself up and saw three warriors and started. Then he realized they were Flatheads.

One came over and squatted down in front of him. He said something in his own language. Cooper shook his head. The warrior asked his name in sign language.

"Hawley Cooper," he said in English.

With signs, the few words Cooper knew of Flathead, some Nez Percé the Flatheads knew, and some English, they were able to converse well enough.

The warrior nodded. "I'm Kills the Bear. What're you doing here?"

"Heading toward Nez Percé country—or their route to rendezvous really. My wife is with them, and I was trying to reach them."

"You're hurt."

"Attacked by Blackfeet."

"They didn't take your hair," he said, stating the obvious.

"Hard to do when they're dead."

Kills the Bear's eyes raised. Over his shoulder, he said something in Flathead. Two of his warriors hurried off. "Why attack?"

Cooper cocked an eyebrow at him. "They're Blackfoot."

The Flathead nodded. "Mean warriors, the Blackfeet."

"Yes. Especially against us American mountaineers."

"And my people too," the Flathead said fiercely.

Cooper nodded. "And just about every other tribe in the mountains or on the plains."

"Yes." He turned his head as his three warriors returned and said something, then turned back to Cooper. "Four Blackfeet dead, scalped. You?"

Cooper nodded. He pointed to the four scalps hanging from the saddle horn on the mare.

"Is good."

"What're are *you* doing here?"

Kills the Bear grinned. "Hunting Blackfeet."

"Why aren't you heading for rendezvous?"

"We will go—after killing some Blackfeet."

"Sorry I killed these four. You might've caught up to them. Their ponies run off. Maybe you can catch them. That'll at least give you something even if they're not scalps."

Again Kills the Bear said something over his shoulder and his fellow warriors hurried off in different directions. They soon returned with the Blackfoot horses. "What'll you do now?" he asked, turning back to Cooper.

The mountain man shrugged. "I'll push on as best I can, hoping I can find the Nez Percé before I go under. If I can find them, maybe they'll be able to help."

Kills the Bear sat there thinking, then said, "We take you to our people. Get help from them. They're heading to rendezvous too."

"What about hunting Blackfeet?"

The Flathead shrugged. "We were going to join our people at rendezvous. This way we find them on the trail a little sooner and travel with them."

"But what about taking scalps?"

"We have ponies now. That's enough. We'll hunt Blackfeet again on the way back to our land after rendezvous."

It was Cooper's turn to sit thinking, then he nodded and offered a smile. "Tell you what, Kills the Bear, for your help, you can have the scalps I took if that pleases you."

"That is good." He continued to stare at Cooper, a puzzled look on his face. He cocked his head. "You've fought Blackfeet before." When Cooper nodded, he continued, "Big fight last winter?"

Cooper nodded, a little uncomfortable wondering where this was going.

"We hear you killed many Blackfeet."

"I did, but I had a lot of help, a fellow mountaineer and a Nez Percé friend."

"Blackfeet are plenty angry. Attack everywhere."

"They're always angry and always attack everywhere."

"But more angry than before."

Cooper shrugged. "That's not my concern. It was either we fight the Blackfeet as hard as we could or we let them raise our hair. We weren't about to let that happen without a fight."

Kills the Bear paused a few moments, then grinned. "It is good many Blackfeet die. Like you say, they are always angry. But now fewer to fight maybe."

"Always a good thing when there are fewer Blackfeet to fight. Be nice if there were none."

"But then we would have to find new enemies."

"Wouldn't be hard," Cooper said with a small laugh. "There are plenty of devils."

"Many, yes."

Cooper nodded, then started to rise but began to topple. Kills the Bear caught him and eased him down onto the ground again. "We go soon. Take you to my people. Can you ride?"

"Don't think so," Cooper mumbled.

The Flathead looked around but saw nothing that could be used as a travois. Finally he nodded and said something to his fellow warriors. Two of the men lifted Cooper onto one of the men's ponies and held him in place until another warrior easily leaped on the animal's back and made sure the mountain man did not fall. Another warrior grabbed the reins to Cooper's mare and the mule. The unencumbered Kills the Bear led the way out of the little sanctuary, moving fast, as the other warrior pushed the Blackfoot ponies ahead of them.

They traveled through the night and all the next day. Just before dusk, they found their people, who had set up a camp for the night.

Kills the Bear called to his wife, Rising to the Sky.

When she saw the warriors lifting Cooper down from his horse, she quickly grabbed a buckskin pouch and hurried to where Cooper had been placed on a buffalo robe. She knelt over him, opened her sack, and began pulling out her healing herbs and powders.

TWENTY-THREE

IN HIS MOMENTS OF LUCIDNESS, which at times were far apart, Cooper became aware that the village had packed up and moved on for the most part. Rising to the Sky fretted over him, worried that her treatments were not working as he had a raging fever, and his wound looked a little sickly. He moaned occasionally in his pain- and fever-racked state. Before he could say anything when he realized the tribe had moved on, he had faded into blackness again. But the next time he awoke, he realized he was shirtless and through still clouded eyes that his shirt, shooting bag, possibles sack, and rifle lay neatly just a few feet away. He called Kills the Bear.

The warrior kneeled beside him on one side, his woman on the other. "You don't look good," the man said with a small smile.

"Don't feel so good either. Where are the rest of your people?"

"Gone on ahead."

"And you stayed behind?"

"Yes. Me, Rising to the Sky here, who has been treating you, and two of my friends, Backbone and Rough Belly."

"You needn't have done that."

"We didn't drag you all the way here just to leave you to die," Kills the Bear said matter-of-factly. You'll get better, then we will go to rendezvous. We can move fast just the five of us."

"The way I feel now, I won't be getting better. Might be best off if you leave me."

"I fix you good," Rising to the Sky said angrily in English. "You not believe me?"

"Sometimes a man's beyond helpin', ma'am. This might be one of those times."

"If what is said about your fight with the Blackfeet last winter, you're a strong man," the Flathead warrior said. "If all those Blackfeet couldn't kill you, one Blackfoot arrow won't put you under."

"I ain't so sure," Cooper said weakly. He paused, almost fading into unconsciousness again, but then roused himself a little. "Blackfeet might show up here."

"Not those four," Rising to the Sky said with a chuckle.

"They have friends."

"We're not afraid," one of the other warriors, who was standing nearby, said.

"Didn't say you were, but if a lot of them come, you'll be outnumbered, maybe by a lot."

"We can handle them."

Cooper shook his head at the warrior's audacity then realized any good fighting man, white or red, who had any faith in himself would say the same. "Why are you doing this? Risking your hair for a feller you don't know?"

"Any man who kills four Blackfeet by himself—and many more with help of only two friends, if stories are true, deserves our help. If you are enemy of Blackfeet..."

"All Americans are enemies of the Blackfeet."

"...you deserve our respect. You are friend."

"I think you're crazy. You..."

"You sleep now," Rising to the Sky said. "I change poultice, then you sleep."

Cooper started to argue, then weakly nodded.

———

"HOW LONG'VE WE BEEN HERE?" Cooper asked when next he woke.

"Nine suns," his doctor said.

"Much too long for you to spend with a dying man."

"Stop talk of dying. You won't die," the woman said in English with only a slight accent and a good command of the language. "I make sure you live."

"But..."

"You say I lie?" The Flathead was angry.

"No, no, I didn't say that." He was still tired and weak and arguing with this woman—or anyone—was wearying. "It's just that I ain't so sure I've got the ability to make it through."

"Hush. You hungry?"

"I'm not..." Then he realized he was. "Yep."

Rising to the Sky fed him, and he found that the nourishing buffalo-infused broth raised his spirits a little. And over the next week, he ate larger and larger meals.

"You eat too much," Kills the Bear said, smiling.

"Well, if you were a better hunter, we'd have more meat in camp and your woman wouldn't have to starve herself so her patient would have enough to eat to help him recover."

"Maybe you should do the hunting."

"Well, maybe you and your friends and Rising to the Sky can eat less. That'll mean I get enough and you'll not have to hunt as much."

Both men laughed.

Cooper's strength began to grow and despite some setbacks, he began to think he really might recover. Within another week he was up and about, moving slowly to be sure, but on his feet and walking. Soon he was able to sit at the fire with the three warriors. "I do apologize, my friends, for keeping you off the trail for so long. Your people are probably at rendezvous by now or will be soon, and wondering where you are. You'll never get there to spend time with them or for the festivities."

The three shrugged. "We will go next year," Kills the Bear said.

Cooper nodded. "Well, I don't know how to thank you boys, and you, Rising to the Sky. You can leave any time, whenever you like. I'm able to get around enough I can make do on my own."

"When we leave, you come with us. You want to find the Nez Percé. They are our friends. We may cut their trail. Or our people's. We get to rendezvous, you will meet the Nez Percé again."

"Rendezvous might be over. Likely it will be."

"Then we look for them on the way back to our country," the warrior said simply. "We know which way they will go, so we go that way. Just the five of us can move fast. We catch up to them soon."

"You sure you just don't want to leave me here to recover a little more while you go and find your people? It's been what, fifteen Suns now."

"I am sure."

The other two warriors nodded.

Cooper shook his head in wonder. "I'll be ready to leave tomorrow. I'm still weak but we should be able to make good time."

"We wait," Rising to the Sky said firmly. Three more suns, then we go. You'll be stronger then, enough to travel."

Cooper decided not to argue. "Whatever you say, Doctor." When she gave him a quizzical look, he smiled and said, "A doctor among my people is a man—among whites, it's always a man—who cures people. After your treatments, I'd trust you far more than any doctor back in the Settlements."

Rising to the Sky beamed.

———

COOPER WAS HALF A MILE DOWNSTREAM, wanting privacy. Kills the Bear and one of the other warriors had gone off hunting, so Cooper had taken the opportunity to drift off. He had not wanted to argue with them, though he did have to do so with Rising to the Sky. She finally acquiesced so he had donned his possibles and weapons, and headed off, walking slowly.

He laid his shooting bag, possibles sack, pistols, and rifle on the ground, then pulled off his shirt and looked at the wound. It was healing nicely, he decided and didn't look too bad. Despite Rising to the Sky's reassurances, he had been worried, but now he felt relieved. He stepped into the stream and began splashing water over himself. He smiled as he washed up, pleased at the feeling of the cold water against his skin.

Suddenly a war cry tore through the air followed by another, then the neighing of frightened horses. Ignoring his shirt, Cooper grabbed his weapons and accoutrements, slug the latter over his shoulder and stuck the pistols on his belt by the metal clips, grabbed his rifle, and ran. He cursed his weakness as he could get little speed, and his breathing came heavy after just a few dozen steps, but he pushed on, ignoring his labored breathing and the new pain that dug into his upper chest.

He burst into the clearing where their camp was. Backbone was lying dead, scalped though not mutilated. Rising to the Sky was gone as was his mare and the two Flathead ponies. The braying mule was off to the north at what seemed to Cooper to be not too far. The sound of running horses came from the east.

"Son of a bitch," he muttered. "Not again." He grabbed a rope rein lying near his and the other two saddles before racing over to the mule. He managed to calm it enough to slip the rein over its lower jaw and leap its back after a few tries. He was not about to take the time to saddle nor bridle it. It took some effort with the animal as skittish as it was. but he did it. Then he kicked the reluctant beast into motion, snapping, "Come on, dammit, move, you four-legged minion of Satan."

They headed up the trail after the sound, Cooper trying to get the mule to move at a faster pace than the animal seemed ready to take. "Dammit," he snapped. "Move. Faster." Exasperation flooded over him. He had visions of the last time Indians had raised his camp and taken off with his woman and their horses. Rising to the Sky wasn't his woman, but she was a friend and his savior, and he was determined that the Indians, Blackfeet he knew from the few signs he had seen in the camp, to make sure they did not carry her to her doom.

"You don't pick up speed, you fractious four-legged walkin' pile of buffler shit, and I'll be feastin' on roast mule come nightfall."

The mule seemed to understand and picked up the pace. They rounded a curve in the trail and Cooper yanked the animal to a halt. Three Blackfeet were less than a hundred yards ahead. Cooper figured they thought they were safe since there had been no one else in the camp and could take it easy once they were a couple of miles away.

Rising to the Sky was lying across one warrior's saddle. She did not seem to be moving, and Cooper figured she was just unconscious and not dead. If the latter, they would have cast the body aside.

He darted into the woods on the side of the thin trail and stopped just off it. He slid off the mule and stepped into the trail. He dropped to one knee, brought the Dickert rifle up, and fired.

"Damn," he muttered as no warrior fell out of his saddle. The Blackfeet had gone around a small curve in the trail, giving him little to really shoot at. He darted back into the woods and reloaded his rifle as he heard the Blackfeet racing away.

He jumped on the mule again and eased onto the trail. He trotted ahead, wary. He didn't think the Blackfeet would turn back and look for whoever had fired at them, They would race away until they felt they were at a safe distance—and likely set an ambush. So Cooper followed at a slower pace.

Several miles away, he stopped. The trail made a sharp curve fifty yards ahead. There was a good chance the Indians were waiting there to see if they had been chased, and they would have plenty of cover in the trees. "I ain't makin' it that easy for you to rub me out, you snake-humpin' sons a bitches."

He pulled off the trail and slid off the mule. He tied the animal to a bush and said, not really hopeful, "I'd be obliged if you were to stay tethered here in case I need you." He patted the animal's neck, then slipped off between the trees. He moved slowly, cautiously, carefully avoiding twigs or anything else that would snap noisily if he stepped on it. The time it was taking to find the Blackfeet, if they were even up ahead, seemed interminable.

Then he heard voices. He stopped and swiped a hand across his sweating forehead, then dried it on a pant leg. He moved forward even more cautiously. Then he saw the three of them watching over the trail. Rising to the Sky was sitting against a tree.

Your time is up, boys, he thought with an evil grin. He brought the rifle up.

TWENTY-FOUR

THE WIND PICKED up just a bit for which Cooper was glad. The rustle of the leaves masked the sound of his cocking the rifle. Without hesitation, he fired. The .54-caliber lead ball tore off a chunk of one warrior's head. Before he had hit the ground, Cooper had dropped the rifle and was reaching for a pistol.

But the warriors didn't hesitate either. Before the wind had carried off the puff of gun smoke, they were in the trees.

"Dammit," Cooper muttered as he reloaded. He had hoped to kill at least one more before they reached cover. Now he had to go find them, and they had gone in different directions. They would, though, circle back to their ponies within minutes, when they figured they had lost whoever had attacked them.

Cooper took one glance at Rising to the Sky. She was still out, though a small moan escaped her lips. The mountain man reloaded the rifle, slung it across his shoulders by the buckskin strap, and headed toward where he had seen the ponies as quickly as he could while doing so quietly. He slowed even more when he heard the animals snuffling, then dropped to a knee behind a huckleberry bush.

After an interminable wait with sweat dribbling down his forehead and his naked back and chest, he spotted movement. Seconds later, one of the warriors crept up to the three ponies.

Cooper pulled a pistol but hesitated. He was reluctant to pull the trigger without knowing where the other Blackfoot was. But he could not let this warrior go. As the Indian leaped on his horse, Cooper fired. The ball caught the Blackfoot in the side. The Indian swayed a moment, then righted himself and kicked the pony into a run.

"Dammit all to hell," Cooper cursed. He dropped the pistol and reached for the other one. Before he could get it off his belt, he sensed someone behind him, and he turned just in time to block the knife thrust of the third Blackfoot. He shoved the warrior aside weakly so didn't have enough strength to do more than block another vicious swing of the warrior's knife. His feet went out from under him and he fell into the bush. He landed painfully on his rifle, and his pistol went flying off to he knew not where. The warrior pounced on Cooper's chest.

Cooper managed to grab the warrior's knife wrist and keep it from plunging into his chest, but he was worried about keeping his grip. He was still quite weak from his arrow wound and he didn't think he could hold out for very long. The only advantage he had, and it was a mighty small one, was that the Blackfoot was a few inches shorter and twenty or so pounds lighter.

Summoning up all the strength he could muster,

Cooper shoved. Surprised, the Indian toppled to the side. Breathing heavily, the mountain man rammed his knee into the Indian's stomach. The warrior's breath whooshed out. Cooper rolled partly up and kneed the Blackfoot in the groin. He climbed on top of the warrior and snatched out his own knife. "You ain't raisin' this ol' chil's hair, you son of a bitch," he muttered as he slit the Indian's throat.

He fell to the side, his breath coming in great gulps, and he became aware of pain in his upper chest He looked down and saw the arrow wound was seeping blood. He managed to get to his knees, and from there he lifted the Blackfoot's scalp. He waited a couple of minutes before he tried to rise. It was difficult, and he was shaky, but he did it. He gathered up his two pistols, staggered into the camp, and stopped next to the first Blackfoot he had killed there. Because the Indian's head had been shattered, Cooper had a little trouble raising his scalp, but he managed to get enough and stuck it in his belt with the other.

He glanced at Rising to the Sky. She was awake but dazed.

The woman looked with bleary eyes at Cooper as he approached, showing some fear. Then she recognized the mountain man and smiled. "You kill 'em?"

"I got two. Wounded the third. He run off on a pony. Don't know whether he went under nearby or if he's halfway back to his village by now." He plopped down next to her.

Rising to the Sky nodded toward Cooper's belt. "You scalp 'em?"

Cooper nodded wearily. The pain and exertion were flooding over him.

"You sleep now," the woman said.

"But the other..."

"I keep watch. Be all right."

"You sure?"

"Yes."

Cooper nodded weakly and handed her a pistol. He pulled the rifle over his shoulder and set it down beside him, then stretched out. Something tickled at his mind but the weariness and pain made his brain cloudy. He closed his eyes.

It was dark when he awoke. He pushed himself up and rubbed his face. A fire was going and Rising to the Sky was watching him.

"How you feel?" she asked.

He bit back a retort, then snorted. "Like all the buffler God ever created are runnin' across my body. How about you?"

"I'm all right. Head is a little sore." She pointed. "I have more work to do on chest."

Cooper nodded. Then the thought that had been niggling at him suddenly coalesced. "Your husband," he said urgently. "We've got to get back. Make sure he and Rough Belly are all right." He paused. "They must be dead, like Backbone," he said, fear for the two other men's lives clutching him.

"They will come."

"How can you say that? We ain't that far from camp. It wouldn't take them long to follow and catch up to us if they were still alive."

"They were hunting. Had to go far as they did the other day. Game was scarce. So they maybe didn't find out what happened 'til much later. Maybe take care of

Backbone, too, make sure wolves don't get him. Then they come after us. They will find us."

"I don't know, Rising to the Sky. Maybe we should go lookin' for 'em."

"We wait. They will come. Was Backbone...?"

"Scalp was taken. He wasn't cut up though." He pushed himself weakly to his feet. I'll go check these two damn Blackfeet, and see if one them has it. If so, we can return it and let his eternal rest be peaceful and pleasant."

Rising to the Sky nodded sadly. "You a good man," she said with a sigh.

Cooper shrugged. "Did you know him well?"

"No, but he was my husband's good friend."

Cooper nodded again and lurched off. He returned and shook his head. "Reckon the other son of a bitch has it," he said as he took his seat. There anything to eat?"

"Small piece of deer. Enough for us."

Cooper cocked an eye at her. "Both of us?"

"Yes."

"I think you're not tellin' me the truth. You best make sure you have some."

"You need it more than me. I'll be fine. You'll see." She rose and took a small hunk of meat from its buckskin wrapping and hung it over the fire. She sat again. "You eat, we stay the night here. Leave in morning."

"You sure you don't want to get back...?"

"I'm sure."

Cooper nodded thanks as Rising to the Sky handed him the hunk of meat on a piece of bark.

"You have some," he insisted.

"No. You need it more. I just have a sore head. You need food for strength to get over wounds."

After a few moments, Cooper nodded. As he ate, he said, "I ain't headin' back toward our old camp, Rising to the Sky."

She looked at him in surprise.

"You take one of the ponies and go. I reckon you'll be safe enough. You'll likely meet your husband and Rough Belly on the trail. If you're right, they're followin' us, but maybe not so close if they were far away on their hunt and took time to care for Backbone."

"What you do?"

"I'm goin' after the son of a bitch and reclaim what's Backbone's."

"You can't go alone."

"I've been alone before."

You wait. Kills the Bear and Rough Belly will find us soon. We all go."

"I ain't waitin'. If those two show up by mornin', I'll be glad to have 'em along. If not, I'll go alone."

"You have no shirt. Even though it's near the Month of Huckleberries, it still gets cold at night."

"I've been in a hell of a lot colder weather than in July and August even up this high. Besides, that feller over there"—he pointed to the dead Blackfoot—"is about my size. His shirt'll fit me close enough. I'll be all right."

"You are hard-headed, as white men say, like my husband. If you go, I'll ride hard, find Kills the Bear and Rough Belly. I'll bring them along fast, catch up to you."

"That'll be fine," he said insincerely; he didn't care whether they caught up or not. He finished eating and wiped his hands on his pants. Then he, with Rising to the Sky's help, got the war shirt off the dead Blackfoot and slipped it on. It was a little short and tight, but it would do. It would have to. Then he went and looked over the ponies. Even though the saddles were primitive ones, they were usable. And he found two buffalo robes. He dragged both to the fire. He dropped one next to Rising to the Sky and placed the other across the fire on the ground and sat next to it. "It'll keep you plenty warm and comfortable."

Rising to the Sky just grunted in annoyance.

IT WAS STILL DARK when Cooper awoke but daybreak was just beginning to slice a sliver of light into the darkness. He had not slept well and finally gave up trying to sleep at all.

Rising to the Sky was still asleep. Cooper reconsidered letting her head along their back trail by herself. The chances of other Blackfeet being around were slim, he figured. But she had been unconscious for most if not all the flight the Blackfeet had made, so she might have trouble finding her way. Though the trail was distinguishable, there were several forks, which might confuse, or at least delay her. Then he shrugged. As a woman, she would not be much of a tracker, but she was a Flathead and so courageous and smart. She would find her way, he decided.

He swiftly, quietly saddled the two ponies. He mounted one and left the other for the woman, then rode out through the darkness.

It didn't take long to find the Blackfoot's trail. Cooper just followed the blood. But as with any wound over time, the blood had begun to coagulate, and the signs of it grew less and less. Like the way to this point, there were twists and turns in the trail as well as various offshoots. When the blood trail dropped off, he had to check every one of these different paths, costing him time.

About midday, with hunger beginning to gnaw at him, he pulled off the trail, found a pleasant little spot where the trees were widely spaced, and sat. He needed sustenance before he continued as the small hunk of meat he had eaten had not filled him. He was weak enough with the wound, it would not help to get even weaker because of a lack of food. He couldn't believe his luck when not long after, a deer drifted into his range of vision, unaware of his presence. With decidedly slow movements, he brought his rifle up and fired. Two minutes later, after having reloaded his rifle, he was butchering the deer, taking as much meat as he thought he could eat in a day or two before it went bad. He quickly started a fire, roasted a large hunk of the meat, and ate it before it was barely heated. He kicked dirt over the fire and wrapped the rest of the meat in a piece of hide. Then he was on the horse's back again and moving on.

More than two days later, he slowed, sensing there was someone not far ahead of him. He hoped it was his quarry. He dismounted and walked the pony into the woods and tied it to a huckleberry bush. Then he cautiously crept up the thin trail. As he neared a curve, to his surprise he heard a mule. Once again he slipped into the trees and snuck forward. He stopped and waited behind a tree. In a very small clearing, sat a Blackfoot. And nearby, stood his own mule. He almost laughed aloud at the thought of a proud, savage Blackfoot riding a mule. He figured that if this was the man he was seeking, the warrior probably had fallen off his pony, which had wandered away. How he managed to catch the mule, which obviously had broken free, was a mystery.

The Indian was sitting at a fire, waiting for some meat to cook. As he waqtched, he wondered for the hundredth time or so on his travel since leaving Rising to the Sky her, why her husband and Rough Belly had not caught up to him. He wondered if something had happened to them. They would not have just ridden off, not without knowing what had happened to Rising to the Sky. And he did not think they would ride off if the woman had met up with them and told them what had happened.

He pushed the thought from his mind. There were more important things to deal with now, like taking care of the warrior in front of him. As a Blackfoot, the Indian was a target under any circumstances. But Cooper wanted to first see if he could tell whether the man was the one he sought.

The warrior shifted, favoring his one side. Cooper smiled grimly. It was the one. He raised the Dickert.

TWENTY-FIVE

THE BLACKFOOT DOVE to the left of the fire, away from the sound when he heard Cooper cocking his rifle, but the rifle ball caught him in the side of the hip.

As he reloaded the Dickert, Cooper watched the Indian trying to rise. He got no measure of joy at the man's lack of success in doing so. He walked out from the trees and rolled the Blackfoot over with a foot. "Where's the scalp you took from the Flathead?" he asked harshly, though he could plainly see it in the buckskin cord holding his breechclout.

The warrior looked blankly at him.

Cooper set the butt of his rifle in the dirt and leaned the barrel against his leg, freeing his hands. In signs, he asked the question again.

The Blackfoot shrugged.

Cooper stamped on the man's lower chest, cracking some ribs. Still no reaction from the Indian.

With a sigh, Cooper laid his rifle down, pulled a knife, reached down, and grabbed the Indian's hair. The

Blackfoot struggled weakly. Cooper slowly, without expression proceeded to cut off the warrior's scalp.

To his credit, the Blackfoot made little sound, though his eyes widened with the pain and humiliation.

Cooper stuck the fresh scalp in his belt. He cut a piece of the warrior's war shirt off, then used it to wrap the slain Flathead's scalp. Cooper placed it in his possibles sack. Ignoring the bleeding, softly groaning Blackfoot, Cooper sat with his rifle beside him and grabbed a piece of the rabbit that was roasting on a green stick spit and tore into it. He finished and ate another. Then he went and cared for his horse. He stretched out the buffalo robe, then dragged the Blackfoot off just into the trees. It was close enough so that Cooper could keep an eye on him in case the warrior somehow gathered enough strength to find a weapon or even to slither off, but far enough so that if the wolves came along, they would not disturb the mountain man too much.

Cooper ate more and then, though there was still plenty of light, he stretched out and fell asleep. When he woke, it was still dark and he was glad that wolves and other scavengers had not partaken in the meal—the warrior had died sometime in the night—he had provided though at least one wolf was sniffing around.

The mountain men finished off the rabbit, saddled the pony, found a rope and ran it around the mule's neck and rode off, leading the latter.

As he traveled, his concern for the Flatheads grew. He knew the warriors would not just flee, especially since the Blackfeet who had attacked the camp were, for the most part dead. They might not know that, but they would know it when Rising to the Sky caught up with them and began leading them up the trail to where she had left Cooper and beyond.

But maybe she never found them, he thought. *Maybe there were other Blackfeet around and she was killed. Or...*

Such speculation was futile. He would keep riding until he either found them or reached their old camp. If he had not found them by then, he might be able to learn what had happened and perhaps pick up a trail they had taken.

Without having to worry about the Blackfeet—though he was aware of the possibility that there were others about—he made good time, and in a day and a half was back at the camp where he had killed the two warriors and found Rising to the Sky. He searched but found no sign that the Flatheads had been there.

Though there was still daylight left, he decided to stay the night. He tended the pony and hobbled it and the mule and let them graze. He waited patiently at the nearby stream and was rewarded when a fat beaver wandered by, a cottonwood branch in its mouth. He shot it and butchered out a little meat, which he was not fond of, and took the tail, which he was. He quickly built a fire and set the meat to roasting. He wished he had some coffee. A coffeepot was still on the rocks near the fire, having been left when he killed the Indians, but the contents had gone sour and was undrinkable. He searched around and found what had been a bag of coffee beans, but it had been torn open and all but a few of the beans were gone, eaten by various animals, he supposed. With a sigh, he sat to his repast.

As he ate, he wondered where his mare had gotten off to. He had not found her or the other horses taken from the Flathead camp. And they had not been here when he had gotten here a week ago. If they ran off, which seemed likely now, he might find her on his journey. That, he thought, would be a good thing. The mare was a trustworthy steed and had been his mount for a number of years now. Man and animal were comfortable with each other. He shook his head in annoyance. He had faced too much trouble in his relatively short life and was tired of it. Then he grinned. The way to get away from all these troubles was to go back to the States, and he was not about to do that. At least not without Goes Far.

Lordy, I miss her, he thought. With pictures of her in his mind, he fell asleep.

———

HE FOLLOWED his nose into the trees from where a foul smell—faint but still unmistakable—emanated and came upon the bodies, or what was left of them, the scavengers having left little. He tied the horse and mule to a tree, disgust and hatred filling him. Sadly, he looked around. The bones of all three had been scattered by animals to various degrees but he could tell who they were and guess what had happened. The remains of Rising to the Sky—with pieces of flesh here and there that the scavengers had left for some reason—lay mostly sprawled spread-eagled near a large pine, the remnants of her chewed over dress spread out as if cut and thrown open. A knife lay near one skeletal hand, and Cooper figured she had fought as best she could. He hoped she had done some damage. The two warriors, each in the same scavenged condition as Rising to the

Sky, were behind what cover they could find. They lay in dried stretches of blood, their bows and tomahawks scattered nearby. They showed signs of having been scalped and mutilated at least somewhat.

"Damn," he muttered, then screamed, "Damn! Damn! Damn!"

He headed for his horse, intent on trying to find the Blackfeet who did this, then stopped. No, he thought, the two warriors and the woman deserved as decent a burial as he could give them.

With only a horn spoon and knife to work with, it took most of the rest of the day to scrape a shallow hole in the earth, grateful that the ground was soft. But he finally got it done. He took his sleeping robe and wrapped the remains of the three Flatheads in it as carefully as he could, then set it into the hole. At the last moment, he remembered Backbone's scalp, and he interred that, too. He shoved the dirt back in with his feet and stomped the hump of soil down 'til it was almost flat. Then he went around finding rocks and piling them on the grave. It was a waste of time considering the condition of the corpses, but he thought it necessary for the Indians' dignity.

Finished, Cooper said a few prayers, including a couple learned from the Shoshonis. Then he stood for a bit, thinking. He nodded, making his decision. He mounted the Blackfoot pony he was using and rode off, moving fast.

He rode 'til after dark, made a quick, cold camp, tended the animals, then slept. He was back on the trail before daylight.

Late the next afternoon, he came to the camp where Rising to the Sky had nursed him back to health. Most of his supplies had remained untouched under a tarp, including his saddle, store of powder and lead, a small supply of pemmican and jerky and, he joyfully noted, a sack of coffee beans. He was glad to find his old buffalo robe and an osnaburg shirt in his horse-carried possibles sack. His traps were there too, and though he wouldn't need them for a spell, he would bring them. Once his new mission was accomplished, he would put them to use.

There wasn't much else in the camp, though there was a musket and horn of powder where Backbone had lain in death. As he prowled around the camp looking for anything else he might use, his mare came out of the woods.

"I'll be damned," Cooper muttered as he patted the horse's neck. He grinned a little. "Reckon the Good Lord—or the Great Spirit—kept you 'round these parts waitin' for me."

The horse snuffled and bobbed its head.

He hurriedly built a fire, heated some pemmican—and coffee—and ate before turning in.

Before daylight, he loaded the mule and saddled his horse, then hit the trail, heading back the way he had come. He rode through the night and got back to where the three Flatheads had died and been buried by late afternoon of the next day. With daylight still left, he prowled the area, looking for signs of which way the Blackfeet had gone. He thought there were seven of them, though some of the prints might have been made by stolen ponies. There was some blood, too, that led off farther into the trees, where there would be no trail. He shrugged. That would not stop him.

After five long days of riding, searching for any

minute sign of which way the Blackfeet had come, and four nights of cold camps, he smelled smoke and the faint aroma of roasting elk. The soft snorting of ponies added to his certainty that the men he was following were ahead.

He tied the horse and mule to bushes, then crept forward, rifle in hand. He stopped behind a tree and gazed at the five Blackfeet. As he had thought possible, some of the tracks leading from the battle scene had been made by stolen horses. The warriors' camp was not in a small clearing, really, but in a spot where the trees were widely spaced. Cooper watched for a bit, taking it all in. One of the warriors had a rifle lying next to him along with a powder horn and shooting bag. The others had bows, though the weapons and the arrows that went with them, lay about. The Blackfeet seemed relaxed, figuring no one had followed them—and after more than a week they had seen no one on their trail.

Cooper wondered why they had not ridden to their village with the stolen horses or moved on to another raid, though perhaps they had already attacked others, but he shrugged. To him, there was no reading a Black-foot's mind.

Cooper looked up through the canopy of trees and judged nightfall to be more than an hour away. He slipped back to where he had left his animals. He plopped down, back against a tree and gnawed absent-mindedly on a piece of jerky, trying to come up with a plan. He could not simply walk into their camp and kill five experienced Blackfeet warriors, but staying hidden and trying to pick them off one by one would not work either. He probably could get two, three if he were lucky, before the others fled. Then they would either come for him or grab their ponies and light out. He might, he supposed, wait 'til they were asleep, slip into the camp and try to kill each one silently with a knife but the chances of success were slim. One of them would make a sound that would wake the others, he was certain.

Then an idea began to form and he let it coalesce. With a nod, he decided it would work. He pulled off his cloth shirt and cut two pieces each nine or ten inches square. He took Backbone's powder horn and poured the contents onto one of them, added a couple of handfuls of pebbles, then wrapped it up and tied it with laces of buckskin taken from the side of his trousers. He waited until just before dark. With the Dickert slung over his shoulder, Backbone's musket in one hand and the package of powder in the other, he made his way silently to a tree where he could watch the camp. Before long, the warriors were asleep.

Now came the hard part, he thought. Leaving his rifle on the ground, he sneaked into the camp, freezing twice, placing a hand on a pistol, when one of the Indians rolled over or let loose a snort. Then he moved on. The one Blackfoot's rifle and accoutrements lay where they had been. Cooper grabbed the powder horn and silently went back the way he came. He poured the powder from the Blackfoot's horn and again added pebbles into the other pieces of cloth and tied that tightly.

Well, here goes, he thought. He crept forward and dropped one of the packages in the fire and darted back to his post behind the tree. Sweat beaded on his forehead as he waited. But it was only a minute or so before the muslin started to burn.

TWENTY-SIX

SECONDS LATER, the gunpowder exploded. The Blackfeet jumped up and looked around in a daze. Cooper lobbed the other package of powder and rocks into the fire, then shot two of Blackfeet with his pistols.

The other warriors went for their weapons and turned to look for their enemy when the second makeshift bomb went off, sending pebbles flying all around. A few almost hit Cooper, but most flew around the camp hitting Blackfeet. One screamed and clutched at his eyes. The other two stumbled, not seriously injured but hurt. Cooper shot those two, one with the Dickert, the other with Backbone's musket.

Cooper reloaded all his weapons while keeping an eye on the blinded Blackfoot. Finished, he strolled into camp, made sure the other four were dead, put his rifle and the musket down, and picked up the one Blackfoot's rifle. He walked, and holding the rifle by the barrel, swung it and mashed the injured warrior in the face with the flat side of the butt.

The Indian stumbled backward a few steps, hit a

rock circling the fire and fell into the embers. Cooper grabbed him by the shirt, pulled him up, and tossed him aside.

Cooper got a rope, cut a short piece off and kneeled beside the Blackfoot. He rolled the Indian onto his stomach and tied his hands behind his back before rolling him over onto his back again. "You and your skunk-humpin' friends here killed some good people, some very good people whose moccasins you ain't fit to lick. And that don't shine with this ol' chil'. No, siree, it don't. I'm almost sad I shot your friends down. They deserved to die a long and painful death. Yours might not be long, but I aim to make it painful."

The warrior grunted something in his own language.

"I don't understand you, hoss, but it doesn't matter. Ain't nothin' you can say that'd save your festerin' hide from the welcome embrace of Satan himself, who's sittin' on his throne just awaitin' for you."

Cooper sliced open the Blackfoot's buckskin shirt, baring his chest, then cut a piece of the garment. He rose, walked to the fire, and gingerly kicked some of the hot coals onto the buckskin. He turned and dropped them on the warrior's naked chest.

The Blackfoot hissed and writhed, succeeding after a couple of minutes in getting the coals off his body.

"That was for Backbone." He cut away the warrior's breechclout, exposing his privates. Then he got another small batch of coals. Ignoring the faint call of his conscience at the brutishness he was displaying, Cooper dropped the coals on the man's genitals.

The Blackfoot screamed.

"That's for your abuse of Rising to the Sky, as fine a woman red or white you could ever find."

The warrior managed to buck and jerk enough to get the coals off him, but he was badly burned and moaned.

"Don't feel good bein' so abused, does it?"

Cooper picked up the long rawhide rope and tied one end around the warrior's ankles. He ignored the man's feeble attempt to kick him. Then he dragged the Blackfoot over to a maple, tossed the other end of the rope over a branch, and hauled him up, feet first until his head was just inches off the ground. He tied the rope, leaving the Indian dangling. He wandered around the camp, checking out the dead warriors. He found what he believed to be the three Flatheads' scalps, carefully wrapped them in another piece of buckskin cut from the dangling warrior's shirt, and placed them in his possibles sack.

He strolled off, still wondering at his ferocity, trying to tell his conscience that it was reasonable revenge for the way the Flatheads had been treated. He almost convinced himself, so he pushed the thoughts out of his head. He got the mare and the mule and brought them into the camp, where he tied them to the picket line along with the Blackfoot ponies before tending them.

Without emotion, he scalped the four dead Blackfeet, then went and did the same to the live one. He tied the scalps together with a buckskin thong and tossed them onto his saddle where it lay on the ground.

He plopped down by the fire. A hunk of elk sat on a piece of buckskin near the file. He stoked the fire, stuck a green twig through the meat, and hung it over the fire. He placed the coffeepot on a rock just outside the flames. Before long, he was wolfing down elk meat and slurping up coffee. Sated, he strolled over to where the Blackfoot hung.

"I ain't as bloodthirsty or as cruel as you and your companions," Cooper said. "Maybe it doesn't seem so, but...well, I don't regret the way I've treated you, but it doesn't make me feel very good inside to emulate such scum as you. So I think instead of torturing you some more, I'll just let you hang there, let you contemplate how long it'll be before some bear or wolf comes 'round to investigate. Now, there's a good chance I might not get into my heaven or your Spirit World after some of the things I've done in my life, but I can say that you ain't gettin' into either place for certain. If you were a white man, I'd tell you to start praying to your Lord and Maker, but since you're a heathen Blackfoot, I don't know quite for sure who to tell you to pray to. But if you got some kind of god—and I ain't so sure the Blackfeet do—maybe you best use your last few hours in suppli-catin' yourself to him."

Cooper stood, rolled out his robe near the fire, and fell asleep. It was not a comfortable or comforting sleep, haunted as it was by demons and skeletons and bodies that only had bits of flesh hanging from them. And there he was facing the devil himself, with the fires of hell burning right behind him, which changed to a frozen wilderness with bitter cold, snow up to a horse's neck, and him with nothing more than a breechclout to wear.

In the morning, Cooper felt wretched. He was exhausted from the poor night's sleep and still haunted by his behavior. But he finally shrugged. He had done what he had and nothing could change that now. He consoled himself somewhat in telling himself that these Blackfeet deserved all he had done, but he was still not in a good frame of mind as he sat at the fire.

Cooper ate the last of the elk and drank the last of the coffee. Finished, he walked over to where the Blackfoot hung.

"Still alive, I see," he said nastily. "You're a tougher critter than I thought you were."

He saddled his horse and loaded the mule with his own small amount of supplies, adding the few things of the Blackfeet that he thought he could use. He tied the Blackfoot ponies in a string, mounted his horse, took the rope to the ponies, and called to the warrior hanging from the tree.

"Can't say it was a pleasure meetin' you, you festerin' pile of snake shit, but remember, I couldn've killed you, but I didn't." He laughed a little as he rode off.

IT WAS TIME, Cooper decided, that he find the Nez Percé and reclaim his wife—if she still wanted him. He had been away longer than he had planned, and he worried that she might have thought he had abandoned her. He was pretty sure that was not the case, but a bit of doubt tingled in his mind on occasion.

He wasn't sure of the date, but he figured it was mid-to-late August, which meant that rendezvous would be over, and the Nez Percé would be on their way back to their homeland. It would, he figured, make his journey a little easier, or at least a little shorter, as he should encounter the People along the way instead of having to ride all the way to Horse Creek where the rendezvous had been held. He held great hope for a quick meeting as he began to angle his way southwest.

But as he rode, he began to reconsider. He wanted very much to see Goes Far and Strong Bow. But the need to find the Flatheads and bring them the sad news of their tribesmen and tribeswoman grew in him seemingly with every mile. He awoke one morning and after finishing what had passed for breakfast, he made up his mind.

"Looks like we'll be takin' us a little detour, girl," he said as he saddled the mare. He loaded the mule, mounted the horse, and grabbed the rope to the Blackfoot ponies. Then he was off, turning more westerly. He figured he could reach the trail the Flatheads would take north at a spot long before they would reach it. Then he would ride south, meeting them along the way, within a few days, he hoped. Once he had spoken to the Flatheads, he would turn west again and hurry toward the Salmon River and go northwest. If he didn't meet the Nez Percé on the trail, or where they usually put their village, he would wait there for them to arrive.

The travel was not hard for the most part, though it would have been easier without the seven Indian ponies. The horses made it difficult to cross some of the roaring streams and rivers, and the animals were often cantankerous. Being Blackfoot ponies, they were not used to being tugged along by a rope and they fought their restraint as often as not. More than once Cooper considered cutting them free and letting them run off. It would be much easier. But he planned to give them to the Flatheads as a minor form of compensation for the loss of the members of their tribe. If they did not want the animals, he would give them to Pale Thunder, the Nez Percé war chief, or whoever had been caring for Goes Far and the baby—as long as he was not a new husband.

Dealing with the horses made traveling slower than he wanted to go, but it could not be helped. Nor could the occasional thunderstorm, hailstorm, and a few times a light snowfall despite it being August. The snow barely made it to the ground on those rare occasions when it came, but it was a harbinger of things to come. And that drove him to push a little harder than he might otherwise considering the limitations posed by the animals. But he had to move as quickly as possible if he wanted to start the fall beaver hunt early enough to bring in plentiful plews. First, he had to find the Flatheads—and the right village—to deliver his gloomy message to them. He figured they would expect him to stay several days with them. Then he would have to track down the Nez Percé, spend some time—though not much—with them, then move on to decent trapping grounds. He figured he would be lucky to be able to start trapping by late September considering how advanced the summer was.

Almost three weeks later, he spotted a Flathead band camped for the night. He rode in and was greeted kindly by the Indians, the Flatheads having always been friendly to the whites. First, there was a meal at the lodge of the civil chief, followed by a solemn smoke.

Cooper chaffed at the formalities and when the first opportunity arose, he asked, "Is this the band of which Kills the Bear was a member?"

He was disappointed when the Flathead chief shook his head.

TWENTY-SEVEN

"KILLS the Bear's band was ahead of us on the trail," the chief said. "They will be to the north, nearer our homeland along the Flathead River."

Dispirited, Cooper spent the night and was back on the trail, this time heading north just after daybreak. But that band, too, was not the one he sought. Growing more disheartened, Cooper pushed on, beginning to wonder about the time. It was early September as best he could figure it, which meant the fall hunt for trappers would begin in a month or so, especially if the weather turned soon. He would be hard pressed, he figured, to meet up with the right band of Flatheads, get to Red Leggings' village to the west, then head east toward where Two-Faces Beaubien, Duncan MacTavish, and the others would be heading for good hunting grounds.

More than once, he considered just giving up on this quest. But each time, his conscience told him that he owed it to the three warriors and the woman. The four had saved his life after he had been wounded by the Blackfoot arrow, and he felt responsible for their deaths. There was, he knew, nothing he could have done to prevent their being killed, but it still ate at him.

A week later, he pulled into another Flathead camp. They were near their homeland here and filled with joy at the prospect of creating their village again, where they would stay put for a while. Of course, they couldn't stay in one spot too long. They had to move as the amount of waste—human and animal—increased and grass for the horses decreased.

Cooper was directed to the lodge of Strange Bull, the civil chief, who was waiting outside, having been told there was a visitor in camp.

Inside, where the chief and mountain man were joined by three other warriors, there were the usual formalities of food and a leisurely smoke. Then the chief asked in his own language, which was translated by one of the warriors.

"What brings you here? White men are always welcome, but not many come alone. You look for a wife, perhaps?"

"No, Chief, I have a wife. A Nez Percé, who is a good wife." He paused, took a deep breath, and said, "I come with news of Kills the Bear, his wife, and two friends. It's not good news."

The warriors' faces grew worried as they waited.

"All of 'em's gone under."

"How you know this?"

"I had a small battle with the Blackfeet. Was wounded bad. Kills the Bear and the others found me. Rising to the Sky nursed me back to health."

"We know of this. They brought you to another

band, who waited around a few days, then left you in Rising to the Sky's care."

Cooper nodded.

"How they die?" the chief asked while the warrior translated.

"I ain't exactly sure." He ignored the hard looks that had dawned on the warriors' faces." He paused. "Let me start early on. I was getting' better and had gone down to the river to wash some of the old blood off. Kills the Bear and Rough Belly were off huntin' somewhere. Backbone and Rising to the Sky were still in camp. The Blackfeet attacked. By the time I got back—just a couple minutes at most—Backbone was dead and Rising to the Sky taken. My horse was gone as were the two belonging to your people. Only my mule was left. I hopped on it and followed. The Blackfeet didn't have much of a head start but they were movin' fast and the mule was not inclined to speed along."

Cooper paused for a sip of coffee. "I finally caught up with 'em. Killed two and wounded the other, but he got away. Rising to the Sky was there. She had been knocked on the head but was all right otherwise. We spent the night there. I took off after the third feller in the mornin'. I had told Rising to the Sky to head back toward the other camp. I figured she would meet up with her husband and Rough Belly on the trail and they could catch up to me."

"So they did and were…"

"Nope, never saw 'em again. It took me a couple days to track that son of a bitch down and sent him along to whatever hell the Blackfeet have."

"You scalped them?"

Cooper nodded. "And the other two."

"Where are they?"

"Just hold on, Chief. I ain't done with the story. Once I took care of that feller, I headed back. Thought I'd catch up with the others. Didn't figure they take off without tryin' to find me."

"They were brave," Strange Bull said harshly.

"Yep. I know that. I was afraid something bad might've happened to 'em. There could've been other Blackfeet about. There were, and it did. I found 'em all right." He shook his head as a new bout of sadness swept over him. "It had been a while, and there wasn't much left of any of 'em. They took out four Blackfeet as best I could tell."

"They were...?" one of the warriors asked, face a mask of fear and hate.

Cooper nodded. "Looks like they were cut up, too from what I could tell lookin' at the bones. Rising to the Sky had been scalped and I figure abused, though not mutilated. I took the time to bury 'em. It wasn't the way you would've done, but it was as close to the way my people do it. I buried Backbone's scalp with 'em."

Stone-faced, Strange Bull nodded. "Then you came here," he said, head still bobbing tightly.

"Hell no," Cooper said vehemently. "I followed those snake-humpin' sons of bitches 'til I caught 'em. Raised hair on all five of 'em."

"You are a fierce warrior," the chief said.

Cooper shrugged. He tossed a bundle of scalps tied together with a rawhide strip to Strange Bull.

"It is good," the chief said. "Would have been good if you had..."

Cooper rose, stepped across the fire, and carefully handed Strange Bull a small buckskin-wrapped parcel.

"Those are from your people who died at the hands of the Blackfeet, except for Backbone's. As I said, I buried his with the others' bodies." He retook his seat. "I thought maybe of diggin' up the grave and puttin' 'em in there, but..." He shrugged. "I decided you might want to care for 'em here in your own way. You want 'em buried with the bodies, I'll take 'em back there and do it."

The Flatheads conferred among themselves, then Strange Bull shook his head. "We will care for them in our own way."

Cooper nodded. "And there're seven Blackfoot ponies outside. They're for you, to maybe help ease the loss of your loved ones."

Strange Bull looked surprised, then nodded solemnly.

"Reckon I'll be on my way." Cooper started to rise.

"You stay," the chief said. "We honor those who are no longer with us. And we honor the man who avenged them, saving their spirits."

"No need for..."

"You stay," Strange Bull commanded.

"I think I'll stay for a spell, Chief," he said with a small, sad smile.

"Good." He spoke to one of his warriors in his own tongue. The warrior left. "He will have someone tend your animals. They will be cared for as they should be— the animals of a warrior who deserves the respect of all the People."

"You're makin' too much of me, Chief."

"No," Strange Bull said with finality. "Tonight we will honor those who are no longer with us. Tomorrow we will have a feast in your honor."

Cooper was about to argue but he saw the set line of the chief's jaw and simply nodded.

"A lodge will be prepared for you."

"Thank you."

COOPER SAT UNCOMFORTABLY through the two nights of feasting and dancing. He was eager to be on the trail. He missed Goes Far more every day, and he worried about finding his friends and getting to decent trapping grounds before October, which seemed to be rushing toward him with increasing speed. And managing to do so seemed to be growing less likely with each passing day.

Three fidgety days after he arrived in the Flathead village, he packed his mule, saddled the mare, and rode away, heading west. As soon as he was out of sight of the village—and had lost the boys who had gleefully escorted him—he picked up speed.

By now, Cooper figured, the Nez Percé should be getting close to their home, so he decided to go near to where they would place their village and then work his way south until he encountered them. The weather was beginning to change. It was evident in the leaves turning, the wild creatures getting fatter in preparation for the cold months, and the decided chill that grew over the country each night. He even encountered snow once, though it did not last and could not even accumulate a hair's depth, but it was a clear sign.

Two weeks later, he stopped on a mostly bare hill and looked to the forest that ran from the bottom of the hill to...well, he couldn't see that far. But it was discouraging. It had him thinking that he still had too far to go to reach Goes Far. Even worse, was the daunting time and distance to travel to find Beaubien and the others before winter set in. If he did not have much trouble in his search. He knew generally where they planned to go, but it could be anywhere within a few thousand square miles, a quest that would resemble a search for a specific twig among several hundred cords of firewood.

If I turn around now and push hard enough, and with a heap of luck, I can get back to my friends by the beginning of October, in time to make a good fall hunt, he thought. *And maybe even help the men make meat for the winter.* But lordy he missed Goes Far, and he had a real hankering to see his son. It left him torn and unusually indecisive. He knew what he wanted to do, but he also knew what he needed to do. He looked up at the gray sky as the first drops of rain splattered on him. "Just what the hell I need," he muttered.

He made his way down the hill and into the trees. He quickly found a spot where the trees were spaced widely enough to give him a small open area for a camp-site. He grabbed his coffeepot and a cooking pot and set them where they would not be under the overhanging trees and then went to tend the animals. The rain increased, which was a blessing and a curse. It made starting a fire more difficult, but it also meant that his pots would fill with water more quickly. Soon, but not soon enough, he groused to himself, he had some jerky hydrating in the pot over the fire, and some coffee going. He anticipated the latter a lot more than the former. He hunched under the low branches of a pine, leaning against the trunk and ate his meager supper, his anger, despair, and annoyance growing with each roll of thunder.

It didn't rain hard, but it didn't let up either, even by morning, not improving his humor in the least. Nor did the duplicate meal he ate. Still uncertain of his decision, he saddled the mare and packed his few supplies and such on the mule. He mounted the horse and rode out of the woods and back up the hill, where he turned and sat, looking toward the west—where Goes Far and Strong Bow would be. He stayed there for a long time, dawdling as his mind wrestled with the decision he needed to make. His wife and son were at least a week's ride ahead, a not unreasonable distance for him to hurry. But his livelihood awaited a month's ride or more to the east.

At long last, he shook his head, sighed, and gently kicked the mare into motion.

TWENTY-EIGHT

AS HE RODE, Cooper fought back the sinking feeling in his stomach and forced himself not to look back, toward the west, toward where Goes Far and Strong Bow were waiting for him. The thought that he was so close, yet so distant, ate at him, and his misery increased with each step his horse took. He stopped once and started to turn back, but then forced himself to keep riding east. He was sure she would accept his explanation when he gave to her at next year's rendezvous.

Or maybe before, he suddenly thought with a slight lifting of the heart. He had faced more than one trip in the dead of winter, including the trek he had made to get Goes Far in the beginning, back when she was still called Butterfly. He had made it to the Nez Percé village that time and the two of them had made it back to Brooks' group. He—and they—could do it again.

With a very slight easing of melancholy, he pushed on a little harder.

IT TOOK MORE than a month of hard riding and searching to find his friends, who had a camp along a small tributary of the Milk River, deep in Blackfoot country. Though it was only midday, Cooper was challenged: "Stop where ye are, boy-o, unless ye want a lead pill in yer lights," Paddy Murphy called.

"Hell, Paddy, it's just me, Hawley," Cooper called back.

"Well, come on in, Hawl," Murphy said. "Glad to have ye back among us. Reckon some of the others will be, too."

"You alone here in camp?"

"Al's with me..."

"Welcome back, Hawl," Alistair Wentworth called from across the camp.

"Thanks."

"All the women and children are here, too. The rest of the men are off seein' to their traps except Bill, who's huntin'," Murphy said. "Most of the boys ought to be back soon. Come and rest a bit, have some buffler, some tea—ain't got coffee goin' right now."

"Reckon I should care for the animals first," Cooper said with a yawn.

Murphy nodded. "I'll take care of the mule while you tend to the mare."

"Obliged."

It didn't take them long, but before they were finished, the other men began straggling in, each greeting Hawley, some with more friendliness than others. One of the first back was Bill White, who rode in with a load of buffalo meat on one mule and elk meat on another.

Well before dark, all the men were back, and Cooper joined his usual messmates at their fire.

"Where is Mam'selle Goes Far?" Two-Faces Beaubien asked, surprised when he did not see the woman. "You leave 'er behind again?"

Cooper grimaced and shook his head. "Had me a run-in with some Blackfeet…"

"Who would've e'er thought of such a thing out here," Duncan MacTavish said. Then his eyes widened. "She ain't gone under, has she?" he asked, face showing worry.

"No. She wasn't with me then. I was still headin' west to get her. Took me an arrow in the chest in the fight, though. Thought I was gone under for sure, but some Flatheads found me and took me back to their camp. They were headin' to rendezvous. The band waited a few days but then moved off. Three warriors and one man's wife stayed behind. The woman, Risin' to the Sky was her name, tended to me well but it took some time for me to get well enough to consider movin' on. A day or two before we figured on leavin', the damn Bug's Boys raided again. I was off a little ways cleanin' up after more than two weeks on lyin' there with blood crusted on my shirt and chest, covered with dust and dirt and sweat. I must've made the worst mule smell heavenly. So there I was when the devils came raiding. Two of the boys was out huntin'. The other was killed and scalped, and Risin' to the Sky was taken. The damn Blackfeet run off our horses, though the mule got left behind. I got on it and chased after them devils."

"I reckon y'all caught up those demons," Bill White said.

"That I did. Took some doin', though. They were movin' fast, and that mule was in no hurry. When I caught up to 'em, I killed two and wounded the third, but he took off. Found Risin' to the Sky there. It was gettin' late, so me and Risin' to the Sky stayed the night there. I left in the mornin', chasin' down the wounded one and sendin' her back down the trail figurin' she'd come across her man and the other warrior. Took more than a couple days to run that bastard down."

"He could nae been that far ahead of ye, lad," MacTavish said, not in derision but in surprise.

Cooper nodded. "Should've been. But it seemed there was a side trail every ten feet, and each had to be checked. I finally found him, though, and sent him to the Spirit World, or maybe not, since I took his hair, as I did all the others."

"What about ze others, your friends?" Beaubien asked.

"I wondered that, too. I knew those boys wouldn't run off. They were good warriors. But that part of the trail also had all kind of side trails and forks and such, so I figured they were just comin' along."

"They weren't, though, were they lad?"

"No, Duncan, they weren't. Found all three of 'em dead, scalped, mutilated some, and havin' been gone over good by the scavengers. Wasn't much left of 'em." Cooper shook his head in sadness as he relived the picture in his mind. "They did take four of Bug's Boys with 'em, though. I buried the three and took off after the ones who did it."

"Taught 'em a lesson, I wager," White said.

"That I did. Even recovered the hair of my friends. Took me a while to run down the right band of Flatheads that the three belonged to. Told 'em what went on, gave 'em the Blackfoot scalps to dance over, and gave 'em the scalps of three of their people—I'd buried the other with the bodies. They held a dance and feast and such the next two nights. I finally got out of there and headed west to try to find Red Leggin's band."

"Didn't find them?" Beaubien asked, surprised.

"Well, I gave up after a spell. I got to thinkin' on the trappin' season comin' up fast and if I was going to track down the right band of Nez Percé, get Goes Far and the child, then hunt for you fellers, I'd miss more than a month of trappin', and I can't afford that, not again, so before I got very close to Nez Percé country, I turned back and came lookin' for you fellers."

"Aye, and found us, ye did, lad."

Beaubien grinned. "You 'ad better do well, *mon ami*. Mam'selle, she will be very angry with you."

Cooper grinned ruefully. "That she will, Two-Faces. Tell you true, there's a good chance she won't have me back."

"Well, if y'all bring in enough plews to deck her out in a buffler's weight in foofaraw, she'll forgive y'all," White said with a laugh.

"I can always hope, Bill." He paused to let the chuckling die down, then said, "Looks like you boys've done all right for yourselves so far."

"Trapping 'as been *tres bien*," Beaubien said. "We are pulling in many plews, good oncs."

"Glad to hear it. Now I can join in the fun." He paused. "That is, if you brought me any supplies." It was a question.

"*Mais oui, mon ami*. I sold your plews for cash money right away, when we did our own. But when we were ready to leave and you 'adn't shown up yet, I decided to get your supplies and bring them with us, thinking you would find us soon after gettin' Goes Far. It seems my t'inking was mostly right."

Cooper nodded. "That it was, Two-Faces, and I'm much obliged for all you did. I owe you anything."

"*Non*. There is nothing left, though, of cash."

"Didn't reckon there would be. Waitin' that long to buy supplies must've come at a dear cost. Worse than usual even."

"That is true, 'Awley. I will give you an accounting of all ze money that came in and all that went out as soon as I can."

"No need, Two-Faces. You've never cheated me before, and I don't expect you did this time."

"*Bien*."

"So what now, Hawl?" White asked.

"Like I said, I get to join the fun now, so you boys best watch it. The best trapper in the mountains is back among you, and your take is gonna diminish considerably from now on."

The men laughed.

THE TAKINGS WERE good for all the men both there and at the other places they stopped for a few days. They trapped an area 'til it was bereft of beaver, then moved on.

Three weeks after Cooper returned, the men found a suitable spot and began making meat. As usual, Cooper did most of the hunting but he also joined in the butchering and the making of jerky and pemmican.

While he worked, and even when he did not, he missed Goes Far, and his thoughts often turned to her, wondering what she was doing, whether she missed him nearly as much as he missed her. He wondered, too, about his child, Strong Bow. It was odd, he thought at those times when his mind drifted toward his son. He had never met the infant, so it was a strange thing for him to realize he was a father. He was a little surprised that he looked forward to being one, and he hoped for the day to come soon for him to take his part in the boy's life.

The days melded one into the next. There was little difference from one to the next as far as real change went. They trapped and hunted, made meat, ate, gambled, argued, cursed, and laughed.

The men got along for the most part despite an occasional tiff among a couple of them. Cooper still had little to do with Dan Anderson and Dave Wheeler, and the two stuck mostly to themselves. More concerning was Colin Leary, who seemed to have not made any effort to become one of the group. He was cantankerous and surly, and the rest of the men wanted little to do with him. The other newcomer, Sam Berryman, however, had become one of the men, an old hand almost now, taking full part in the chores and learning the trapping trade quickly and well. None of the other old-timers had any concerns about working with him. Now that Cooper was back, he sometimes joined Bill White and Berryman, though he often went alone. Beaubien and MacTavish trapped together, as did Paddy Murphy and Alistair Wentworth and Anderson and Wheeler. Leary kept to himself.

Cooper kept a wary eye on Leary and was

unabashed about confronting the belligerent young man, especially when it came to trapping. More than once he caught the young man trying to set his traps in an area Cooper had staked out. Cooper put up with it twice, but the third time was more than enough.

Coming up silently behind the young man, Cooper clubbed him in the back of the head, knocking him into the cold stream.

Leary came up sputtering and screaming. "You son of a bitch," he yelled, charging toward Cooper. "Why I ought to..."

Cooper knocked him down again, then once more when Leary tried to stand. "What you ought to do, boy, is keep away from me. And my traps. I catch you tryin' to horn into my trappin' ground again and I'll raise your hair, and don't you doubt I can do it. I've faced a lot of fellers a heap tougher than you and come out on the winning end. You won't cause me any trouble. Now get back to the camp or go find yourself somewhere else to trap before you make me angry, which'd be something you'd regret."

Leary stormed away, tossing various imprecations against Cooper, who would have laughed if he weren't so angry.

"I'm surprised you ain't sent that fool packin', Two-Faces," Cooper said that night. "That young buck is nothin' but trouble."

"I've told him the same thing, but he'll nae listen to me," MacTavish said.

Beaubien shrugged. "I 'ave considered it, 'Awley, but it does not seem right to send even an 'orse's ass like 'im off on 'is own in Blackfoot country, though I am beginning to regret not 'aving done so. 'E gives us much more trouble, and I will send 'I'm away."

"He crosses me again, Two-Faces, you won't have to concern yourself about it."

Beaubien stared at him for a few moments, then grinned. "That would not offend me, *mon ami*."

TWENTY-NINE

COOPER AND BEAUBIEN spotted Duncan MacTavish stomping angrily around the camp.

"What's doin'?" Cooper asked, amused.

"I canna find me squaw," the Scot snapped.

"Likely she's just found herself a Blackfoot with a bigger pizzle than yours," Cooper said with a laugh.

"I dunna find that funny, lad. Nae, not at all."

"I do."

"*Moi aussi*," the half-breed threw in.

"Bah to both of ye."

"Ah, hell, Duncan, she'll show up in a bit, I reckon. Might be just takin' care of business in the bushes or some such."

"I dunna care. The wee ones are squawkin', and I canna stand the noise. It's her doon's to care for the critters. Their wailin' has me wishin' they were Blackfeet so I could raise hair on the buggers."

Cooper and Beaubien laughed as MacTavish stormed away.

The Scotsman was still grumbling around the camp

an hour later, and Cooper looked at Beaubien. "Something ain't right here, Two-Faces," he said.

"*Oui.* Slow Calf 'as nevair been neglectful of 'er duties, especially 'er children. Something 'as 'appened to 'er."

"That's what I'm thinkin'."

Beaubien looked around. "Everyone is 'ere—except Leary, Sam, and ze woman."

"I noticed that too. It don't bode well, I'm thinkin'."

"*Oui. Mes amis,*" he called, "we need to search for Slow Calf. She 'as been missing a long time."

"Ah, I say she's just wandered off to be by herself, mate," Alistair Wentworth said.

"*Mais non.* She would not be gone so long for no reason. Me and 'Awley t'ink something is wrong. You and Paddy search south along ze creek and onto ze others that way. Dave, you and Dan search to the southwest. And Bill, you look to ze northeast. 'Awley and I will look north and west."

"I'm going' wi' ye and Hawley, Two-Faces," MacTavish said.

"*Non, mon ami.* You will stay 'ere and be 'ere if she comes back."

"I dunna like that idea, lad."

"Doesn't matter, Duncan," Cooper said. "Two-Faces is right. You need to be here in case she returns. Maybe she's gotten hurt or something and is makin' her way back here. We might miss her while we're searchin' one stream while she's near another."

"Och, ye lads bedevil me when ye make sense. Off ye go then lads to find my woman. And be quick aboot it."

As Wentworth, Murphy, White, Wheeler, and

Anderson headed off on foot, figuring to be able to cover spots not accessible by horse, Beaubien hurriedly talked to his two women, who went straight off to care for MacTavish and Slow Calf's children, who were still crying. Then he and Cooper were on the move.

More than an hour later, Wheeler, Anderson, Murphy, and Wentworth as well as Beaubien and Cooper had returned and were anxiously awaiting Bill White.

The Black mountain man staggered in, practically carrying a sagging, seriously wounded Sam Berryman.

"*Mon Dieu*," Beaubien exclaimed. "What 'appened?"

"Don't know yet, ye half-breed idiot," White snapped. "He ain't said a word since I found him."

"Quick, take him into your lodge," Cooper said as Beaubien yelled for Dancing Water, one of his two wives.

The woman looked out of the lodge, took in at a glance what was happening, and moments later rushed out with her sack of herbs and other remedies.

All the other men in the camp had crammed into White's lodge, along with his wife and two children, and squatted around the fallen mountain man.

Dancing Water rushed in, kneeled, and cut open Berryman's shirt. His chest was covered in blood from three knife wounds. The woman gently examined the wounds, then looked at her husband and shook her head.

"You can do nothing?" Beaubien asked.

Dancing Water shook her head again, rose, and left.

"What happened, *mon ami*?" Beaubien asked quietly. "Can you tell us?"

Berryman's words came out in fits and starts, whispers and gasps. "I was headin' toward my traps. I was almost to where I'd set 'em when I saw Colin draggin' Slow Calf away from the camp. She didn't seem to be strugglin' much..."

"She was goin' along willingly?" MacTavish asked, surprised and angry.

"She didn't seem to be, no. Seems more like she was dazed or something, like maybe she'd been hit on the head." Berryman paused, struggling for air, the light in his eyes fading some before recovering a little of their luster. "I asked him what was goin' on, and he said something about her wantin' to be shed of Duncan and he was takin' her away."

"Why that..." MacTavish fumed. "I canna believe..."

"And you shouldn't, *mon ami*, I t'ink," Beaubien said.

"Two-Faces is right, Duncan," Berryman continued, coughing up some blood. She said, 'I no go with him,' and looked like she was gonna scream. He clouted her hard on the head with a fist. Knocked her down."

"Why that dastardly son of a bitch," the Scot growled.

A grumble of assent rippled throughout the other men.

"I didn't like that he'd treat a woman that way," Berryman gasped around bloody coughs. "Even if she was a squaw." His eyes widened, then looked ashamed. "Sorry, Duncan, I didn't mean..."

"Dunna worry yer head on it, lad. Is that when he stabbed ye?"

"Yessir. I went after him, figurin' I'd clout *him* a few

times and teach him a lesson." Berryman weakly shook his head. "Never thought a cousin'd take a knife to me." He seemed to be fading.

"Did he say what he was plannin' for my woman?"

"No." The young man's voice was barely a whisper. "He threw her on my horse, mounted his own and rode..."

"Which way, man?" MacTavish demanded urgently.

"He's gone, Duncan," Cooper said.

"But how're we gonna find the bloody bastard?"

"I will find 'im, *mon ami*. And your *femme*," Beaubien said.

"How can ye be certain of that, lad?"

"I am ze best tracker 'ere, maybe in ze whole mountains," Beaubien boasted, not without good reason.

"Then let's go."

"*Oui*." Beaubien rose, as did MacTavish and Cooper.

"You need to stay here, Two-Faces," the latter said.

"*Mais non*. It is my duty to track down this critter."

"Like I've told you before, Two-Faces, in case you forgot, is that as captain of this bunch of fellers, it's your duty to watch over all the folks here, men, women, and children. Havin' you runnin' 'round the mountains lookin' for some pissant miscreant ain't doin' so. 'Sides, you bein' the captain, you'll be needin' to see to Sam."

"But..."

"Me and Duncan'll go."

"But I am ze best tracker, as I say."

"Yep. It's the truth, too. But I ain't so bad at such doin's. If I can't track him down, it's likely you couldn't either."

Beaubien looked ready to take umbrage at what he considered an insult but bit back his retort. "Take what you need from my supplies, zen, and be gone. *Vite!*"

"Don't need much. I don't expect we'll be gone long." He turned to White. "Where'd you find him, Bill?"

"Be easier if I just took y'all and the Scottie there."

"Duncan?" Cooper asked.

"I'll nae turn down his help, lad. Be glad to have ye."

"Saddle up, then, Bill, while we do the same."

Fifteen minutes later the three men rode out, moving fast. It didn't take long to reach the spot where White had found Berryman. They dismounted. MacTavish and White waited, the former impatiently, shuffling nervously as he fought to keep his anxiousness in check as Cooper painstakingly searched.

"C'mon, lad," the Scot said in irritation before too many minutes had passed. "It canna be hard to find their tracks. Unless ye're nae the tracker ye claim to be."

Cooper ignored him. He knew how worried the man was and eager to be on the move to rescue his woman. He had felt much the same thing when Black Moon Woman had been taken. So he saw no reason to retort, nor even to address the man, knowing it would do little good.

Ten minutes later, MacTavish pressed again, he and White having followed Cooper as he had moved forward and now stopped in his search for sign. But this time White stepped him saying, "Patience, Duncan. Y'all need patience. We know you're desirous of catchin' that skunk and gettin' your woman back, but to go off without really knowin' which way won't do no good."

"Och. It ain't easy."

"Reckon it ain't. But it won't help…"

"Let's go," Cooper said, leaping into the saddle. He moved off slowly, MacTavish following him and White bringing up the rear.

It was not long before the Scot began agitating for more speed in a steady stream of angry imprecations, warnings, and worries.

Finally Cooper had enough. He stopped his horse short, and MacTavish almost ran into him. "I've had enough of your nonsense, Duncan, and I ain't about to put up with it anymore."

"But it ain't your woman…"

Cooper's eyes blazed red as he glared at the Scot. Behind MacTavish, White gasped. All the men knew of Black Moon Woman, and to hear the Scot say something so egregiously unthoughtful was surprising even under the circumstances.

"Just slap your trap shut and keep it that way, Duncan," Cooper said through a tight slit of an angry mouth, "or I'll knock you down, hogtie you, and have Bill haul your useless ass back to camp."

MacTavish realized, finally, how troublesome he had become and how close to making an enemy of a good friend. "I'm sorry, Hawley," he said apologetically. "I'm beside meself wi' worry. I've nae had a woman of my own, not a steady one, and one wi' children, and I'm…"

Cooper relented a little. "I understand quite well, Duncan. I've been through this my own self, as you know."

"Aye, that I do, lad, and how ye e'er kept yer sanity through it all is something I'll nae be able to understand. Or maybe e'en do."

"We'll find her, Duncan, don't you fret." He turned back to the trail and rode on, not wanting to mention that when—or even if—they found her, she might not be alive or even untainted.

A short while later, MacTavish rode up alongside Cooper. "I hope I'm nae botherin' ye, Hawley, but where could this fiendish critter be goin' wi' Slow Calf?"

"Haven't got any idea, Duncan. It don't make sense. Far's I know, the only folks he knew out here other than us, were El, Farley and Sam, and now all of 'em are gone, one of 'em at his hands. Far's I know, too, he ain't had any contact with tribes where he could've made friends and aims to live with. I'm figurin' he was plannin' to ravage Slow Calf, then put her under so she couldn't say anything and come back to camp playin' the innocent. But he panicked when Sam found and challenged him. Best thing I can think of is that in his panic, he just took off not knowin' where to go or what to do."

"Y'all know we might never catch him, don't y'all?" White called from the rear. When MacTavish whipped his head around, the Black said, "We're still deep in Blackfoot country, and those dammed savages might just find him first. Would serve him right." He paused. "But that wouldn't be good for your woman."

"I did nae need to hear that, Bill, ye devil."

"Just a possibility to keep to mind."

Dark was coming fast, and they soon reluctantly made camp, such as it was. They had no food other than jerky and no water other than what they had in canteens. They simply tended their animals, gnawed on some jerky, spread their robes and slept, none of them very deeply, MacTavish having the most difficulty.

In the morning it was a few more bits of jerky, some canteen water, and then they were back in the saddle.

Before midday, Cooper suddenly shouted, "Cache!"

THIRTY

THE THREE MEN darted into the trees. An arrow knocked a few fringes off Cooper's pants, one took White's hat and nailed it to a tree, two others sank into MacTavish's side. He grunted as he fell into the bushes.

"Damn bloody savages," he shouted as he struggled up, pulling out a pistol as he did. His horse had trotted off when MacTavish fell, taking the mountain man's rifle with it. "Show yersel's, ye spineless devil's spawn." He coughed.

"You all right, Duncan?" Cooper called.

"Aye, right bloody goddamn fine. Better than I e'er been." He coughed again, this time spewing a little bloody phlegm. "Can ye nae tell, lad?"

"Well, y'all sound as cantankerous as usual," White said.

He and Cooper were within a few feet of each other and glanced the other's way. "Ain't good, Hawl," White said quietly.

Cooper nodded. "We need to find these sons a bitches and rid the earth of 'em so's we can get Duncan back to the others. Maybe Dancin' Water can do something for him."

"Ain't gonna be easy."

"Never is. You have any indication of where any of 'em are?"

"Nope. Arrows don't give much indication of such."

Cooper glanced at White with an eye roll. "I didn't realize that, Bill," Cooper said, sarcasm thick in his voice.

"Ah, hell, Hawl, y'all know I'm just talkin' to be talkin'." He paused. "But from the way those arrows hit Duncan, leastways the little I was able to see, I figure I know where one of 'em is."

"Go raise his hair then."

"Aim to." White slid off through the trees.

"Duncan, move off a little and then stay where you are. Bill and I'll hunt down the fractious sons a bitches."

"I canna stay put when there's hair to be raised on Blackfeet."

"You ain't in any condition to go roamin' about. Stay in one spot, conserve your strength, and pick off any of those bastards who come along your way."

"Ye ain't no fun, Hawley Cooper." He coughed again, and to Cooper it did not sound good.

"Be glad to rob you of some fun, hoss, if it'll keep your worthless hide on this side of the dirt."

"Bah. Go raise hair, then, whilst I take a nap."

"Do so." Cooper slipped through the trees, moving silently, every sense alert. He had no idea where the Blackfeet were and didn't want to accidentally wander into a nest of them. He froze when he heard soft voices. He quickly realized one was speaking English, the other hesitatingly responding in the same language. He was certain it was Colin Leary and Slow Calf. He was only a little surprised that they were still alive. The two would provide much sport whenever the Blackfeet got them back to their village. Cooper felt sorry for the woman but thought it would be fitting for Leary.

A shot came from MacTavish's direction, then a shout by the Scotsman, "Got ye, damn ye, ye foul bastard."

Before he had finished his sentence, there was another shot. Cooper hoped it was from White. Regardless, the two gunshots forced action. Cooper kneeled and fired his Dickert into a bush that had had some unnatural movement.

A Blackfoot rose, his face a bloody mask, screamed a strangled war cry, and collapsed on the hackberry bush.

"How's them apples for you, hoss," Cooper said as he hurriedly reloaded his rifle. He moved forward slowly, silently, heading toward the voices. He stopped when he saw the would-be mountain man and the Nez Percé woman tied to two trees a couple of feet apart. He waited, eyes searching, trying to see if there were any Blackfeet lurking about. He decided there were none.

Slinging his rifle across his back, he drew his knife and moved quickly up behind the woman. "It's Hawley," he said softly as he sliced the rope holding her. "Your man is hurt, maybe bad, but I ain't sure where he is. Make your way back about a hundred yards to the southwest. Hopefully me and Bill's horses are nearby if they didn't wander off too far when the ruckus started. Stay there, and keep yourself hidden, 'til me, Bill, and Duncan can rid the world of these bastards."

"I find husband?" she asked hopefully.

"No," Cooper said with a shake of the head. "Too dangerous. Duncan's on the other side of the trail, and I ain't sure where. Can't have you runnin' around more than necessary. So get back to the horses, if you can find 'em, and keep under cover. If you can't find the animals within a few minutes of gettin' where we left 'em, just stop where you are and find someplace to hide. Understand?"

"Yes."

"Before you go, how many of these damn savages are there?"

"Seven."

"If the three of us were lucky, we've taken three of 'em down. Shouldn't be long before we care of the rest of 'em," he said with a confidence he was not entirely sure was justified. "Their horses?"

"Just behind bushes there." Slow Calf pointed.

Cooper nodded. "Now go. And be careful."

She took a few steps, then stopped and looked back. "You help husband soon?"

"Soon's me and Bill can."

The woman hesitated only a few moments, then turned and moved off warily.

Cooper started heading to where the woman had pointed to where the Indian ponies were.

"Hey, dammit, what about me?" Leary demanded.

"What about you, hoss?" Cooper said, stopping and glaring at the man.

"Cut me loose, dammit."

"Ain't got the time, boy."

"What d'ya mean ain't got the time? You had time

to cut that damn squaw loose and talk to her. You sure as hell got time to set me free."

"Right now I'm busy, boy. I'll come back for you when I can." He grinned viciously, "'Less the Blackfeet come get you first."

With Leary's imprecations filling the air, Cooper headed for the Blackfoot horse herd. He cut most of the animals loose from the picket rope and sent them running. He trotted off a few yards and forced himself through some bushes, then kneeled behind a tree. He waited.

It was not long before two Blackfeet came running up, yelling angrily when they saw that several horses were missing.

"Got a lead pill for each of you," Cooper muttered. He fired his rifle, taking down one Blackfoot, dropped the rifle, grabbed a pistol and put the other warrior down before he could even respond to his comrade's death.

As he reloaded his rifle, he heard a commotion not far away. "Bill?" he called worriedly. "That you?"

"Sho' is, hoss. Got me another. That's two."

"Duncan?" Cooper yelled, reloading his pistol. "You still with us, boy?"

"Aye. Got me one, too." His voice was low and sounded as if the Scot had to struggle to say it.

"One more, then," Cooper called. "Maybe he's chasin' the ponies I set loose."

"Did ye see Slow Calf?" MacTavish asked, struggling even more to talk.

"Yep. Set her free. She's back where me and Bill left our horses. Ain't sure the animals are still there, but she ought to be somewhere in the vicinity if they ain't. Go find her. Me and Bill will..."

The seventh Blackfoot slinked up to where the remaining ponies were. As he prepared to leap on one's back, Cooper fired the Dickert. The warrior went down missing half his skull.

"Hawl?" White called. "Y'all all right?"

"Yep. And if Slow Calf's number of Blackfoot was right, we're rid of the vexatious devils. Let's gather where our horses should be."

On his way, Cooper cut Leary loose.

As the man stood rubbing his wrists, he said, "I need to get my weapons. Reckon they're over near the ponies."

"You won't need 'em," Cooper said flatly.

"Like hell. I..." He shut up when Cooper slammed a forearm across the side of his head.

While Leary was down, Cooper grabbed some rope, tied the young man's hands then looped another piece of rope around his neck.

"What the hell?"

"Get up."

"I ain't goin' nowhere 'til you take these ropes off me."

"Then I'll drag you. And if that's too much of a burden on me, which it likely will be, I'll grab a horse and have it do so."

Fuming, Leary stood. Tugging him along, Cooper headed to where the others would be gathering. White had managed to find MacTavish's steed as well as his own and they were there, as was Cooper's mare, which had not wandered far.

The Scotsman was lying, blood still oozing from the

two arrows in his side. Slow Calf was kneeling next to him, face contorted with sadness.

"We best get Duncan back to the others," Cooper said.

White shook his head. Moving up next to Cooper, he said, "He ain't gonna make it another ten minutes, let alone a hard trip back to the camp."

"Nothin' we can do?"

"Don't reckon so. I suppose we could get the arrows out, but we got nothin' to use as a poultice or any way to stop the bleedin'."

"Got to try, Bill. If he's as bad off as you figure, it won't make him any worse, and maybe the Good Lord'll look down and smile and it'll help."

"Ain't likely but reckon it won't hurt none."

Cooper gently pushed Slow Calf out of the way, and the two men knelt beside MacTavish. The former pulled his knife and gently touched one of the arrow shafts, then the other.

MacTavish groaned. "Ye canna do anything, lad," he said weakly. "I'm gone under certain, and there's nae anything anybody can do to change that." He coughed up a little blood.

Cooper hesitated.

"Don't ye fret, lad. Just give me a good burial." He took a deep breath that was labored, then said, "And make certain Slow Calf and the young'uns are taken care of."

Slow Calf elbowed Cooper aside and took one of MacTavish's hands in her. Tears rolled down her dusky cheeks.

"Bless ye, woman."

Coop sheathed his knife. "We'll get you back to the

camp, where we can put you to rest in the presence of the others."

"Aye, that'd be a good thing."

"Think you can travel?"

"Might be hard." He offered a weak smile. "But I reckon I'll be in the Spirit World long afore we get there so it won't matter none."

"We'll make the goin' as easy as we can on y'all," White said.

"My thanks, lad. I..."

But he was gone.

"Damn," White said as Slow Calf began to wail.

Both men ignored it.

"At least he won't be sufferin' on the way back to camp," Cooper said. He turned and smashed as forearm across Leary's nose, shattering it and knocking him to the ground.

"What the hell'd you..." Leary started as he rose.

Cooper promptly slammed the heel of his hand against the young man's forehead knocking him down again. He prepared to smash the young man again, but White stopped him. Cooper turned angry eyes on his companion. "You aimin' to stop me, dammit?"

"Yep," White said tightly. "I can't let y'all have all the fun." When Cooper looked quizzically at him, he added, "Duncan was my friend, too. I've known him longer than y'all have." He turned and pounded the side of a hard fist against Leary's teeth, knocking a couple out and loosening some others.

As Leary slowly struggled up, White kicked him under the jaw.

White went after him again, but Cooper stopped

him. "Let me go, Hawl," White rasped. "I ain't done with this critter yet."

"Yes, you are, my friend." He grinned a little at the fire in White's eyes. "You were right, hoss. I shouldn't be the one havin' all the fun. You shouldn't either."

"What's that mean?" White asked, confused.

"You and me ain't the only ones who were friends with Duncan. Paddy and Al were too, but most of all, Two-Faces was, and he deserves to deal some of his ire on this wretched son of a bitch."

White nodded, the anger ebbing a little. "We leavin' soon?"

"Soon's we get everyone mounted. I'd be obliged if you was to get the horses Slow Calf and Leary were usin'."

White nodded and hurried off. Cooper slid his rifle through the loop behind the saddle horn, then turned to Slow Calf. He gently tugged the woman up. "You need to stop this wailin' woman. I know you're in pain, but that noise might bring other Blackfeet if there's any around. We've got to take care of your man, get him back to the camp for a proper burial."

The woman stood, wiping at her tears and swiping a buckskinned sleeve over her snotty nose.

Cooper lifted MacTavish's body and gently laid it across the Scot's saddle, gritting his teeth against the indignity in death it presented. As he was tying the Scot's body down, White returned with the other two horses.

Cooper turned to Leary, who was still lying on the ground groaning. "Get up and get on your horse."

"Can't."

Cooper took the long rope, still wrapped around

Leary's neck and tied it to the man's saddle horn. "This'll help."

"Ain't necessary," Leary said in panic, words garbled a little coming out of a mouth with some broken and missing teeth. "You'll have to help me into the saddle, though. I can't do it with my hands bound."

Cooper nodded. "You try anything foolish and I'll break a couple of bones."

White collected MacTavish's rifle and pistols, stuck the former through his sleeping robe behind the saddle and the others in his large possibles bag.

Cooper looked around. Everyone was mounted. "Time to ride."

THIRTY-ONE

THE MEN in the camp were silent and grim as the sad procession rode in. The newcomers stopped in front of Two-Faces Beaubien's lodge outside of which the half-breed stood. His face was stony. The other men in the camp gathered behind the new arrivals, all looking gloomy.

"Blackfeet?" Beaubien asked.

"Yep."

"You make them pay?"

"Yep."

"*Bien.*" He cast flinty eyes at Leary. "'E was ze cause?"

"Reckon so. Bug's Boys caught him and Slow Calf. Had 'em trussed up against trees, ready to take 'em back to their village for sport."

"It weren't my fault," Leary protested, his voice shaky. "Them Blackfeet..."

White clubbed him on the side of the head. "Shut up."

"You could do nothing?" Beaubien asked.

Cooper shook his head.

Slow Calf's two children came out of the lodge she and MacTavish had used. They stood, looking confused and scared.

Dancing Water, Beaubien's Nez Percé wife, who had been watching, helped Slow Calf off her horse, then took her and the two children into the MacTavish lodge.

"He did take one of the red devils with him, though," Cooper said.

"*Bon*." He stood in thought for a few moments. "You were on ze trail long with 'im?"

"Day and a half, a little more. In the fall coolness, his body ain't goin' bad yet."

Beaubien nodded. "We will bury him tomorrow." He called to Little Fox, his other wife, a Flathead. "You will raise a lodge for Duncan, eh."

"He has a lodge, Dan Anderson said.

"*Oui*. But that lodge is for 'is grieving wife and children. This small one will be just for our longtime friend, eh."

Everyone nodded.

"Bill, you will 'ave your woman 'elp?"

"Of course."

"*Bon*."

"What about that son of a bitch?" Paddy Murphy asked, pointing at Leary.

"'E will spend ze night tied to a tree. If a wolf or a bear don't get 'im, 'e will face our justice after ze funeral." He glared at Leary, putting off any argument from the man. "Dave and Dan, take care of these 'orses.

Paddy, Al, watch over Duncan's body until ze lodge for 'im is up, *s'il vous plaît*."

The two men nodded. They looked at each other, then Murphy said, "I'll watch over him tonight, too, Two-Faces. Make sure nothin' bad happens."

Beaubien nodded. "*Merci.* 'Awley, you and Bill come into my lodge after you find a good tree that ze *fils de pute* may call 'ome for ze night. We will talk."

"After I tell my woman to help Little Fox," White said.

"Go on, Bill," Cooper said, dismounting. "I'll take care of shit pile there." He grabbed the rope around Leary's neck and jerked him out of the saddle onto the ground. When the young man make no effort to rise, Cooper tightened the rope around his neck. The younger man rose. The older mountain man tied the younger one to a stout maple that stood in view of the entire camp.

———

"'OW DID THIS 'APPEN, *M'SIEURS*?" Beaubien asked when he, Cooper, and White had gathered in the former's lodge.

"Don't use that tone with me, Two-Faces," Cooper snapped. "If it weren't for Leary snatchin' Slow Calf and killin' Sam, we'd never had to have gone after him. And that means Duncan would be alive now."

Beaubien nodded. "You are right, 'Awley. I am angry and so spoke harshly."

"We're all angry, Two-Faces, and I reckon we'll all talk harshly about what's happened. But you needn't make it sound like you're accusin' Bill and me of some doin's that brought this on."

The half-breed nodded once more. "Again, I am sorry. Duncan was a friend for a long time. 'E and I, we rode together before we joined with El."

"I know you were friends for a heap of time," Cooper said. He grinned without humor. "It's why we brung him back here."

"Eh? What do you mean?"

"Means we could've killed that son of a bitch out there and saved us all some trouble," White said. "I wanted to. But Hawl kept him alive so y'all could have a say in what his punishment will be. I reckon that does not include a long and fruitful life after another day or so."

"That is true, *mon ami*. *Merci* for bringing 'im 'ere for justice."

"No need for thanks, Two-Faces," Cooper said. "Like I said, we knew what the length and strength your friendship with Duncan was."

"'E said nothing about why he did this?"

Cooper shook his head. "Nope. It don't make sense no way, no how. He was just a fool, I reckon, and maybe thought he could get away with abusin' Slow Calf. If that's so, maybe he was gonna bury her, and come back into camp prertendin' he never saw her. I just don't know. And right now, I don't give a good goddamn. The son of a bitch has been nothin' but a plague since El brought him on."

There was silence for a bit as the three men nibbled on jerky and sipped sweetened coffee. Then White said, "The question now is what do we do with Slow

Calf? She's been made a widow now twice." He smiled dourly. "By the damn Blackfeet both times."

"I need time to think of this," Beaubien said. "If you 'ave ideas, tell me them."

"I might have a couple things in mind, but I need to think those over too," Cooper said.

The half-breed nodded. "All ze men will meet 'ere after ze work is done and we will decide then maybe."

THE LODGE, which was not a full-size one considering this was just a temporary trapping camp, not one for wintering, was cramped with all the men but Murphy crowded in. Little Fox was also there to serve food and coffee, while White's wife was helping Dancing Water care for Slow Calf's children.

"Seems like there's two things to be decided here," Cooper said. "What happens with Leary. And what's to be done with Slow Calf. As Bill said before, she's been made a widow twice. She wasn't fond of Jacques, but it seems she was very fond of Duncan. Now he's gone, what's to become of her?"

"Here now, mates, I might be overstepping things here, but I'll take her in if she'll have this ol' chap," Alistair Wentworth said.

"It's a kind offer, *mon ami*," Beaubien said. "And it may be welcome. But I don't think so. I think she is done with any man for at least a short time. This is not a situation like she 'ad with Jacques. I don't think she will want to go with someone else right away. We all saw what 'appened when El took in Morning Song too soon."

Cooper cringed remembering that it was Zeke Potts' will that left Morning Song to Elson Brooks and Goes Far's decision to put the two together too soon.

Wentworth nodded. "I understand, but if she does want another man, I'll offer myself up—if she would want me."

"Ain't but two other choices I can see," White said. "She stays here and we all care for her, maybe let the other women tend to her. Rest of us can provide her with food if she needs it, care for her animals, well, the ones that belonged to Duncan with no men annoyin' her..."

"Unless she wants it," Wheeler said with a snicker.

Everyone ignored him.

"Though if she wants to take on a man, that'd be her concern."

"What about all his possibles?"

"When we get to rendezvous, we can sell off his animals and plews and anything else and split it all up among us, unless we decide to do so beforehand."

"What about Slow Calf?" Wentworth asked. "She gets nothing?"

White shrugged. "We send her back to her people when we get there. She'll marry herself a warrior and be all set. She won't need any of his plunder or the money we might get from it."

"Seems a might harsh, mate."

White shrugged again. "It's the way of things out here, Al. Y'all know that."

There was some silence before Beaubien asked, "And ze other?"

"We set her free. Give her a horse, one for the

young'uns and maybe a mule to carry food and what-ever necessities she might need."

"Damn, Bill," Wentworth said. "That's even harsher. Ye expect a young woman—a grievin' one who might not be of the best mind—travelin' hundreds of miles in the winter on her own? With two young'uns? How'd ye like it if we was to treat your woman that way if ye went under?"

"Reckon if I went under I wouldn't be around to give a damn or not." There was no humor in the state-ment, just fatalism.

"I've never heard ye act so cold toward squaws before."

White shrugged.

Cooper, watching, thought White was not comfort-able with his idea but could see no other way.

"There's another way," Cooper said into the silence that had grown. When all eyes turned toward him, he said, "We could send her back to her people…"

"That's what I already said," White noted.

"You didn't let me finish. Send her back with an escort."

"You volunteerin'?" White asked. "I sure as hell ain't, and I reckon none of these others will either."

"Hadn't planned on it."

"Then it is not a real idea, *mon ami*," Beaubien said.

"I've done more than my share of travelin' from one place to another out here in winter."

"It ain't winter yet," Wentworth said.

"Will be soon enough."

Again silence fell across the group. After some uneasy minutes, Wheeler asked, "We ain't decided the other thing either. What's gonna happen with Leary?"

"Y'all lookin' for mercy for the son of a bitch?" White snapped.

"Nope."

"Y'all ought to know what's gonna happen to that snake-humpin' bastard."

"Reckon I do. Just was wonderin' the how of it, I suppose."

Everyone but Anderson looked at Wheeler. He had never been friendly with MacTavish, nor any of the other old-timers in the group. Wheeler shifted uncomfortably and looked down.

"Listen to me, *mon ami*," Beaubien said in a cold, hard voice. "You 'ave not been friends with many of ze '*ommes* 'ere. Maybe you 'ave become close to Leary, eh. Maybe not. But it seems maybe is possible. Now, I tell you, *m'sieur*, that if you try to 'elp 'im, you with either join 'im or take 'is place depending on if 'e is 'ere. And if you 'elp 'im to escape and go with 'im, I will 'unt you down."

"As will I," Cooper said immediately.

"And me," White added.

"Me too," Wentworth said.

Only Anderson said nothing but he had a look of terror on his face.

"Do you understand, what I say, *m'sieur*?"

Wheeler nodded, afraid that his voice would not work if he tried to speak.

"*Bon.*"

"So how do you plan to make Leary pay for his perfidy?" Wentworth asked, a half-smile showing he was interested, not challenging Beaubien.

"I 'ave given some thought to this matter, though not much because 'e 'as not been back 'ere long. Maybe

I could cut 'is throat." He shook his head. "But, no, that would be too easy. And too kind to ze *fils de pute*. Maybe I shoot 'im. Many times. Not to kill, just wound. I reload slowly each time, watch as 'e bleeds more and more. Maybe I catch a heap of rattlers and throw them at 'im." He shook his head. "But no, ze snakes, they are slumber now."

"We could strip 'im down to the way he came into this world," White said, "and leave him ten or twenty miles from here, even closer to Blackfoot country than we are now."

"That is worth consideration," Beaubien agreed.

"Or maybe treat him the way we did that one feller we caught who had stolen all our plews and horses."

"Not a good way to go under, that is certain." Beaubien sighed, then grinned. "So many ways to treat such an evil man."

"Maybe," Wentworth said slowly as if developing the idea as he went, "we could do something like that. We move real stealthily, drop him down just outside a Blackfoot village, or even better, a camp of warriors on the warpath. They will enjoy the surprise, I'm thinkin'."

Several of the men laughed, but Cooper said, "Too dangerous for the rest of us. I don't know about you fellers, but I've had more than my fill of temptin' Blackfeet to take my hair."

The men chuckled, though it was underlain with nervousness. They remembered the previous winter's clash with the horde of Blackfeet in the valley where they were wintering. Many was the man here who thought he'd be wolf bait that time.

"I will think on it some more," Beaubien said. "Now it is close to robe time for this *'omme*."

The others got the message and rose, heading for the flap.

"Not you, 'Awley," the half-breed sad. "I wish to speak with you more, eh."

Eyes wide in surprise and question, Cooper planked his rump back down.

THIRTY-TWO

BEAUBIEN TOOK out his small clay pipe, filled it, and lit it with a burning twig from the fire.

Cooper did the same, chaffing at the delay. He wanted to know just what the half-breed had in mind. Finally he had waited long enough. "What'd you want to talk to me about, Two-Faces?"

Beaubien puffed a few more times.

Cooper pulled the pipe from his mouth and started to rise. "I ain't got the time or the willingness to sit here and try to guess why you asked me here. Reckon I'll be goin'."

"Sit, *mon ami*." He offered a small smile. "You stay 'ere with us all ze time. You 'ave nowhere else to go."

"Bill will take me in. Or I can share the lean-to with Paddy and Al."

"True. I ask again, sit, *s'il vous plaît*."

Cooper settled back down. "So talk."

"I don' like ze idea of just sending Slow Calf back to 'er people on 'er own, but I do like the idea you 'ad of escorting 'er there."

"And?" Cooper was beginning to suspect what was coming.

"You would be ze best choice to take 'er, 'Awley."

"Why? 'Cause I've been unfortunate—or foolish—enough to make such treks?"

"Unfortunate things you cannot do anything about, *mon ami*." He grinned. "But foolish? That you can. And you chose to do that twice, once to fetch Goes Far as your wife, a woman you 'ad 'ardly spoken a dozen words to."

"Yep. Pretty damn foolish that one." Then he, too, grinned. "But it's worked out all right."

"'As it?"

"Why sure."

"Then where is Goes Far? Is she 'ere sharing ze robes with you, eh? *Mais non*, she is very far away, wondering where in 'ell 'er man is and what 'e is doing. She might t'ink you 'ave gone under. There are many dangers on ze trail as we know."

"Never thought of that," Cooper said, surprising himself.

"Or maybe she t'inking you 'ave another woman and won't come back to 'er."

"You know that ain't true."

"But of course. But does she know that? 'Ow is she to know you will come back for 'er. She worries like many squaws that many white men treat their Indian wives poorly."

"Many do, that's for certain. I don't."

"You 'aven't before. But now? 'Ow is she to know. Maybe she thinks you are a good man to bring 'er back to 'er people so she can find a warrior to marry instead of just casting 'er out at rendezvous or some trading post?" He paused, watching the various emotions flicker across Cooper's face.

"You 'ave an eye for ze femmes, *mon ami*. Maybe not an eye, but a soft spot most men don't 'ave for women, especially squaws. El was mistreating Morning Song, so your woman, she knows what kind of man you are, she asks you to 'elp 'er friend."

"I..."

"So what do you do? You do what your wife asks and take 'er friend back to 'er people where she will be safe. And when do you do this? In ze winter."

"But Elson was..."

"As I told you, and others did too, the way a man treats 'is woman is 'is business, not someone else's."

"It was my doin', and Zeke's will that I was enforcin' that brought about those troubles," Cooper said defensively.

"That doesn't matter, 'Awl. When you interfered, Morning Song was El's woman. You should not 'ave intruded, no matter what ze cause. And because of that, what 'appened, eh?"

Cooper sat with a clenched jaw, refusing to respond.

"What 'appened is you 'ad to kill an old friend and another man. True," he added with a bob of the head, "that one deserved killing and 'e was not a friend. So you do that and take ze woman back to 'er family maybe or to friends to 'elp 'er. But you took your woman there, too. And where is she now? She is still in 'er village many miles from 'ere."

"I was plannin'..."

"*Bien sur*. But you didn't. You are a strange man, *mon ami*. Different than most white men. You stick your nose in doin's that you should not, often because there is a woman involved. I love ze ladies. *Mais oui*! But you, you not only love them, you 'ave a soft spot for them."

"Reckon I do. What makes me different is that I don't think that's a sin."

"That makes you a rare man among mountaineers, 'Awley."

"Maybe, but I ain't about to change. Hell, I couldn't change the way I am even if I wanted to."

"I'm not sure that makes you a better man than most of us others or a damn fool." He smiled crookedly. "What I say in all this is that you bring troubles on yourself sometimes with these notions that are strange to most of us others." He held up a hand to forestall any protest from Cooper. "What also makes you different from us others is that you 'ave courage beyond most others. Courage in battle, which most of us possess. But you 'ave the courage to do things you think are right when you do them, no matter ze consequences. Like that time last year with the run-in with the Shoshonis. You did what you thought was right at ze time to 'elp all of us survive, and to hell with the consequences. As a result, you lost your Shoshoni family and great friend. That, *mon ami*, is real courage, more than any other man I know in these mountains."

"You're startin' to confuse me, Two-Faces. First you tell me I'm wrong for interferin' where most say it's not my concern. I do it because I think it's right. Then you tell me, I'm a courageous feller because I do things I think are right at the time even though they could have poor consequences. And in between, you tell me I'm a fool for much of what I do. It don't make sense, none of it."

"But it does. All men do brave things, all men do foolish things, all men do things they think are right that maybe aren't."

"So maybe I'm all these men in one at the same time unlike others. Doesn't make a difference. I am the man I am. There ain't no changin' that. I do what I think is right at the time, no matter how dangerous, how poor the consequences might be for me, no matter how foolish."

Beaubien smiled. "That is what makes some men follow you. You are unafraid of anything. That can't be said of many men."

"Hell, there's plenty of things I'm afraid of."

"Besides your woman, what things, eh?" He smiled.

"Like what'll happen to me if the fur trade dies. And what'll life be like without Goes Far all the time."

"And is she with you?"

"No, but..."

"I t'ink you make that suggestion about what to do with Slow Calf because you t'ink it's the right thing. To 'ave someone take that woman to 'er people. To protect 'er from all ze dangers of ze mountains. Things that will kill any man other than 'Awley Cooper."

"Now you're really talkin' nonsense."

"*Mais no, mon ami.* You fought dozens of Blackfeet last winter, took many scalps then, or could 'ave. You were counted coup on dozens of time, maybe more. You were left with nothing many years ago by that scum called Jeremiah Weeks, left to find yourself through the winter with no weapons, no cloak, nothing. You survived all of this. And zia fall, you were shot near ze 'eart with an arrow. Did you die? *Mais non.* Any other man would 'ave. But you lived, raised 'air on those that wounded you, then raised hair on ze ones who killed your new friends. You are a blessed man, my French countrymen might say. Or you 'ave strong, powerful medicine, my Sioux friends would say."

Cooper shook his head in confusion and disbelief. Much of what Beaubien had said was true, at least of the incidents. But of him being special? Hogwash as far as he was concerned. "All of what you're sayin', Two-Faces, is claptrap. Pure buffler shit. Ain't no sense to it, ain't no reason in it. Just words comin' out of your mouth like shit from a feller with dysentery."

"That is not true. Maybe you don't know it. Maybe you don't believe it, but I speak ze truth."

"Fine, if that's what *you're* thinkin'. I think you've gone mad like El but in a different way." He took a deep breath and let it out. "You said when the others were here that it was close to robe time for you. I reckon that time has come. And the same for me, though I reckon I'll be spendin' my nights with Paddy and Al if Bill's woman won't have me."

"A few more moments, 'Awley. I suppose I say too many things to you, things you don't believe even if they are true. And ze French side of me makes me talk too much."

"That's a goddamn fact I can believe."

"All of what I said 'ere I should have not bothered and just came out and said what I wanted to say."

"And that is?"

"That because of ze man you are, you made ze suggestion because you do want to take Slow Calf back to her people. Because you t'ink it's right."

"More nonsense."

"And you want—need—someone to convince you that it is what you want to do."

"No," Cooper said with a shake of his head. "No, you got it all wrong, Two-Faces. I'd not like to...she ain't nothin' but someone else's woman...she..."

"Now it's you who are speaking nonsense. You know it is ze right t'ing to do." He grinned for real this time. "But if you don't want to believe that, there is another reason for you to do this."

"And what is that?"

"Goes Far."

"How's she enter into this?"

"Slow Calf is a Nez Percé. She is from another village, *oui*. But she is Nez Percé. And that means 'er village cannot be too far from Red Leggings'. And you know who is there, *ne'cest pas?*"

"Goes Far," Cooper said, shaking his head to clear it. With everything that Beaubien had been throwing at him, he had not connected that fact. He wished Beaubien had done as he just admitted and left out all the gibberish about his bravery and such and just told him that if he took Slow Calf back to her village, it would be easy to find Goes Far's village and be with her.

"*Oui!* You were close enough to 'er early this fall but turned back because you were missing out on the trapping season. That, you thought, was ze right thing to do at ze time, even if that meant leaving your woman behind. Now, you will miss more trapping perhaps, but you will do what is right in taking Slow Calf home and going to get your woman. When you get back, you will take up trapping again. Maybe it won't be ze same, and maybe you won't 'ave nearly as big a catch, but you will 'ave done something that is good, and you will 'ave your woman beside you. She is a good woman, and she will not be too put out that you 'ave 'ad a poor hunt because you 'elped a friend of 'ers—another friend of 'ers. And I bet that first friend you 'elped is not so melancholy now that she is with 'er people."

"You're a connivin' son of a bitch, Two-Faces. A devilish, schemin', evil shit pile."

Beaubien laughed. "*Oui*. And you will thank me for it one day, I t'ink."

"Not as long as I'm on this side of the grass, you bastard." But he too laughed.

———

COOPER DID NOT WAIT to see Colin Leary's demise. Not long after daylight, well before the method of Leary's death was decided upon, Cooper, Slow Calf, towing a pack mule loaded with supplies provided by all the men in the camp, and her two children, both on one pony, rode out of the camp. Cooper decided Beaubien had been right—he was doing what he thought was right. He just hoped it was also wise. And most of all, that Goes Far would be waiting for him.

THIRTY-THREE

THOUGH WINTER WAS ALMOST upon them, the weather remained relatively mild, which suited Cooper. The longer he could avoid the storms and bitter cold of a mountain winter, the better. He occasionally thought as he rode that it would be nice if real winter held off until he was in Red Leggings' village. Or even better, until he was back with Two-Faces Beaubien and the others, with Goes Far at his side. The foolishness of such thoughts kept his spirits light much of the time, though it brought on bouts of melancholy when the reality of the nonsense crept over him.

Slow Calf was, as Cooper had expected, no trouble on the trail. She was a seasoned traveler having been with Jacques Dubois for a few years and then Duncan MacTavish for the past few months. Each night, as Cooper tended the horses and mule, Slow Calf would, despite her sadness, efficiently gather firewood, start a blaze, put on whatever meat they had to cook and a pot of coffee. When he had time, Cooper would kill fresh game—elk and deer mostly. It would last several days in the cold air, easing their travel a little. The woman would use some herbs and wild spices she carried with her to make the meals even more palatable, something that both pleased and saddened Cooper, pleased because the meat was better, saddened because it reminded him of Goes Far. Amid all that work, she also took care of her children—a five-year-old girl named Spotted Deer, and a three-year-old boy named Curved Horn. And she did it all without complaint.

Each night, Cooper would build a basic lean-to for Slow Calf and the children. If the weather was bad, he would throw up an even cruder one for himself. They were serviceable at best, and with their hasty construction of whatever trees were around, they provided only a minimal protection from the storms that were becoming more frequent.

Slow Calf was quiet around Cooper, rarely speaking to him other than concerning the necessities. Knowing that she was grieving, Cooper did not pressure her. But as time went by, she began to open up a little under his coaxing, quiet questions about her life with Jacques Dubois and Duncan MacTavish. It amused him a little to hear her use a pastiche of French and English, in neither of which she was perfect.

"Old Man was mean," she finally said one night as they ate, speaking of Dubois, who had been considerably older than she and well-known as a cantankerous curmudgeon.

Cooper nodded, knowing it to be true.

"I not like him." She sighed. "But he gave father several horses for me, so I was his." The distaste for that situation was strong in her voice.

"And Duncan?"

She smiled through her sadness. "He was good man. Make me laugh many times. Treat me good."

"He cared for the young'uns?"

"Yes. Much. Not like Old Man. The children, they like him but were afraid of father."

"Jacques wasn't very likable that's certain. You're right, though, Duncan was a good man. He was a good companion to the rest of us fellers, and I ain't surprised he was good to you and the little ones."

Slow Calf started to weep, and Cooper let her be, not knowing what, if anything, he could do for her. He had never been any good at dealing with women in such a state, even with Goes Far or Black Moon Woman before her. But her unhappiness saddened him, and the feeling was worsened when he saw the children's despondency as they huddled around her mother. He thought of trying to comfort them somehow, but he did not know how and was certain they would be afraid of him because they didn't know him. He figured they would be confused, having had an unwelcoming father but a welcoming one in MacTavish. It also had him worried about how he would be able to care for his son, *Maybe*, he thought more than once, *I ain't cut out to be a father*.

Two and a half weeks out, the weather began to change. Cold started to settle in for real, and snow cropped up a few times, though not much. Until a storm swept over them one afternoon when they were caught in a flat. Cooper's mind flashed back several winters ago, when he and Black Moon had been caught in a similar situation, and he roared in anger. He had survived that winter, and others as bad, as had his women, and he vowed he would come through this all right—with the woman and children in his care unharmed and healthy.

As the snow grew stronger and thicker, he rode back, picked up Curved Horn from the horse he shared with his sister, and handed the child to his mother. She nodded thanks and wrapped the already swaddled child into her buffalo robe. She glanced worriedly back to Spotted Deer.

"I'll see to her," Cooper said into the growing wind. He rode back, grabbed the girl and plunked her on the saddle in front of him, having taken his rifle and slung it across his back. He pulled his capote around her with him as best he could.

The child stiffened in fear

"It's all right, girl," he said softly. She was still tense, so he asked, "You liked your new father, Funny Talker?"

"*Oui*," the girl whispered, the soft little word whipped away into the wind.

"He was my *ami*. My friend. He wasn't like nasty Old Man. He was a good man, and I'm like him."

Still no favorable response.

"I've been nice to you while we travel, yes?"

A small nod almost lost in the confines of the thick wool coat.

"Then you're safe with me, little one. Don't be afraid. We'll find a place soon where we can let the storm growl and blow and act nasty but can't hurt us."

Spotted Deer said nothing, but she did relax a little against his chest.

The storm kept building, but before much longer, Cooper pulled them into a large stand of cottonwoods, which cut the wind considerably even though they were mostly bereft of leaves.

Cooper slid off his horse, then helped Spotted Deer down, setting her on the ground, where she ran to her mother and hugged her legs.

"She scared," Slow Calf said apologetically of her daughter.

"Me, too," Cooper said with the slightest smile on his face.

Slow Calf's eyes widened in shock. She had seen this man in battle and knew he was afraid of nothing. Then she saw the tiny smile and one of her own appeared briefly.

"Besides, havin' a big, ugly ol' feller like me wanderin' around don't help make her any easier," he added with a wink. "Now, make sure the young'uns are tended to right off. I'll gather up wood and get a fire started."

"*Mais non*," she said firmly. "Not man's job. I do." When Cooper hesitated, she added, "You tend to animals. *Les petite fils* will be all right."

"You sure?"

"*Oui*. Children will help me get wood."

Cooper nodded and headed off to his chores. He didn't know how Slow Calf did it, but by the time he had tended the horses she had a fire going, with a pile of firewood nearby, a hunk of frozen elk warming in a kettle of melted snow, and a coffeepot near the flames. He sat and nodded thanks for the cup of coffee the woman handed him.

"Though the storm's easin' considerably, I'll build you and the children a lean-to soon's I eat," Cooper said.

Slow Calf nodded. "You good man, Haw...Awl..."

"Just Haw is all right," he said with a chuckle. "Or you can call me Hairy Face like Goes Far does." Saying her name brought a dash of unhappiness over him, but he fought it off.

They soon dug into the boiled meat, eating quietly. Cooper sat on an old log, legs outstretched before him, his feet near the fire. But as they ate, the two children edged a little closer to Cooper, then some more. With his mind still lingering on Goes Far, he did not notice at first but smiled to himself when he became aware of it. He noticed, too, that Slow Calf was about to admonish the children, but he gave a barely perceptible shake of the head.

Finally Spotted Deer was right next to one of his knees. She looked up at him with sad, though curious eyes. "Are you our *nouveau pere*?" she asked.

Cooper was taken aback. "Your new pa? No, little one. I'm just a friend of your ma's and your papa Duncan."

"Oh." Tears crept into the girl's eyes.

Not sure he was doing the right thing, he stroked her hair. "You'll have a new papa soon after you get back to your people. You'll see, He will be a good man, like Duncan." He looked at Slow Calf helplessly, not knowing what else to say.

The woman smiled sadly at him. She had no answer either.

The boy edged close to Cooper's other knee. "You smell like *Pere* Dunca," Curved Horn said.

"Reckon I do. We both trapped and hunted and butchered meat." He tried to restrain a grin without much luck. "And mostly we're full of piss and vinegar." He paused at the confused looks on the children's faces.

He glanced over and saw that Slow Calf was aghast. Then she realized that the children had no idea of what the words meant and she let loose with a giggle. It was a very small one, and very short-lived, but it was real.

When the boy and girl saw that, they laughed too.

"Now you don't say such a thing to anyone else," he mock scolded. "These are just for silly men to say." He set down his cup and tousled their hair.

Sensing they wanted more attention, Cooper pulled a child up into each arm and just held them, their heads covered by the hoods of their capotes. Minutes later, they were asleep. Uncertain of what to do, Cooper looked at Slow Calf. The woman seemed to be at peace, so he said nothing.

———

SOMETHING'S WRONG, Cooper thought as he slowly came awake, though he did not yet open his eyes. It was nothing threatening or he would have snapped awake and been in motion before his eyes opened. But there was definitely something out of the ordinary here. His face was cold but he felt no snowflakes settling on him. The wind had quieted, too. He opened his eyes. Looking at the sky, he realized he had slumped back off his seat on the log, legs half over it, and fallen asleep— with the two children still in his arms. Slow Calf had covered them with a buffalo robe against the frigid night. He was confused, not knowing how to feel. And he was afraid to rise lest he awaken the children. Then he saw Slow Calf looking at him—with a shy smile on her face.

"Yes, you good man, Haw," she said. "Come, children," she said in Nez Percé. "Wake now."

The boy and girl stirred, then pushed aside the robe and stood, sleepily rubbing their eyes.

Cooper rose, still wondering at this strange situation, and headed for the bushes. When he returned and sat at the fire, Slow Calf handed him a bowl of boiled elk and a mug of coffee and said quietly, "*Merci.*"

"For what?"

"Caring for children. Letting me sleep without worry."

"Wasn't much. Besides, I never did build you a lean-to."

"No need. Storm stopped."

"That it did."

TWO WEEKS LATER, accompanied by several warriors who had trotted out to greet them, Cooper, Slow Calf, and the two children sat on a rise and looked over Slow Calf's village, a different one from that led by Red Leggings. It was several days' travel east of where the latter's village was according to the people here.

The travelers had endured only one more snowstorm on their journey—though it lasted almost three days. The weather otherwise, except for the bitter cold, was almost favorable. As the children grew more comfortable with Cooper, the traveling became easier and they progressed more quickly.

They entered the village to a warm welcome, with a

feast and a dance planned despite the frigidness of the temperature. Cooper chaffed, wanting to be on his way. He was, once again, within a few days' ride of Goes Far, and he was determined not to be forestalled in his return to her this time. But he endured the two days of celebrations before he saddled the mare, loaded the mule, and rode off, waving farewell to Spotted Deer and Curved Horn. There was a tinge of sadness in it as he realized he would miss them. "Won't be long now, Goes Far," he muttered as he left the village amid a light snowfall.

THIRTY-FOUR

IT WAS SNOWING. Again. And Hawley Cooper was sick of it, tired of the never-ending blanket of whiteness and of the cold. It seemed that every year he made a midwinter trek. He had had far worse ones than this one, but his present trip was rather tedious despite its expected pleasant culmination. Perhaps it was time, he thought with increasing frequency, usually accompanied by a sigh, that maybe it was time for him to leave the mountains. It might not be much warmer or bereft of snow, but Missouri had the benefit of having houses in which to stay warm and out of the storms. But he always shook his head. He had no idea of what he would do in a civilized setting. As a boy, he had been part of a farming family, but that had never appealed to him and was one of the reasons he had fled home. He had no trade other than trapping. He supposed he could do some scouting. People would, he suspected, start heading across the plains to places like Oregon country. The coming of the white missionaries—and two white women with them—at the last rendezvous signaled the beginning of change that Cooper was sure he would not like. There were places, he had heard, farther south of Missouri, where it was warm year-round, places like New Orleans or even one called Florida Territory. But he knew little of those places, other than that they, as well as Missouri, he realized, favored slavery and he was not sure he could countenance that after having served with Bill White for the past half dozen years or so.

So he continued to plod along, knowing that the mountains and forests with their rivers and streams teeming with beaver, and the meadows and plains crowded as far as the eye could see with buffalo, were the only places he would feel comfortable. Its hardships were many and the dangers even more so. But they were part of his life now; had been for more than a decade. These Shining Mountains were home. There was no getting around that fact.

But the melancholy was irregular, coming in fits and starts, usually dispelled quickly. Thoughts of Goes Far and being with her again within a few days kept him going.

IN ONE OF the brief moments that the thick white cloud parted a bare few hours into his day, he saw a figure riding toward him. He was about to pull his rifle but stopped and grinned. Even with the intermittent lifting of the curtain and the little distance, Cooper knew there could be only one figure as bulky as the one he saw. He just hoped the warrior would recognize him in time to prevent violence.

Ten minutes later, the two men stopped next to each other, one facing southwest, the other northeast.

Cooper pointed to the thick buffalo robe the warrior had wrapped around him, the bow and quiver of arrows, the well-cared-for hair. "Huntin' Blackfoot, I reckon, Sits Down?"

The huge Nez Percé grinned. "Why you say that?"

"Easy. Your get-up ain't your usual slovenliness."

Sits Down's grin widened. "You're smart, Hairy Face. Yes, I go to fight Blackfoot."

"Not really that smart. It's just that when you're alone you're the real you, not the fat, lazy critter you pretend to be in front of the others."

"Maybe," the warrior said cryptically.

"Besides, you're too far from home to be huntin' buffler."

The warrior nodded. "Where you go?"

"To get Goes Far." He paused. "If she'll have me. There's a good chance she thinks I abandoned her and has forgotten about me. She's likely gone and married some warrior and is livin' happily with him."

"Not true. You work things out. You see. She pines for you. I think she will have you back. Don't know why she cares for a crazy, hairy-faced white man." This time he laughed. "Might take one mighty heap of foofaraw, though."

"That might be a problem, seein' as how I ain't had much of a trappin' season and am one poor devil of a feller."

"I had camp not far back. Maybe we go there? Talk, eat buffler—if the wolves ain't ate what I left there."

"It's still mighty early in the day," the mountain

man said, a smile spreading across his face, "but that shines with me, Sits Down. Let's go."

Before long they were sitting at a large, warming fire, a few slabs of buffalo ribs sizzling over the flames near which a coffeepot was getting close to percolating.

"Why you not stay with the others, trap, take plews, winter in one place maybe, get Goes Far at rendezvous?" Sits Down asked. "Would be smarter than another winter trip across mountains."

"Long story, my friend."

"I listen."

The mountain man hesitated. "You remember ol' Jacques?"

"Yep. Not likable man. Treated his women and children bad."

"That's him. He was killed by Blackfeet down to rendezvous. You weren't around."

"No loss."

"That's a fact. Nobody missed him, not even his woman. But it left Slow Calf and the children alone. So Duncan took 'em in."

"He is good man, though he talks funny," the Nez Percé said with a grin. "Funnier even than other white men."

Cooper did not return the smile. "Yep, he was a good man."

"Was?" Sits Down asked, a question in his eyes.

Cooper nodded. "Blackfeet got him about a month ago. Another feller Elson had hired on went bad, boy named Colin Leary, stole Slow Calf and killed another feller that had joined us at rendezvous. Me, Bill White, and Duncan went after him. Blackfeet ambushed us. Duncan took a couple arrows deep in his innards. Me and Bill managed to raise hair on the damned devils. We found Leary and Slow Calf trussed up. Bug's Boys were plannin' on havin' some fun with 'em, I reckon. Took 'em both back to camp."

"You didn't just raise hair on this Leary?"

"Figured Two-Faces and the others would want a part in seein' to it considerin' they were longtime friends of Duncan's."

Sits Down nodded.

"Slow Calf was grievin'. She didn't care none for Jacques and didn't miss him when he got put under. But she favored Duncan considerably and was bereft at his passin'. So we decided she should be back with her people."

"And you say you will take her?" Sits Down said. He didn't really need to see Cooper's nod before adding. "Another dangerous trip in winter. For a man who is braver than anyone I know, you have soft heart."

"I've been told that before," said with a self-effacing smile. "I left her at her village a couple days ago and was headin' for Red Leggin's village to get Goes Far."

"She will be glad."

"I hope so." He ate a little, then asked, "What about you, Sits Down? Still livin' the same?" The mountain man was surprised when the Nez Percé hesitated, looking uncertain. "Sits Down?" Suddenly he laughed. "Everyone knows about you now, don't they? And you got to live like the real warrior you are? That it?" he asked with a hoot.

Sits Down nodded glumly.

"Don't be so gloomy over it, hoss," Cooper said, still laughing. "You deserve the peoples' respect."

"Now people expect much. Want much."

"Reckon they do. That why you're out huntin' Blackfeet?"

"Yes. Like old days, A warrior on own."

"You'll have to go back sometime."

"Yes," Sits Down said sourly.

"Well now maybe you can find yourself a woman, have children, get fat and sassy." Cooper burst out laughing again. "Well, you're already fat and sassy so that won't be nothin' new."

"I should've known you're as bad as all white men. Think funny. Act funny."

The mountain man was about to say something but caught himself and let himself think a moment. Then he said in shock, "You're scared, ain't you?"

The warrior's eyes grew large and angry, and he looked like he was about to attack Cooper. Then he gritted his jaw and nodded.

"Ain't nothin' to be ashamed about, Sits Down. It ain't like you're afraid of an enemy. You're the strongest, bravest warrior I ever saw. But facin' people who have known you as a slacker all his life, well, that could put any feller off. It's like facin' spirits you can't see or some- thing, where you ain't sure how to act. You'll be fine, my friend."

"You not afraid of anything."

Cooper smiled. "Ah, you're wrong there, hoss. You'll see that sure as hell if the day ever comes when there ain't no more trappin'. Facin' a life without the fall and spring hunts, without takin' plews to rendezvous..." He shook his head. "And if there's no more trappin', what'll I do? Go live in some wretched town some- where? Be a farmer? No, sir, my friend, such things make me afraid."

"I say again, you're a strange man, Hawley Cooper. White men can do many things that Nez Percé can't."

"Maybe there are things are available to us that ain't to you, but that don't make 'em desirable. The thought of sittin' in a wood or stone house in a rank town, scrubbin' in the dirt hopin' I can raise some corn or something ain't a life, Sits Down. Nope. Not when compared with the fresh air of the mountains, runnin' buffler, feastin' on ribs and fleece and hump meat."

"No danger in city."

"Like hell. Bad people there, too, and they're all cramped together 'stead of spread out like in the mountains here. Makes 'em bad-tempered. And there's disease and all sorts of plagues. No, Sits Down, I'll take the dangers of mountain weather, bloodthirsty Bug's Boys or even starvin' times out here than a miserable existence in some flatlander place."

"You braver than me," the warrior said thoughtfully.

Cooper shook his head. "You just have different things to concern you now. It ain't fear so much, just caution about what's in store for you. You don't know how to act in this situation 'cause you've never had to—or, rather, wanted to. Now you have to face a different world, and that can be a scary thing. Don't mean you're not brave. You don't think I'm scared fightin' Blackfeet? I sure as hell am. But I put it aside, just like you do. Hell, the thought of becomin' a father makes my innards knot up. I reckon I'll get over it. It'll just take some gettin' used to."

Sits Down was silent for quite a while, filling his mouth with buffalo and coffee instead. Then he nodded. "I am glad you are a friend, Hairy Face. Good friend."

Cooper nodded slightly, embarrassed in his turn.

———

"YOU STILL PLANNIN' to go huntin' Bug's Boys?" Cooper asked in the morning as the two men sat to break their fast.

"I think yes. Why?"

The mountain man laughed. "I was thinkin' I need someone to protect me." When the Nez Percé looked at him as if he were insane, he grinned. "Hell, talk about bein' afraid, the thought of facin' Goes Far scares me all the way down to the bottom of my mocs."

A rumbling laugh bubbled up from Sits Down's throat. "I'm too small for you to hide behind when you face *that* strong woman."

"Well, damn, maybe I should turn tail and run back to Two-Faces and the other fellers. Maybe wait 'til rendezvous to talk to her. With all the boys around, maybe she won't be spittin' fire at me."

"Be worse. She have all those folks—mountaineers, Nez Percé, Flatheads, maybe Crows even—watchin'."

"That would be embarrassin'." He sighed in mock resignation. "Then I'll just have to ride up and hope she ain't primed to raise my hair. You'll be there to hold me up in case I feel the need to swoon, won't you?"

"Don't know. That seems even scarier than bein' a warrior in front of all my people."

Both men laughed.

"So, how far is it to the village?"

"Three days, though maybe more if the weather stays bad." He glanced up at the sky. "Snow still comes, so maybe take longer."

"Travelin' in snow bother you?"

"No. But may be bad. Maybe not. It's snowin' hard now. But maybe will stop soon."

"So when do we leave?"

"Soon as you load the supplies."

THIRTY-FIVE

THOUGH IT WAS as cold as a demon's heart, the sky was cloudless and the sun dazzlingly bright when Cooper and Sits Down rode into Red Leggings' village. Cooper was glad it wasn't snowing—he was decidedly tired of snow—but at the same time, he wished the precipitation was there to at least partially hide him when he got to Goes Far's lodge. He had never been as nervous as he was now as he neared the time when he would face her, as he was deeply worried that the Nez Percé woman would cast him aside after he had been gone so long.

The mountain man and the large warrior stopped in front of Red Leggings' lodge, where the old chief, as well as Pale Thunder, waited, each wrapped in thick blankets against the cold.

"Come inside," Red Leggings said. "We eat, talk, smoke."

Cooper dismounted. He did not look forward to this. While he was nervous about meeting with Goes Far, he wanted to get it done, so he could find out where he stood in her eyes. But it would be an insult to the two great Nez Percé if he refused to do as they wished. He followed Sits Down, who had followed Red Leggings and Pale Thunder, into the dim lodge.

The warmth was welcome as Cooper and the others shrugged off their capotes, blankets, or robes, and sat. Red Leggings' two wives, both younger than the old chief but looking ancient, served up bowls of boiled buffalo and tin mugs of coffee before fading into the background.

"So you have come home, eh?" Pale Thunder said with a grin.

"Yes," Cooper mumbled.

"Come to reclaim your woman?"

"Yes," the mountain man grunted.

"You've been gone a long time. Maybe she won't want you."

Cooper's head snapped up, and he glared, worried, at Pale Thunder, who did not blink. "Has she said something?" he asked, voice strangled.

"Why would she say anything to me?" Pale Thunder asked.

"Because you have become her father unless you have turned her out." His voice had grown hard.

"She is sad. She has missed her man."

Cooper gulped.

"But who can tell a woman's mind?" the war chief said.

Cooper gritted his teeth, set down his bowl next to his mug, and rose. "Obliged for your hospitality, Red Leggin's, as usual. But I got business to take care of." He grabbed his capote and put it on as stalked out, then stopped to regain control of himself. But to put it off a little longer, he went and tended his two animals. Then, with a chill growing in the pit of his stomach, he headed for the lodge that Goes Far shared with her mother, Bright Eyes. He stopped at the flap and stood a few moments to compose himself. He was disgusted with himself for being so nervous. He had faced hordes of Blackfeet, starving times, and brutal winters, but had not been this concerned. This was different, though. He knew he could find another woman—including one in this village—if Goes Far no longer wanted him. But she was his woman, and he wanted her back at his side. He did not want another woman. He took a deep breath and let it out, watching the vapor fade into the sunlight, then called for entrance.

He entered when given permission and sat at the fire, slipping the rifle off his shoulder and setting it down beside him. He was not offered food or even coffee, and a vision of his rejection by Cheyenne Killer and Cuts Throat flickered through his mind. That had gone badly, and he was sure this would do so as well. Goes Far sat across from him cradling an infant in her arm. In the flickering firelight, she did not look happy. Her mother hovered in the background.

Cooper nodded sadly. He started to speak, then thought it useless. He rose, picking up his rifle as he did. Goes Far's voice stopped him.

"Why you not come back for so long?"

"Needed to get back to trappin'. A man's got to make his way in the world and he can't do that without working for some recompense. At least white men can't."

"Trapping more important than me?"

"Nope. But sometimes one thing needs to be

thought of first, no matter how much it might hurt a feller on the inside. It wasn't an easy thing for me to turn away and head away from you."

"You not want me anymore," the woman said in an accusatory voice. "You want Slow Calf."

"Where'd you get that notion?"

"Sits Down says you brought her to her village…"

"When did he tell you this?"

"Just before you come. He said you traveled with her for weeks in winter."

"I did. She needed to get back to her people, and I brought her. Just like I did Mornin' Song."

"You share robes with her, keep from cold at night."

"That's an even more foolish notion than you thinkin' I want her more than you."

"But you travel many nights."

"Of course. It took many days and nights to get to her village. Just like it took many days and nights to get here when we brought Mornin' Song."

"Why you take Slow Calf?"

"Doesn't matter, I reckon, with you feelin' the way you do. But think of this, woman—if I wanted her more than you, why would I have left her at her village and come to get you here?"

"Maybe she tell you to go away. Maybe you want to take me to her village and make me your second wife."

"You've let bad spirits take over your mind, Sally. I had no such plan. I had no plan to be with Slow Calf."

"Then why you make trip in bad winter with her?"

"She needed to be with her people."

"Why. She had husband."

Cooper hesitated before answering, then realized she did not know what had happened. "Jacques was killed by Blackfeet at rendezvous if you remember. Slow Calf didn't like him much so saw no need to grieve him. Duncan took her as his woman."

"Yes. I remember. He good man. Not like Old Man."

Cooper nodded. "She was happy with him. Then Colin Leary, one of those fellers who had joined us at rendezvous last year went and killed one of the other men who had joined us then and run off with Slow Calf. Me, Bill, and Duncan chased after him. Blackfeet had caught the two of 'em, but before they could practice their savagery on 'em, we came along. Killed them Blackfeet off to the last one." He sighed. "But the Blackfeet got Duncan. Alistair offered to take her and the young'uns in, but she was s grievin' too much. We all decided she'd be best off bein' with her people."

"And you say you take her?" When he nodded, she asked, "Why? You have many bad times traveling in winter."

Cooper smiled sadly. "That's a fact. But I took Mornin' Song to safety here with the People, so I figured I'd do the same for Slow Calf. Besides, when I left her with her clan, I'd be only a few days from you, I figured, so I thought I'd come get you. But it seems I've lost favor with you. So I'll be on my way. I hope you get a good man who'll take good care of the child."

"You not want to see him?"

"It'd be nice, I reckon, but I can't see no reason now. I'll miss you, woman." With a sinking heart, he turned and headed for the outside, hoping in those few steps that she would call him back. But she didn't.

"SHE SEND YOU AWAY?" Sits Down asked the next morning as Cooper was loading his mule with what supplies he had left, supplemented by some given to him by Pale Thunder.

The mountain man simply nodded.

"I'm surprised."

Cooper shrugged. He felt bad enough that talking about it would only make it worse.

"Where you go? Back to the other trappers?"

"Reckon so. They've got my traps and whatever plews I've taken. I'll spend the spring hunt with 'em and head to rendezvous with 'em. After that..." He shrugged. "I might just move on by myself. Ain't gonna be much the same with El and Duncan gone under. And Zeke, of course. Paddy and Al are all right fellers but not so close friends as the others. Dan and Dave, well, they ain't ever been what I'd call friends."

"Maybe you find new friends at rendezvous."

"Maybe, but it ain't likely."

"I go with you maybe?"

Cooper looked at the Nez Percé in surprise. "Doubt I'd be very good company, at least for a spell, Sits Down. Besides, you're needed here. The Blackfeet are always a threat to the People. And now that the People know how great a warrior you are, they'll be countin' on you to help protect 'em."

"I told you having people know me would be a curse as you say."

"We all have our crosses to bear."

"Eh?"

Cooper smiled a little. "Words from some of the white men's religion. Means every man has hardships to deal with in life, often ones that he feels might crush him under their weight."

"White men's religion is strange."

"White men say the same about yours." Cooper tightened the last knot on the pack saddle, grabbed his apishemore, and tossed it on the mare's back.

"I visit at rendezvous."

"That'd be a welcome thing, Sits Down. Zeke was likely the best friend I ever had," he said, sadness putting a hitch in his voice, "except for Cuts Throat maybe. Two-Faces and Duncan and El before his mind went bad were close friends too. And after what you and me been through together, I consider you a damn good friend too."

"I'm glad, Hairy..." Sits Down slapped his mouth shut when he saw Cooper's growing melancholy. "Maybe I ride with you for a way?"

"I ain't so..."

"You go soon?" Pale Thunder asked, walking up.

"Yep."

"You would go without sayin' goodbye?"

"Was plannin' on it. Figured it'd be too difficult to say farewell the way things are."

"Not like you to be cowardly about such a thing."

"Ain't cowardice, Thunder. More like gloominess. Ain't every day a man loses a woman he cares for deeply. Maybe your notion of lovin' and havin' a woman by your side is different from a white man's or just from mine, but..."

"Not so different maybe in feelin's. Maybe way we show is different, maybe not. Man needs a woman, though he might think he doesn't." He grinned. "Not so sure woman needs man except to feed her." He laughed.

"Could be. I had—have—deep feelin's for Goes Far, and it ain't gonna be much of a life without her at my side, especially after all we've been through together. But that's my burden to carry, I suppose." He tossed his saddle on the horse's back, hooked the near stirrup onto the saddle horn, and reached under the animal's belly for the cinch.

"You weren't gonna say goodbye to Mornin' Song either?"

"Also too painful. Give her my regards, Thunder."

The Nez Percé nodded. "You'll come back?"

"Maybe. If so, it won't be for a spell."

Pale Thunder nodded. "You have enough supplies?"

"With what you gave me, yep." He tightened the cinch and dropped the stirrup back down. He walked to a nearby tree, grabbed his rifle and slid it through the loop behind the saddle horn. He turned. "You boys've been as good a friend as a man could have, always willin' to help, to stand by me in tough times. I'm obliged." He held out his hand and shook with each. Then he pulled himself into the saddle. Looking down, he said, "I'd be obliged, Thunder, if you were to keep lookin' after Goes Far, at least 'til she finds herself a husband."

"I will."

"Farewell to you both. You've been shinin' friends. We'll meet up again someday." He grinned crookedly. "Even if it's in the Spirit World after some damn Blackfeet put us under."

"Never happen," Sits Down said with a strong rumbling laugh.

"With you, I don't doubt it." He rode off, now looking back.

———————

TWO HOURS of leisurely travel later, he was pulling out from a line of trees onto a short meadow when he saw movement to his left. He pulled back into the trees far enough to not be seen but not so much that he couldn't observe. And what he saw made his heart pound. He turned around and raced away, pushing the mare as hard as he could, dropping the rope to the mule when the animal couldn't—or wouldn't—keep up, hoping he would be in time.

In less than an hour at his pace, he thundered into the village, bellowing, "Blackfeet! Blackfeet coming!"

THIRTY-SIX

COOPER SLID his horse to a stop in front of the lodge used by Goes Far and her mother. The former was holding the infant, looking around, not in a daze but in a calculating manner, trying to decide how best to handle the situation. She could see the large Blackfoot war party moving quickly toward the northeast edge of the village.

The mountain man made the decision for her. He leaped off the horse, grabbed his woman and tossed her into the saddle. He grabbed his rifle and yelled, "Go!"

The horse bolted, joining other animals and most of the women and children in heading for a long, thick band of trees along the river's steep bank, which would help protect them. Several warriors were heading there, too, ready to protect the vulnerable.

Goes Far's mother looked a little worried.

"Don't you fret, Bright Eyes," he said.

A teenage boy hurried by, heading for where the warriors were taking up positions behind trees or lodges, but Cooper grabbed the rope rein. "I need this horse, boy," he said. "Now go on with the others to safety."

"I want to fight."

"Then get yourself a weapon and join the warriors. I hope you have good medicine."

"Me too," the youth said seriously.

Cooper handed the rein to Bright Eyes and lifted her onto the horse's back. "Off you go." He smacked the horse's rump, then hurried to where the ragged line of warriors was. Sits Down and Pale Thunder were in the open, ten or fifteen feet apart, defiantly waiting for the approaching enemy, daring the Blackfeet to take them. Cooper rushed to join them. As he ran, he saw Red Leggings in a vulnerable position next to his lodge. Cooper stopped and grabbed the arm of the youth from whom he had taken the horse. "You want to be a warrior, go protect your chief." He pointed to Red Leggings. "He must not be harmed, understand?"

Looking worried though not particularly scared, the teenager rushed to stand beside the old chief.

Cooper trotted the last few yards until he was between Sits Down and Pale Thunder. The former glanced at him and grinned, looking forward to the battle.

"We make damned Blackfeet come as you say," he said in his rumbling voice.

"Certain we will. I..." He stopped as Blackfeet started charging into the village. He dropped to one knee, raised the rifle, and fired. A Blackfoot wearing an elaborate headdress went down, dead.

Three more Blackfeet died with arrows from Sits Down's bow in their chest. Moments later, others fell as more Nez Percé warriors fired their bows. Cooper shot again and brought down another enemy.

Several foes swept past Cooper, Sits Down, and Pale Thunder, none of whom had been hit by Blackfoot arrows. Cooper spun and fired again, the lead ball plowing into a warrior's back. As the latter two stayed facing more incoming Blackfeet, Cooper and several Nez Percé raced toward the enemies who were heading for the trees. Cooper reloaded as he ran.

The Blackfeet had jumped off their ponies and were invading the woods on foot. Cooper and his friends charged in after them. He slid the rifle over his shoulder, then plowed into one from behind. He grabbed the Indian's hair and jerked his head back. "You ain't gettin' these women and children," he muttered. "Not today or ever." He slit the warrior's throat.

Yells, screams, and war cries split the cold air as warriors went after each other. Enraged by having to face another horde of Blackfeet, Cooper was a wild man. He relentlessly hunted down Blackfeet, racing from one to the other, hacking them down, slicing throats, gutting enemy warriors, breaking limbs.

Finally he realized there were no more Blackfeet around him. He stood, breathing heavily, wanting more enemies to kill. He wandered toward the edge of the woods and looked out.

"Lord al-goddamn-mighty," he whispered when he saw Sits Down, Pale Thunder, and a few other Nez Percé holding off a circling mob of Blackfeet. "You Blackfeet are some stupid bastards," he mumbled as he ran toward them. "Goddamn fools for wantin' to count coup instead of just killin' those boys. You'll pay for it, damn you!"

With the noise the attackers were making, as well as the wind still whistling through the camp, the Blackfeet did not know there was a man as savagely bloodthirsty as they coming at them until he hacked three of them down with his tomahawk.

Sits Down glanced at him and grinned, relishing the fight. "About time, Hairy Face," he called.

Cooper just nodded and chopped the neck of another Blackfoot.

Several foes broke off their siege of the Nez Percé and turned their attention to Cooper. "No, goddammit," he snapped, "you ain't poundin' me like last time, you bloody damned devils." He let out a roar and leaped forward.

He hacked one across the side, the tomahawk blade tearing a wide swath from side to stomach. The warrior screamed.

Another warrior raced at him, arm raised high, blade in hand. Cooper ducked and brought his shoulder—the one opposite where the rifle barrel rose— and jerked upward, tossing the Indian up and over. He spun and stomped on the warrior's back, then cleaved his head. A knife slid across his side rather than puncturing his innards as he spun. He snatched out a pistol and blasted the Blackfoot as the Indian came at him again.

He slammed the flat side of the 'hawk against another warrior's cheek, then raced forward, seeing a Blackfoot creeping up on Sits Down's back. He grabbed the warrior's head and jerked him back, flinging him to the ground, then stamped on the man's throat, crushing it. It didn't kill him, but the warrior would fight no longer.

Sits Down glanced over his shoulder and grinned. "Thanks, Hairy Face."

"It's nothing." Cooper charged to where two Blackfeet were closing in on Pale Thunder. He tackled one, rolled him over, then split his forehead with the tomahawk.

He stood in time to see Pale Thunder jam a knife in the other warrior's stomach and gut him. He nodded.

The Blackfeet were fleeing. Again Cooper stood breathing heavily. "Damn!" he suddenly yelled as an arrow thudded into his leg, much closer to his privates than was comfortable. Moments later another struck him in the side, just under the ribs, and tore out through the back. He staggered a little but remained on his feet. He watched as Sits Down and two other Nez Percé punctured the Blackfeet with their own arrows. Then he started to sag but Sits Down caught him, careful to avoid the arrowhead sticking a little way out Cooper's back.

"Put me down, Sits Down," he protested. "I'm all right."

"You lie. Shut mouth now."

Pale Thunder took the tomahawk from Cooper's hand and slipped the rifle off his back.

As Sits Down started carrying him away, Cooper heard Red Leggings shouting in Nez Percé, "Follow them. Let none live. Gather their ponies." He smiled a little at the chief's order. Twenty years ago, Red Leggings would have been the one leading the charge after the fleeing Blackfeet.

Pain started to course through him and he gritted

his teeth. *Yep,* he thought, *might be time to head back to the Settlements. I've had enough of fightin' Blackfeet and takin' arrows from those damned savages.*

Sits Down brought him to Pale Thunder's lodge and laid him down, mostly on his side, braced by a folded buffalo robe. The two warriors and a few others stood around wondering what to do. The war chief's wives hovered over Cooper, examining him and discussing what to do.

Suddenly Goes Far burst into the lodge unannounced and shoved everyone aside to kneel at Cooper's side. "You're hurt," she said rather than asked.

"Would seem so, yep," he said, not really knowing how to respond to the woman he loved but who had spurned him just the day before.

Goes Far looked up over her shoulder at her mother, who had followed her in and stood with a hand on her shoulder. The older woman nodded.

Goes Far stood. "Take him to my lodge," she ordered.

"That's not a good idea," Pale Thunder said in Nez Percé.

"Don't argue. Just do."

Pale Thunder looked at Sits Down. The huge warrior shrugged, knelt, and easily lifted Cooper. Minutes later, he was laying the mountain man down on a buffalo robe, again keeping the arrowhead from hitting the ground and maybe being pushed back in.

"All go," Goes Far commanded, pointing at the tipi's exit flap.

"No," Sits Down said. Goes Far looked as if she were going to slap him, but he said, "You need help getting arrows out. Especially one in the side."

Goes Far thought for a few moments, then nodded. "Rest of you go."

Reluctantly Pale Thunder and two other warriors walked out, leaving Goes Far, Sits Down, and Bright Eyes alone with Cooper.

Moments later, Morning Song entered. "He is all right?" she asked tentatively.

"Bad hurt," Goes Far responded. "But I fix."

"I help," Morning Song said. "I fetch my things." She hurried out.

"Does it hurt much?" Goes Far asked, frightened, as she knelt beside Cooper.

"No worse than last time." He tried to grin but was not very successful. "You best have Sits Down get these damn things out. You didn't do so good last time."

"I'm stronger now."

"And angrier at me, too, I reckon. Might give you joy to go tuggin' on these arrows, maybe cause me some pain."

"Maybe so." But she had a wan smile. "We wait for Mornin' Song." While waiting, she sliced open Cooper's pants around the arrow in his leg and his shirt around the arrow shaft in his midsection.

It wasn't long before Morning Song came back. She put out pouches and gourd bowls and got a dipper full of water. She nodded.

"Get them out, Sits Down," Goes Far said.

The huge warrior kneeled. "I try to be gentle," he rumbled, "but it still hurt."

"I know. Just do it and be quick about it."

Sits Down took the arrow shaft at Cooper's back and snapped it as if it were a twig.

Cooper gasped and his chest heaved. After a few moments, he nodded. "Get it done, my friend."

Sits Down grabbed the arrowhead and yanked. The bloody shaft slid out, making Cooper buck and groan. Sits Down's powerful hand held him down.

Before the mountain man could get settled, Sits Down jerked the arrow out of Cooper's leg.

Cooper moaned, and his eyes bulged. It took several minutes, but he finally calmed some. "Thanks," he mumbled.

"Is good, Hairy Face." The huge warrior rose and walked out.

Morning Song had been making poultice salve and quickly slathered it on all three wounds, then awkwardly bandaged the wounds with calico Goes Far had lying around.

"You sleep now," Goes Far said, wiping the sweat off Cooper's brow with another piece of cloth.

Cooper started to respond, then closed his mouth and simply nodded.

IT TOOK several minutes to push aside the grogginess when he awoke. Goes Far was sitting next to him making a new pair of moccasins for their child. "How long I been out?" he asked through a dry mouth.

"Two suns." She rose and got some water and kneeled beside him again. Helping him to keep his head up, she let him drink his fill. Finally he nodded and lay back down. Eventually he asked, "Why're you doin' this?"

"You're my man."

"I thought you cast me over. That's what you did the other day."

"I thought then that you not want me anymore. Or maybe Slow Calf didn't want you, so you come back to me. I not like that."

"I can't imagine you would."

"But then I think that you came back to fight Blackfeet here—and you take care of me and Mother first. I think then that maybe I was wrong. Maybe you still want me." There was hope and expectation in her eyes.

"Ever since Black Moon Woman went under and I met you, you're the only woman I ever wanted."

"That true?"

"Yes, ma'am."

Goes Far smiled. "I like."

"Then you still want me?"

"Yes. Now, would you like to meet son?"

"Yes, Sally—Goes Far—I most certainly would."

IF YOU LIKE THIS, YOU MAY ALSO ENJOY: BUCKSKIN COUNTY WAR

COLORADO TERRITORY BOOK ONE

BRODIE PIKE IS ONE AGAINST MANY—THE ODDS ARE NOT IN HIS FAVOR.

Brodie Pike knew he shouldn't get involved. It would somehow turn out bad, as seemed to happen too often to him, but he couldn't watch four gunmen bully a small-time rancher. The next day, the man he had helped is found beaten to death. Though he knows he is responsible for Dunn's death, he refuses to help the group of small ranchers who know that the Buckskin County Cattlemen's Association will be coming for their land soon.

Months later, he reads that the association has started its campaign of terror against the small ranchers. Against the odds, he decides to throw in with them, facing the association's horde of hired guns, risking his life in the bloody, violent Buckskin County war, where death is always just one bullet away.

AVAILABLE NOW

ABOUT THE AUTHOR

Though it might sound strange for someone who has published more than sixty Westerns, John Legg was born and raised in New Jersey. An Air Force veteran, he has traveled much of the West, having been a news-paper copy editor for more then twenty-seven years in Phoenix.

He currently works for a major newspaper's editing center in Florida and has a BA from William Paterson College (now university) in Wayne, N.J. and an MSJ from the Medill School of Journalism at Northwestern University. He has two grown children and two young grandsons.

Made in the USA
Las Vegas, NV
22 May 2024

90230197R00204